the Tenth Power

Kate Constable

Arthur A. Levine Books

AN IMPRINT OF SCHOLASTIC INC.

I would like to thank Rosalind Price and Jodie Webster from Allen & Unwin for all t
Lyn Tranter from Australian Literary Management for her support; Jan, Bill, and Hila,
Joy Taylor, and Richard Evans for allowing me extra time to work, and Richard for the wh
Heather Evans and Oslem Ozmetin, for the dancing; and Michael Taylor, as always, for believing.

Library of Congress Cataloging-in-Publication Data
Constable, Kate, 1966-
    The tenth power / by Kate Constable. — 1st American ed.
       p. cm. — (The chanters of Tremaris trilogy ; bk. 3)
    Sequel to: Waterless sea.
    Summary: Having lost her magical powers of chantment, eighteen-year-old
Calwyn searches for the missing half of the broken Wheel of the Tenth Power with
the hope of stopping the plague and endless winter that have fallen on her world.
    ISBN 0-439-55482-9
    [1. Magic — Fiction.   2. Fantasy.] I. Title.
PZ7.C7656Ten 2006
[Fic] — dc22
                                                                    2005018716

10 9 8 7 6 5 4 3 2 1   06 07 08 09 10
Printed in the U.S.A.
First American edition, March 2006
Book design by Elizabeth B. Parisi · Map illustration © 2005 by Matt Manley

To Michael

Contents

Moondark

The autumn night was chilly, and the skies over Antaris were black. The three moons had turned their faces away, as if they could not bear to watch the scene below. Even the stars were hidden behind a bank of cloud, and the priestesses stumbled in the uncertain flicker of torchlight.

If the procession had led to the sacred valley there would have been music. The initiation of novices would have been accompanied by solemn, joyful songs, by chimes and drums. But on this night, there were no songs; there was no ritual music for what they were about to do.

The Guardian of the Wall led the way, torch held high. Her plait swung heavy down her back, black and silver intertwined, and her thin lips were pressed together. The sisters followed in silence. The hems of their wide yellow trousers were splashed with mud, dark as bloodstains.

At last the Guardian halted and turned. Behind her towered the Wall, the impenetrable barrier that protected the community of Antaris from the world outside. It was made of ice, high as three

I

men, and wide as the nearby river. The Guardian raised her torch, and the Wall reflected glints of fire in its depths: cold fire, without heat or warmth.

The silence of the sisters deepened and widened. Just as they sang together in their rituals, so now they were silent together, and the silence of many was stronger and more dreadful than the silence of one alone. The spit and hiss of the torches seemed unnaturally loud.

The Guardian beckoned, and one of the priestesses stepped from the crowd. She was a strongly built woman of middle age; the flames picked out gleams of red in her dark hair. Her skin was very pale, her face stiff and expressionless, as if carved from white marble. As she moved toward the Guardian, someone sobbed, *"No!"*

The Guardian uncorked a small earthenware vial. With unsteady hands, the other priestess took it, tilted back her head, and swallowed the liquid within. When she lowered the vial, her lips were stained black. She closed her eyes, and swayed; she reached back and unbound her long hair, shaking it loose around her face in the traditional gesture of mourning. Without a sound, she crumpled to the ground. The little vial rolled away, a few drops of dark bitterthorn brew trickling from it.

The Guardian nodded, and two priestesses wrapped their hands in their cloaks and propped the fallen woman carefully between them.

The Guardian raised her hands in a movement that was more challenge than entreaty. For the space of a breath, two breaths, there was no sound but the crackle of torches, the distant hoot of an owl in the forest, and the rushing of the river. Then, unsteadily, one priestess began the chantment of unmaking.

One after another, the sisters took up the song. Behind the forbidding figure of the Guardian, the Wall began to melt, revealing the deep dark of the forest outside as it dissolved. Some priestesses averted their eyes, from the black night beyond the Wall, or from the pale, slumped body of their sister, or both. Hidden in the center of the crowd, someone was weeping.

When the breach in the Wall was large enough, the Guardian held up her hands to halt the chantment. The two sisters clumsily maneuvered the limp body into the gap. The Guardian sang a swift chantment, and a husk of ice swam up to enclose the body and hold it erect. Without pausing in her song, the Guardian gestured to the assembled sisters to begin a new chantment.

The spell of strengthening was faint and reluctant at first. But as more of the sisters joined in, the ice slowly thickened, and the body of the red-haired priestess was sealed in the very heart of the Wall. The Guardian lifted her hands, and the chantment ceased.

"It is done." Her low words fell like stones into an icy pool. "Now let us sing the song of mourning for our beloved sister Athala. We sing the song for those who die in childbed, giving life. Our brave sister has given us all the gift of life, this night."

The Daughters of Taris loosed their hair around their shoulders and took up the lamentation, singing now with their whole hearts, drawing comfort from the familiar ritual. Many of the sisters wept and covered their faces with their yellow shawls. The procession turned, with the Guardian at its head, and wound its way swiftly back toward the Dwellings.

Only one priestess lingered, the chill breath of night on her face as she gazed at the lifeless body within the ice. "Taris, Lady Mother!" she whispered. "Deliver us from this darkness!" She scanned the sky, but the lowering clouds still veiled the stars. Winter was coming. Shivering, the priestess rubbed her hands together. They were so cold — and her feet were cold too.

The priestess stifled a sob, and she stumbled after the others along the path to the Dwellings, where she had always known safety and welcome. But her home was safe no longer.

Bitterthorn

The forest was a sheet of white, streaked with charcoal and daubed with blue shadow. Snowdrifts were heaped beneath the trees, and each twig was outlined with a silvery coat of frost. Day after day the freeze had continued, and the sky was a clear, crisp blue. Here and there, the tracks of birds and burrowers marked the coverlet of snow, but bears and other animals dozed, waiting for the sun's warmth to wake them. They could not know that this winter had lasted too long, and the time for spring's return had already passed.

The only sign of movement in the vast silence of the forest came from three small figures, stark shadows against the snow, their breath puffing in the air.

Calwyn tucked the end of her dark plait securely into the hood of her fur-lined cloak and kicked snow over the remains of the fire. Smoke and steam rose with a hiss. It was midday, but the sunlight was weak and watery where it filtered through the trees.

Calwyn's face ached with the cold, and her eyes were sore from squinting into the glare. Under her cloak, she wore a padded jacket, thick trousers, and several layers of woollen undershirts and tunics. A sharp hunting knife hung from a sheath at her belt, and she wore a small wooden hawk on a silver chain around her throat. Rabbit-skin mittens protected her hands, and a woollen scarf partly hid her face. Her dark eyes stared out beneath straight eyebrows, level and watchful. Calwyn did not often smile these days.

Balanced on iron blades strapped to her boots, Calwyn crunched across the snow to where her companions squatted by the bank of the frozen river. She was taller, stronger, and, at eighteen, a little older than her two young friends. This was her journey. She was taking them to the place she thought of as home: Antaris, locked away behind its great Wall of Ice. They had been traveling for more than twenty days, almost a turn of the moons. They'd been lucky with the weather; in all that time the freeze had held, and there had been no snowstorms. But even so, the journey from the coastal city of Kalysons had not been easy: They had skated along the shore of the Bay of Sardi — frozen across for the first time in living memory — then upriver through the mountains.

Calwyn watched as Trout and Mica, heads close together, struggled with Mica's skate blade. Trout looked tired, and when Mica glanced up, Calwyn saw the bruise of shadows under her eyes.

"You see the moons last night, Cal?" she asked eagerly. "It were the Whale's Mouth."

It was the formation that the priestesses of Antaris called the Goat and Two Kids. "Yes," said Calwyn. "The middle of spring."

"So why's it still winter?" Mica shivered. "It ain't right. I don't like it. Remember when you sung up ice for me that first time, Cal, and I got so excited? Reckon I've seen enough ice and snow now to last me all my life."

"I remember," said Calwyn shortly. Mica's face fell.

"Don't wriggle, Mica." Trout frowned with concentration as he tugged at the leather thong that fastened Mica's skate to her boot. He was seventeen now, a serious young man, no longer the nervous boy that Calwyn had met almost two years before. But his blue eyes were still round and questioning, and his thatch of brown hair still flopped untidily over his forehead. As usual, his bootlaces were strung through the wrong holes, and one of his coat buttons dangled by a thread. He sat back on his heels. "There, that should hold it."

"Trout, it's too tight! My foot'll fall off!" Mica winced as she wriggled a finger through the lacings. She too had grown up in the past year; she had become a striking young woman, with her golden eyes and thick, honey-colored hair. But she looked miserable now; her nose was red and swollen, her lips were chapped, and her eyes streamed with the cold.

"Better too tight than too loose," said Trout mildly. "You'll twist your ankle again if you're not careful."

"Look." Calwyn opened her mittened hand and showed them a prickly sprig. "It's bitterthorn. Ursca uses it to dull pain and help bring sleep. It grows near the Wall."

"So there ain't far to go?" Mica's face brightened.

"We'll reach Antaris by nightfall."

"At last!" muttered Trout fervently. "Hot baths, clean clothes, a proper bed!"

"The beds in the Dwellings are hard, Trout," said Calwyn. "The sisters of Antaris live simply. Don't expect luxury."

"But they have mattresses?" Trout squinted through the glass lenses that perched on his freckled nose. "We won't have to sleep on the ground?"

"Of course not," said Calwyn irritably.

"Antaris must be like Emeran, where me and Grandma lived," said Mica wistfully. "Like when all the men went out to sea, fishin', and all the women was left behind together. Even better, cos there ain't no pirates. We had good times, peaceful, all singin' and that, with no men racketin' around."

"What's wrong with having men around?" asked Trout, slightly hurt.

"I don't mind *you*. Boys is all right."

Trout screwed up his face and hauled Mica to her feet. Born in the Isles of Firthana, where snow and ice were unknown, Mica was far from steady on her skates, though her skills had improved greatly since the start of their journey.

She slid out onto the frozen river, whirling her arms wildly. Layers of wool and fur made her as round as a little barrel, and only a few strands of tousled hair poked out from her knitted cap. In the middle of the river, she wiped her nose on her sleeve and began to sing a high, lilting chantment of the winds. The snow-drifts, fallen branches, and the slush of dead leaves on the ice blew aside, clearing a path for them.

"Mica! Don't forget the Clarion!" called Trout. He held out the precious, golden Clarion of the Flame, the last relic of the Power of Fire. At first, Mica had been wary of using such a powerful artifact, almost too nervous to bring it to her lips, but now the slim little trumpet was an old friend. Without the magic of the Clarion to keep them warm, to start their campfires, to clear the snow from their snug tent, and to light their way when the dark drew in every afternoon, the three travelers could not have survived this journey. Even when it was not being played to summon the chantments of fire, the Clarion glowed with a steady, comforting warmth. Mostly, Calwyn and Trout let Mica hold it; she had to be warm to sing her chantments, and she suffered from the cold more than they did.

Mica skated back, grabbed the Clarion, and tucked it inside her jacket. "Brr, that's better! This'll stop my throat-ache." With a brave grin, she wobbled away again.

Trout was a better skater than Mica. As a student in Mithates, he had skated every winter. He'd told Calwyn and Mica about skating parties on the River Amith, with races and picnics and dancing on the ice. That was strange to Calwyn. In Antaris, where each novice must cross the black ice of the sacred pool to become an initiated priestess, skating was a skill to be exercised with respect, not a matter for fun and games.

But Trout was not reckless. He was a sturdy, dependable skater who never showed off. Now he and Calwyn tugged on the pack harnesses and set off in stride together.

"Wait for us, Mica!" Calwyn called. "How many times do I have to tell you, it's not safe!"

With a tremendous effort, Mica halted her headlong glide. "You say that every day, but the ice ain't broke once yet!" she yelled, her breath a white cloud.

"You don't know the signs of thin ice, Mica. Keep to the edges."

"Don't be cross with me, Cal," said Mica plaintively, but in truth she was tired, and relieved to drop behind the others.

For a time, the only sound was Mica's high, eerie song of chantment, and the steady swish of blades on ice.

"Calwyn," said Trout in a low voice. "Don't be too harsh with Mica. This journey hasn't been easy for her, you know."

"It isn't easy for any of us," snapped Calwyn. "You think it's easy for me?"

"No, no — I mean — I know why you're in such a bad mood all the time. . . ."

"If you know so much, then why talk about it?"

Scowling, Calwyn tucked her chin into her scarf and scanned the river ahead. Once, if she had seen a crack in the ice, she could have sung a swift chantment to seal it. Once, she would have made this journey singing softly all the way. And as Mica sang to clear their path, Calwyn could have sung to strengthen the ice beneath them.

Not so long ago, Calwyn had been a chanter, a gifted chanter. Most chanters of Tremaris could sing the chantments of only one of the Nine Powers. Calwyn had been taught the Power of Ice by the sisters of Antaris, and then she had learned the chantments of the winds from Mica. She had also sung the songs of the Power of Beasts, which tamed animals. And in Merithuros, half a year ago, she'd begun to learn the chantments of ironcraft, the power that moved everything of the earth except air, fire, and water.

It was all gone. All her gifts of magic were lost. *Merithuros stole them from me*, she thought bitterly, though at the time she had given herself freely to try to heal that dry and troubled land. But the task had overwhelmed her — and now this never-ending winter seemed a cruel joke at her expense, reminding her every day of what she'd lost. Her fists clenched hard, and the crushed fragments of the bitterthorn twig crumbled and blew away across the ice.

Trout ventured a change of subject. "Steel blades would be better than iron. Stronger. Lighter too. Do you ever use steel skate blades in Antaris, Calwyn?"

"We have steel knives," said Calwyn, dragging her thoughts from her own misery. "But metal's very precious in Antaris: The traders have to carry it to us all the way through the mountains. We use bone blades for skating."

It felt strange to Calwyn to say *we* of the priestesses of Antaris. Almost two years had passed since she had run away with Darrow, the Outlander who had breached the ice Wall. So much had happened in that time. She had traveled across oceans and through deserts. She had seen the fabled Palace of Cobwebs and walked the desolate streets of Spareth, the city abandoned by the Ancient Ones. She and her friends had fought Samis, the most dangerous sorcerer Tremaris had ever seen, and they had defeated him — or so they'd thought.

There were reports that Samis was alive and hiding in Gellan. Certainly his half sister, Keela, believed so; she had fled from Merithuros to join him there. Now Darrow, with Tonno and Halasaa, had traveled north to the Red City.

The thought of Darrow was, as always, bittersweet. Darrow had carved the little wooden hawk that Calwyn wore at her throat. He had become her friend, then more than a friend. But now she was not sure what they were to each other. What had happened to Calwyn in the deserts of Merithuros had changed everything. Darrow was Lord of the Black Palace, the ruler of all Merithuros. And she, Calwyn, was nothing.

After the loss of her chantments, she had pushed Darrow away. She knew that had hurt him deeply, but her despair and her misery were so great she couldn't bear anyone near her. Sometimes she thought she almost hated Darrow; at times, she hated herself. She wouldn't have blamed Darrow if he'd begun to hate her too. It might even be a kind of relief if he did. But mostly she was numb, beyond feeling.

Now Calwyn was returning home, as an injured animal crawls back to the safety of its den. She was sure of only one thing: Marna, the High Priestess, would be glad to see her. Remembering Marna's smile, the twinkle in her faded blue eyes and the gentle touch of her hand, Calwyn spurred herself to go faster. Her skates bit smoothly across the ice, one long stroke after another.

In one way, it was lucky for the travelers that this fierce freeze had lasted so long. They had skated upriver across the plains and through the mountains, making their journey much quicker than if they'd walked all the way. Calwyn had never known the rivers to freeze so hard, nor so late in the season.

"Cal! Cal!" Suddenly Mica swooped past them. "Come on! Can't you feel it?"

"Mica, *wait*! For the sake of the Goddess!" shouted Calwyn, but as she and Trout rounded the bend, she saw why Mica was so excited.

Ahead, spanning the width of the river, shone a steady, impervious gleam, a shimmer like a vast mass of diamond. The great Wall of Antaris reared over them.

Calwyn's breath caught in her throat. How many times had she stood beside this towering barrier? How many days had she walked along it, singing it into being with chantments of ice-call? She knew it better than she knew the shape of her own face. She knew the Wall in the hot sunshine of high summer and the mellow dusk of autumn, in the clean fresh light of spring, and as it appeared now, in the blue shadows of winter.

But something was different. It wasn't just that she viewed the Wall from the outside now. What was missing was her awareness of the magic that had built and sustained the mighty rampart of ice, the living power that hummed through it and crackled all around it. Mica was a chanter: Mica had sensed strong chantment even before the Wall came into view. Once Calwyn too would have known that they were close to the Wall. It would have called to her, just as it had called to Mica.

But Calwyn felt nothing. The Wall appeared to her as it did to Trout, who stood gazing up beside her, openmouthed. It was a marvel, yes, a wondrous sight. But it was dead, lifeless, no more than a slab of frozen water. It was Mica who shivered, Mica who heard the call of the Goddess, Mica who shied instinctively from the shimmering surface. "Anyone'd feel safe, with *that* protectin' 'em," she murmured in awe.

Trout reached out to the Wall, but Calwyn struck his hand away. "Don't! It'll kill you! It's death to touch the Wall, the chantments that flow through it are so strong."

Trout shook himself. In Mithates, chantment had been outlawed generations ago. And though Trout had been the unwitting finder of the Clarion, the only relic of the Power of Fire, which the people of Mithates had renounced, he still had to be reminded of the possibility of magic. He had a practical mind, interested in how things worked, and making them work better; he had built the direction-finder that they'd used to steer their course. (Mica called it his "which-way," and the name had stuck.)

Calwyn stood staring at the Wall. Then she curled her thumb and forefinger into a circle, as the villagers of Antaris did when they approached the immense shining barrier, and she made the sign that they made, touching the circle to her forehead, her throat, her heart. This was the way the common folk made reverence to the Goddess Taris, Mother of the priestesses. Calwyn could no longer count herself as a Daughter of Taris. She had lost the most precious gift the Goddess had given her.

"Cal?" asked Mica timidly. "We goin' in?"

"Yes," said Calwyn, without moving, and the two girls remained motionless, side by side, gazing upward. Trout waited for a breath or two, then, still balanced on his skates, he tottered up onto the riverbank to explore the Wall as it curved farther into the forest.

A moment later the girls heard a shout. They hurried to where Trout stood by the Wall with his eyes averted, pointing mutely.

Mica and Calwyn didn't scream; they had seen enough horrors to prevent that. But Mica turned away with a shudder, and bile rose in Calwyn's throat.

There was a body inside the Wall. It was a woman; long reddish hair swam around her like a gossamer scarf. Her back was to them, her face hidden, but she wore the yellow tunic and shawl of a priestess. Shafts of blue light trapped the body like the bars of a cage; brilliant diamond cracks in the ice seemed to target the bloodless flesh like arrows.

"You never told us you put dead people into the Wall," said Trout accusingly.

"We don't!"

"Then how did she get there?"

"It must have been an accident —" Calwyn faltered. "Quickly, Mica, the Clarion! We have to set her free!"

"She's dead, Calwyn," said Trout bluntly. "It's too late to help her."

"We don't know that!" cried Calwyn. "A little village boy lost his way in a snowstorm, and we found him, blue and cold, not breathing. But the sisters brought him back to life. Mica, quick!"

Mica pulled out the Clarion and breathed through it as gently as she could. She was the only chanter among them; only she could call forth the power that the Clarion held. As she played, a clear note rang out, and the golden Clarion glowed brighter.

Slowly the ice of the Wall began to melt. Chantment met chantment, fire breathed to ice, as the music of the little horn unfurled. The thick, curdled ice became transparent; puddles of water formed around their feet. "Careful!" cried Calwyn. "Don't burn her!"

They were not skilled at using the last artifact of the Power of Fire; the Clarion's power was far greater than their ability to control it. Mica had grumbled that it was "like tryin' to ride a sea serpent." They had learned through trial and error which notes made heat and which made light, when to breathe through the Clarion gently and when to play a fiercer blast. Calwyn tried to guide Mica, and Trout observed and remembered. Sometimes the Clarion did as they intended; often it did not. After one or two nearly catastrophic accidents, they had learned to be cautious.

"Play it like when you're starting a campfire," suggested Trout.

Mica blew a succession of rapid, staccato notes. Calwyn watched in an agony of impatience as the ice dripped and melted, until the thinnest possible crust of ice remained around the body. "Stop!" she shouted, and simultaneously Trout yelled, "Watch out!"

The head lolled, and the woman's body smashed to the ground, stiff as a wooden doll. A faint blue tracing of veins was visible beneath her pale skin, and her calloused hands were large and strong. Calwyn rushed forward, dragging off her mittens with her teeth. "Give me the Clarion!" The trumpet still pulsed warm with the afterglow of chantment, and Calwyn held it to the woman's breast, her hands, her belly, as she would have held a hot poultice. The priestess's hazel-green eyes stared up unseeing; her mouth was wide, stained with something dark, and one strand of hair was caught between the cold lips. "It's Athala," said Calwyn as she worked frantically over the body. "She's our shoemaker."

Trout looked at Mica and shook his head. Mica, who still had great faith in Calwyn, set her mouth stubbornly. She picked up Athala's cold, stiff fingers and rubbed them between her gloved hands. When Calwyn placed her cheek close to the cold face, she felt no stir of breath or pulse; when she breathed into the blackened lips, there was no quickening response. When she lifted her mouth away, her own lips felt numb, and she tasted the unmistakable aniseed flavor of bitterthorn. So Athala had been drugged, or drugged herself — perhaps the bitterthorn was disguising the presence of the spark of life.

Along with her chantment, Calwyn had lost the special awareness she'd gained with the help of her friend Halasaa. He was one
of the Tree People, the first inhabitants of Tremaris, and he was
gifted with the Power of Becoming. He could heal injuries and illness, and speak with animals.

Half a year ago, Calwyn would have known, without this blind,
desperate groping, whether this woman was alive. She folded
Athala's hands around the Clarion and held it to her throat, willing the blood to pump again through the ice-cold body.

She couldn't have said how long they crouched there while the
early winter dusk gathered around them. At last Trout touched
her shoulder. "It's no use, Calwyn. She's dead."

"It ain't your fault, Cal." Mica slipped an arm around her
friend's waist. "You tried your best."

Calwyn shook her off. "I could have done better than that,
once," she said bitterly.

"Not even Halasaa could have helped her," said Trout. "She
was dead, Calwyn, dead a long time, I'd say. She was past healing."

Calwyn closed the hazel-green eyes and drew the yellow shawl
over Athala's face. "Her body should be burned, and the ashes
scattered under the blazetree in the sacred valley. We can bring her
inside the Wall ourselves, but we'll have to send people to carry
her back to the Dwellings." Calwyn pulled on the mittens she'd
discarded while she tried to revive Athala; her hands were stiff
with cold. "It'll be dark soon. We should go in."

Trout examined the breach dubiously. "Is that gap big enough?"

"Yes," said Calwyn shortly. Part of her was horrified at the blasphemy of melting a hole in the sacred Wall. The voices of her childhood echoed in her mind: *The first duty of every priestess is the care of the Wall.* And now she had mutilated it.

Trout and Calwyn dragged Athala's body inside the Wall and laid it down gently. Mica threw the packs one by one through the gap. Once they were all safely inside, they trudged back to the river and skated on. For some distance, the river and the Wall diverged, but after a time the river veered toward the rampart again. It was so dark now that Mica held the Clarion to her lips. A stream of golden light, warmer than any lantern, flowed from the mouth of the little trumpet and cast a pool of brightness around the travellers.

Suddenly Trout gasped and put out his hand to halt the others. The three huddled together, staring.

Body after body was ranged inside the Wall, a line of the dead as far as the light of the Clarion could reach. Perhaps three dozen of the sisters were held upright in the ice, all robed in yellow, their unbound hair swirling about their frozen bodies.

"Oh, no — *no!*" whispered Mica.

Calwyn covered her face with her hands.

Trout said, "What's happened, Calwyn? Why?"

"How should I know?" said Calwyn sharply. "There must be a reason. Perhaps — perhaps the way to the sacred valley is cut off, and Marna decided to keep the dead bodies here until they could hold the proper rituals." Even to her, that sounded absurd.

"But why so many?" Trout persisted. "Didn't you say about two hundred sisters lived in the Dwellings? There must be thirty or forty here."

Calwyn shivered. "Perhaps it was Samis. Darrow and I escaped, but maybe the sisters . . ." She swallowed. Never in her darkest thoughts had she dreamed that Samis might have destroyed Antaris; never had she imagined returning home to a wasteland.

"Samis done this?" whispered Mica.

"I don't know. Perhaps. It might have — amused him —"

Calwyn turned away, too afraid to examine the faces of the dead. "Take off your skates. We can walk to the Dwellings from here."

None of them wanted to skate past that silent, dreadful file. They thrust their skate blades into the packs, then turned their backs to the Wall and crunched across the hard-packed snow toward the Dwellings.

Snow-Sickness

Dusk had darkened into night before they reached the stone bridge at the foot of the orchard. As the three trudged uphill through the snow, struggling under the weight of the packs, Calwyn pointed out a cluster of domed shadows near the river-bank. "Those are the beehives."

Mica and Trout both knew that Calwyn had kept the hives in Antaris; she had spoken of it often. "These are our apple trees, the sweetest apples in Tremaris. There's the Bee House. That's where I — where the beekeeper stores the frames for the hives, and the smoke-lanterns." This stream of talk about safe, ordinary things did not reassure her companions; Calwyn's voice was nervous. "There are the Dwellings. That building with the tall windows is the great hall. That's where the sisters eat, all together. And we sing there after dinner every night in winter."

"There ain't no singin' now," whispered Mica.

Calwyn paused. The looming hall was dark and silent. No lamplight glowed in the windows, and no clatter of plates or murmur of voices floated into the night. A cold hand clenched Calwyn's heart.

"Dinner must be over," she said abruptly.

"Think they'll find us some leftovers?" said Mica. "Ain't you hungry, Trout?"

Trout grinned briefly; they had all been hungry for days. But his voice was serious. "It's awfully dark, Calwyn. And quiet."

"Somethin's wrong, ain't it? Somethin' big." Mica coughed violently and clutched the Clarion to her chest.

"Marna will explain everything," said Calwyn, too quickly. "Let's find her, before we see anyone else." She bent her head and trudged off across the snow.

Mica trotted after her. "You ain't shy of 'em, Cal?"

"It's not that. Marna will understand when I tell her who you are, but the sisters don't welcome strangers." That was an understatement. "They'll be very suspicious of you two."

"But we ain't strangers," said Mica. "We're your friends."

"You can't blame the sisters for being careful," Trout said. "The last person who came across the Wall was Samis, after all, and who knows what *he* did while he was here —"

"But there ain't no need to be scared of *us!*"

"Come on!" urged Calwyn. Even if they couldn't find Marna first, she wanted to avoid Tamen, the Guardian of the Wall, second in rank to the High Priestess. When Darrow arrived in Antaris, Tamen would have sacrificed him to the Goddess if she'd had her way.

Calwyn's heart was beating hard as they skirted around the jumble of outbuildings that clustered near the Dwellings: the milking sheds, the duck houses, the goat pens and woodpiles. With every step, Calwyn's sense of foreboding grew stronger. She could smell the familiar rank odor of the goats and hear faint bleats and muffled bells. But there was no lantern light, no muttering from the sheds. Goats must be milked, eggs collected, clean straw forked into the pens. Where was everybody?

"Stay close," said Calwyn softly. "In case we meet any of the sisters. And Trout, cover your head. The men of the villages never come so close to the Dwellings."

Near the kitchens lay the walled gardens where the herbs and vegetables grew. They were fallow now and blanketed with snow. And beyond that —

Calwyn drew in a sharp breath. She had forgotten. She had seen the collapse of the infirmary herself, from high in the branches of an ember tree, as she and Darrow fled. But it was a shock to see the blackened ruins, the fallen beams and toppled stones, all thick with snow. One lone wall stood, with a row of bare hooks where Ursca had hung her bunches of healing herbs.

"Was there a fire?" asked Trout in a hushed voice.

Calwyn nodded. "Samis destroyed it so we could see the power of his chantment. I thought they would have rebuilt it by now."

They were standing in the open yard bordered by the ruins of the infirmary and the rear of the Middle House, where the sisters and the older novices slept. From high inside the building came the sound of a racking cough, quickly suppressed. At least *someone* was alive, thought Calwyn, allowing herself to admit her worst fear only as it was proved false.

But as the muffled coughing stopped, another sound began: a desolate sobbing. On and on, the lonely crying echoed around the yard, fading at last into the darkness.

Mica clutched Calwyn's hand. Trout wrapped his arms around his body. His eyes were hidden behind his lenses, but his mouth was set in a firm line, as if he was trying to stop himself from crying too.

Calwyn gripped Trout's elbow and squeezed Mica's fingers. "Marna's rooms are this way. She'll explain everything, you'll see."

The High Priestess would send for food and a basin of warm water so they could wash, and Calwyn would sit on the low stool by the fire, with her Lady Mother's hand resting on her head as if she were still a little girl. Marna's eyes would crinkle with that serene smile. *There's nothing wrong here, little daughter. Nothing but a long winter. Yes, Samis was here. It was a terrible time. But he is gone.*

Perhaps Marna had given her up for dead, just as she'd grieved for Calwyn's mother, Calida. Calida had run away from Antaris too. She'd returned in the depths of winter, bringing her baby daughter, Calwyn, to be raised by the sisters. But Calida had caught a winter fever and died before dawn on the very night she'd returned.

Calwyn pulled herself back from her thoughts and hurried on. She had been damaged by her adventures beyond the Wall, but she was alive, and she wanted to show herself to Marna. But when she turned the corner, she stopped and stared up at the darkened windows, frozen with disappointment. Mica and Trout watched her, their breath drifting in clouds of mist, waiting for her to decide what to do next.

"We'll go to the kitchens," said Calwyn at last. "There's always someone there, day and night, to tend the fires."

"And we can get some food," said Trout.

Calwyn herself was no longer hungry. What could have happened? Dead bodies locked inside the Wall, the buildings dark and deserted, the animals untended. Where was Marna? And that hopeless, miserable weeping . . .

The kitchens were on the eastern side of the Dwellings. Wisps of smoke unfurled into the murky dark, and there was a smell of burned bread and rotting vegetable scraps. Calwyn slowed her pace. The kitchens had never smelled rotten before. Durtha, the head cook, was scrupulous about keeping the larders and sculleries clean and fresh. The novices on kitchen duty always complained about how much scrubbing they had to do.

Cautiously Calwyn beckoned her friends through the storerooms: the fish room with its long stone tanks, the room where the sausages and salted meats hung from their hooks, the mead and honey room. They were in the dairy, lined with shelves of milk jars and hard round cheeses, when the sound of voices startled them.

"No, no, I've already checked the cellars —"

"But Durtha said —"

"— doesn't matter — Tamen said the Bee House —"

The three held their breath until the footsteps died away.

"Wait here!" whispered Calwyn. "I'll go in alone." She crept up the steps into the main kitchen. It was deserted, as though everyone had been suddenly called away to some more urgent task. The sisters hadn't had their dinner after all. Piles of scrawny vegetables lay chopped on the long table; a spoon sat propped in a bowl of batter. At the far end of the room, cauldrons bubbled over the massive hearth that took up the whole of one wall.

A movement caught Calwyn's eye. One of the sisters was sitting in a chair beside the hearth, half-hidden in the shadows. The woman leaned forward, and Calwyn saw her broad face suddenly lit with firelight. She was holding a small knife, and her lap was filled with potatoes. "Don't be afraid," she said in a dry voice. "I can't chase after you."

"Lia?"

Lia was one of the most senior and respected priestesses, the Guardian of the House of Mothers, a revered midwife and milk-healer. Why was she hiding away here in a dark corner of the kitchens?

"Calwyn." Lia's knife scraped, a potato fell into the bucket at her feet. "Tamen knows someone breached the Wall tonight. She has turned the dwellings upside down hunting for the intruder. She's ordered everyone out to search."

Calwyn let out her breath. "But once she knows it's only me —"

Lia stared at her sharply. "Once she knows it's you, she won't rest until she's fed you to the Goddess. You and your Outlander must find a place to hide."

"My Outlander?" It took Calwyn a moment to realize who she was talking about. "Darrow isn't with me."

Lia gestured with her chin. "And who are they, if not Outlanders?"

Trout and Mica had crept out of their hiding place. "We heard voices," said Trout. "We thought — is everything all right?"

"All right?" Lia gave a bitter laugh. "Nothing has been right in Antaris since the sorcerer came."

"I told you two to wait for me!" said Calwyn angrily, but Mica had pushed closer to Lia.

"The sorcerer? You mean Samis?"

"The Merithuran, yes. He came to steal our chantments, but instead he stole our health and our contentment. And now he's taken spring from us, too."

Calwyn frowned. "What do you mean?"

"After he left, our sisters began to fall ill with the snow-sickness. It's a disease that afflicts chanters, only chanters. First the skin turns pale, then all feeling in the limbs fades away. Then the gift of chantment disappears. After that, death follows swiftly. There is no cure."

Calwyn swallowed. "The bodies in the Wall — they had the sickness?"

"You've seen them, then?" Lia's face set like a mask, and the little knife scraped and scraped against the potato's flesh. "That was Tamen's work. She believes that putting the sick ones into the Wall will prevent infection; that the ice will stop the disease from spreading. She believes that some must be sacrificed, for the sake of us all. And it must be said, many of the sisters think she's right."

"What about Marna?" cried Calwyn. "I can't believe Marna agreed to anything so monstrous!"

Lia gave Calwyn a swift, burning look. "Marna is not our High Priestess anymore. Tamen is High Priestess now."

"Marna is . . . Marna is dead?" Calwyn whispered. She groped behind her for the bench, to hold up her shaky legs; she felt sick and hollow. Suddenly she knew that Marna was the real reason she had come back to Antaris: not the sisters, or the bees, or the orchard, or the singing in the great hall. Somewhere inside her, a last candle-flame of hope snuffed out.

"Oh, Cal," murmured Mica.

Lia said, "Everyone in Antaris lives in fear. The sick are too frightened to ask Ursca for help, in case Tamen puts them in the Wall. So the illness spreads."

"Why don't you stop her?" cried Calwyn. Rage swelled inside her, filling the hollow place. "How can you just sit there so calmly, peeling potatoes?"

"I have no choice." Lia's voice was calm, but her dark eyes burned into Calwyn's. "I broke my back the night the sorcerer came. I have not walked since."

The night the sorcerer came . . . Calwyn remembered the terrible clash in the courtyard: all the sisters and their magic of ice-call, and Darrow with his songs of ironcraft, against Samis and his chantments of iron and seeming. Samis had made the priestesses believe they were crawling with snakes and spiders, and in the confusion, one of the sisters had fallen from the gallery. "It was *you* who fell!" Calwyn cried. "I'm . . . I'm sorry . . ."

"Don't waste your pity on me," said Lia crisply. "Save it for Rina, and Athala, and Damyr, and the others Tamen put into the Wall."

"Damyr?" Calwyn had been apprenticed to Damyr, the old beekeeper. It was she who had taught Calwyn the songs of the bees, never knowing that they were the long-lost chantments of the Power of Beasts. Calwyn would have liked to tell Damyr that.

A sudden noise made them all turn. From the shadowed doorway, a tall figure glided into the kitchen. A deep, grating voice said, "Calwyn. I might have known it was you." Tamen's dark eyes glittered, and her hair was coiled on top of her head, as Marna's had been.

Calwyn swallowed, but she stood her ground. "Tamen," she said, her voice matching in harshness. There was no love between the two women, and Calwyn knew that she could never bring herself to call Tamen *Lady Mother.*

Tamen stared at Trout and Mica with icy contempt. "I see you have not learned your lesson. How dare you bring Outlanders here a second time? Haven't you caused enough harm already?"

"These are my friends!" Calwyn's temper flared, as it had always flared at Tamen's rebukes. "And how can you blame me for what's been happening here? You are — *abominable!* Shutting our sisters inside the Wall!"

"Our sisters sacrificed themselves willingly," said Tamen in a low voice.

"You liar! Athala was drugged with bitterthorn, I tasted it on her lips! She was still alive when you put her into the ice!"

Tamen stared at her. "You touched Athala's body?"

"It's not forbidden to touch the dead."

Tamen gave a short, bitter laugh. "Not forbidden, no. Nor is it forbidden to dive down the well, nor to leap from the western tower. But it will kill you all the same."

"What's she sayin', what's she mean?" cried Mica, turning pale.

Lia said in her dry voice, "The snow-sickness is spread from skin to skin, chanter to chanter. If Calwyn has touched her —"

"If Calwyn has touched her, she will reap a fitting punishment for what she's done," said Tamen. "It was she who helped the Outlander Darrow, when she should have left him to die by the Wall, as the Goddess intended. And Darrow brought the Merithuran sorcerer after him, who has cursed Antaris with the plague and this endless winter."

"Samis was a powerful sorcerer, and he has done great damage here," said Calwyn, with a glance at Lia. "But the plague, the winter? I can't believe even *he* could do all that."

"I know what I know! How dare you question me!" Tamen's voice trembled with passion. "How dare you show your face here?

Get out of my sight, get back to the Outlands where you belong, and take *them* with you!"

Calwyn tried not to quail before Tamen's fury. Something flashed into her mind that Marna had told her long ago: *Tamen is afraid of you. She knows that your gift is stronger than her own.* Calwyn was no longer a chanter. But Tamen did not know that.

Calwyn drew herself up tall. But when she spoke, though she tried to sound calm and steely, her voice shook like that of a frightened little girl's. "I won't leave. This is my home, and these are my friends."

"For shame, Tamen," said Lia, and Calwyn caught a glimpse of her quiet authority. "This is our sworn sister. She and her friends have journeyed far. They need food, and rest, and shelter."

Tamen turned on her. "I will give them nothing!" she hissed. She swung back to Calwyn. "This is not your home. You are no Daughter of Taris. You are an Outlander, by birth and by blood. We should have cast you out years ago. But no matter — what was left undone then may be done now!" Tamen raised her hand, and her sleeve fell back. Despite herself, Calwyn shuddered with fear.

Tamen's lips parted, and she began to sing. Trout gave a strangled cry, which was abruptly cut off. "Tamen, *no!*" cried Lia.

Calwyn whirled around. Trout's face was frosted with a mask of ice. He clawed frantically at his nose and mouth, sealed by the thickening ice. Instinctively, Calwyn opened her mouth to counter the chantment. Then she remembered. She was helpless.

Quick as a heartbeat, Mica pulled out the Clarion. There was no time to be careful, to measure her breath, and Mica was angry. She blew a ringing call, and flames roared through the kitchens. The long table and benches blazed, and the fire in the hearth flared up over the mantel. Lia screamed, and so did Tamen as flames licked her long robes. Calwyn sprang forward, tore off her own heavy cloak, and threw it around Lia. "Go! Go!" Lia cried, batting at her burning robes. The room was choked with heat and smoke, and Trout's face was wet with melted ice.

As Tamen sang a rapid chantment to damp the flames, Calwyn dragged Trout and Mica outside. Their clothes and packs were smoldering too, though thick wool and leather and rabbit-skins burned less readily than Tamen and Lia's robes. Calwyn pulled her friends down beside her into the deep snow of the courtyard. As soon as the sparks were quenched, she stared about wildly for a place to run. The western tower? It was the most inhospitable corner of the Dwellings, and her favorite bolt-hole when she was a novice. Black smoke rolled from the kitchens; soon Tamen would call for help.

"This way!" Calwyn cried, but before they'd stumbled twenty paces, a dumpy figure darted out in front of them.

"Dear child! Praise the Goddess!"

Calwyn almost groaned aloud. The very last thing she needed now was to be detained by Ursca. But the infirmarian had seized her arm. "Come. Hurry now!" When it was necessary, Ursca could move as briskly as anyone, and she propelled Calwyn and

Mica across the courtyard, through a narrow doorway into a dark corridor. "You'll be safe with me. Come along!" This last remark was addressed to Trout, who stumbled along behind them. "Oh, dear," Ursca sighed under her breath. "A young man!"

Calwyn's sharp hearing caught the sound of voices close by. The searchers Tamen had sent to find the intruders were returning to the Dwellings. Ursca halted at the end of the corridor and put her finger to her lips until the voices had passed.

"We can't stay here!" Calwyn whispered. This passage led from the House of Elders to the Middle House and served as a storage space for spare linen, broken looms, and boxes of candles. It was seldom used, but hardly a safe hiding place. Trout brushed a cobweb from his shoulder and peered about nervously.

Ursca shook her head to silence Calwyn, then eased open the door. "The way's clear. Calwyn dear, you know the old barn beyond the duck ponds?"

"The one that was struck by lightning? But the roof's gone!"

"Only half gone, dear, only half gone, and it's been searched already. Quickly now! Sing a chantment to fill our footsteps."

"But I —"

Ursca was already hurrying over the snow, beckoning them to follow.

"I'll do it, Cal," whispered Mica. At once she sang a high, eerie chantment of the winds that blew soft snow into the gashes of shadow that marked their tracks. Calwyn tried to feel grateful to Mica, but a pebble of resentment lodged in her throat.

Past the apple shed and the New Barn, the little group darted from shadow to shadow. Behind them, one window after another lit up, golden dots in the darkness of the Dwellings.

The Lightning Barn stood on the far side of the ponds. The blackened scar on its roof was clearly visible, and one wall was gone, exposing the raw beams and the hayloft. There was a sudden whirr of feathers and a rush of wind above their heads. Trout yelped, and Ursca gave him an exasperated look. "It's only a white owl, young man — it won't hurt you!"

"Ursca, we can't —" began Calwyn. Trying to shelter inside the empty shell of the barn would be almost as bad as camping in the open, especially now she'd lost her cloak. But Ursca tutted and shepherded them along.

"This way, dears. You too, young man. Go on, up the ladder, into the hayloft. There you are, you see? Snug as a burrower's den!"

Calwyn clambered up the ladder and was surprised to find a cozy space, walled with bales of hay. There was a gap above the hay bales where the icy wind still whistled through, and the hay-lined room smelled of must and damp. A single candle-lamp faintly lit the loft, and a tiny stove sent out a fitful warmth. Mica shrugged off the heavy pack and sank to the floor, utterly exhausted.

"This isn't so bad," said Trout. "Once we fill in that gap —"

Ursca clucked. "That's as high as I could reach, young man! We're not all as tall as dear Calwyn!"

But Calwyn wasn't listening. "Marna! Oh, Marna!" She flung

herself down beside the blanket-wrapped bundle that lay in one corner protected from the draft.

"Careful, dear." Ursca drew her away. "Our Lady Mother is sleeping. Don't disturb her. And you know, of course, you mustn't touch her skin."

Calwyn couldn't tear her gaze from the small, frail figure of the old woman, wrapped in layers of quilts and blankets. The long, silver-topped staff of the High Priestess lay on the floor at her side. "But Lia told me —" She stopped. No, Lia had not said that Marna was dead.

"Safer to let you think the worst, dear. I told Tamen that Marna had died and been buried, may Taris forgive me, a turn of the moons ago."

"What did she say?"

"Do you know, I think she was relieved? Yes, I think even Tamen, bold as she is, would have been unwilling to close our Lady Mother into the Wall, when it came to it. She was glad to have the decision taken from her." Ursca sighed. "Only Lia and Gilly and I know the truth."

"Gilly?" Calwyn remembered Gilly as an empty-headed, silly young novice, more interested in flirting with the village boys than in chantment or her duties to the Goddess.

Ursca smiled sadly. "Gilly has changed. These dark days have changed us all." She leaned over Marna and smoothed her blankets. "Our poor Lady Mother was weakened by the battle with the Merithuran — you remember, dear. She was ill for a long time after that. She was just beginning to recover when she caught the snow-sickness. How it happened, I don't know. I nursed her myself. I have wondered whether Tamen . . ." Ursca's voice faltered.

"Tamen?"

"Only Tamen and I tended her, you see. Someone who was already ill must have touched Marna's skin, it's the only way to pass on the snow-sickness. And certainly that never happened while I watched over her. So Tamen must have permitted — or perhaps even *forced* — But there, I mustn't speak evil where I don't know the truth." Ursca looked around, her manner suddenly brisk and efficient. "Calwyn, dear, would you sing a chantment to melt the snow in those buckets?"

Calwyn opened her mouth, then closed it.

"Well, go on, dear! You'll need water, and I know Taris will excuse the use of magic for such a simple thing, in these dreadful times! I daren't haul the buckets up and down that blessed ladder as well as everything else!"

"Cal's too tired, ain't you, Cal?" Mica looked up quickly. "I'll melt the snow with the Clarion."

But Ursca had heard only the first part of what Mica said. "Of course, my dears, you must all be exhausted." She laid a hand on Mica's head. "This little one is ready to drop! Have you eaten?" She rummaged in a corner of the loft and produced a round of stale cheese, some old flat-cakes, some spander nuts, and a handful of dried apple pieces. "Our dear Lady Mother can't swallow much more than bitterthorn brew now, but I always keep a titbit or two here to tempt her." She looked ruefully at the unappetizing morsels. "Never mind. I'll have Gilly bring you some stew when she comes in the morning. Though Taris knows, there's not much to put in it. Calwyn dear, you must eat and rest. And your friends too."

Trout needed no more prompting. "Thank you," he said fervently, tearing one of the flat-cakes in half.

"Thank you!" echoed Mica.

Calwyn accepted a piece of flat-cake, but she didn't eat it. *I can't even sing up a bucket of water,* she thought bitterly. *Not even that.*

"Oh, dear, there aren't any spare blankets," fretted Ursca as she stoked the tiny stove.

"We got our own sleepin'-furs," said Mica. "Don't you worry 'bout us."

"Shouldn't you go now? Won't they miss you?" said Trout.

"Yes, I mustn't stay any longer. I'm glad you'll be with our Lady Mother, Calwyn dear. Her mind is troubled. I can't be here as often as I'd like, and I fear the Goddess may take her soon. Now remember, so long as you don't touch her skin, you've nothing to fear, no matter what Tamen says. Your friends can tend to her, they'll be quite safe."

Calwyn said, "Mica is a chanter."

"Oh! But — she's an Outlander."

"I were born in the Isles of Firthana," said Mica. "My grandma were a windworker, and so am I."

"Well, fancy that," said Ursca blankly. "A windworker."

"I'll take care of her," offered Trout.

Ursca looked at him doubtfully. "Dear me! Still, I suppose we've no choice, and with Calwyn to watch over you . . . She has a gift for healing, this one! Sleep tight, my dears. Gilly will come to you in the morning. Best pull up the ladder when I'm gone."

Ursca's curly gray head disappeared down the ladder, and presently they heard a faint thread of song as Ursca sang a chantment to fill her footprints with snow. Then the only sounds were Marna's labored breathing and the rustle of mice in the hay. The three looked at one another, subdued.

"I'll see if I can plug that gap." Trout clambered up and started wrestling hay bales into position.

"Cal?" said Mica in a small voice. "I ain't goin' to die, am I?"

"Don't be silly, Mica, of course not. Your skin didn't touch Athala — you were wearing gloves."

There was a silence.

"Calwyn?" asked Trout over his shoulder. "Chanters know other chanters, isn't that what you and Darrow always say? So why can't Ursca and Tamen tell that you're not a chanter anymore?"

Calwyn took a sharp breath, and it was Mica who answered. "There's too many chanters here, Trout — too many!" she repeated with wonder. "S'pose you was sittin' in the middle of a whole flock of gulls, all squawkin' away, and then one goes quiet. You'd never know, would you?"

"I suppose not," said Trout doubtfully as he shoved the last bale into place. "There! But it's still freezing in here."

"Want me to give the Clarion a blast, Cal?"

"All right," said Calwyn dully. "A small one. We don't want to set all this hay alight. And Mica —"

"Mm?"

"You saved us tonight, with the Clarion. But I don't think we should use it as a weapon. It wasn't made for that."

"It were to save Trout!"

"I know, I know. But you could have burned Lia —" With a pang of guilt, Calwyn realized that she hadn't asked Ursca to make sure Lia was all right. How selfish she had become. The disgust in her voice was more for herself than Mica as she said, "We should find another way."

"There weren't no other way!" cried Mica, tears springing to her eyes.

"All right, never mind," said Calwyn sharply. "There's nothing to cry about." Suddenly she was unbearably weary; her bones ached with tiredness. She pulled a sleeping-fur from the pack and made herself a nest in the hay, close to Marna.

She could hear Mica and Trout murmuring to each other; perhaps they were grumbling about her, and the fine welcome Antaris had given them. Mica blew gently into the Clarion. The little horn glowed golden, and a soft, clear note filled the cramped hayloft. At once, the room grew warmer; the lingering smell of damp began to disperse. Calwyn sank down into a dark, warm place, and she slept.

The Dark Chantments

When Calwyn woke, it was still night. The candle-lamp burned low, but Mica had set the Clarion in the middle of the hayloft, where its slow-fading heat could reach every corner. Winds gusted around the barn, shaking the ruined timbers, but they were safe and snug inside. Mica was curled under a fur on the far side of the loft, and Trout snored beside her.

Close by, Marna stirred, muttering in her sleep. Calwyn gazed down at the High Priestess, her features softened in the gentle light. *Don't touch her,* Ursca had warned, but Calwyn was safe. Tentatively she rested her hand on Marna's thin white hair, in the same gesture Marna had so often made. The High Priestess sighed deeply and opened her faded blue eyes.

"Marna, Lady Mother!" whispered Calwyn.

The old woman smiled at her with love and laid her trembling hand on Calwyn's bowed head. "Little daughter," she murmured. "You've come back at last. Calida, my daughter, welcome home."

"Lady Mother, it's Calwyn! Calida died long ago."

The old woman's eyes were closed, almost hidden in a web of wrinkles. Her white hair, which had once shone like a silver crown, hung in damp wisps around her pale, sunken face. "Calwyn, my little daughter," she murmured, and tears seeped from beneath her eyelids. "The Merithuran stole her from me."

"No, no, Lady Mother! I'm here, I've come home. Please, don't cry!"

"Old eyes water," said Marna distinctly. Suddenly her eyes opened. She stared directly at Calwyn, half humorous, half sorrowful, and Calwyn knew that she recognized her. Marna struggled to lift her head. "Help me . . . to sit up. Careful. Give me your sleeve."

Calwyn eased her upright and propped the pillows behind her. The High Priestess was light and fragile in her grasp.

"Calwyn, my child, why did you wait so long? So much . . . to tell you." Marna had to pause after every few words, fighting for breath, and her voice was so faint that Calwyn had to lean close to hear her. "The secrets of the Goddess . . . must not be lost. I should have taught them to Tamen, but . . ." Marna grimaced, leaving the words unsaid. "I waited for you, child."

Calwyn hesitated. She couldn't tell Marna that she had lost her gift of chantment, not now, as she was dying. The knowledge would break her Lady Mother's heart. But was it right for the High Priestess to pass the secret lore to someone who could never use it? Cravenly, Calwyn seized on another way out. "Have you forgotten, Lady Mother? I've never been initiated, I have no right to hear the Goddess's secrets."

Marna smiled. "I have not forgotten. Yes, in strictness, this lore is . . . forbidden to novices. But in dark times, some rules must be broken, so that more important ones may be kept. You have survived the Outlands . . . come back to us. That is initiation enough."

Calwyn swallowed. "I'm not worthy, Lady Mother," she whispered. "Please, don't tell me anything."

Marna's faded blue eyes flashed with their old fire. "There is no one else to tell, child! You must not shirk your duty to the Goddess, to your sisters, to Antaris . . . and the world beyond." The old woman fell back on the pillows and smiled faintly. "There, little daughter. I didn't mean . . . to scold you."

Calwyn whispered, "I would rather be scolded by you than praised by anyone else, Lady Mother."

"No time for flattery," murmured Marna, but Calwyn thought she seemed pleased. The High Priestess shifted against the pillows. "There is a sickness in the fabric of the world, little daughter. . . . Broken, but it can be mended. . . . The Wheel, you must find the Wheel. The Wheel holds the answer. But you will need the Tenth Power to unlock it."

"The *Tenth* Power?" Calwyn stared at her in alarm. There were only Nine Powers of chantment. Marna must be delirious. Almost in tears, Calwyn clasped the High Priestess's hand.

"Secret," whispered Marna. "Secret lore . . . The Wheel . . ."

"The Wheel? Is it — is that an object of power? Like the Clarion?"

"Object of power . . . the Tenth Power, yes." Marna's voice faded; she seemed to be losing her strength. "The Wheel is safe . . . with your friends." She let out her breath in a soft hiss between her teeth. Her eyes closed, and her head lolled back.

"Lady Mother? Lady Mother!"

But the High Priestess was deep in sleep, and Calwyn was reluctant to rouse her. She lowered Marna and tucked the quilts around her. Then, stiff with cramp, she crept back to her corner. Trout and Mica had not woken, and it was the steady rhythm of their breathing that lulled Calwyn into a troubled sleep.

Ursca was right to say that Gilly had changed. If Calwyn hadn't been expecting her, she would not have recognized the girl who appeared at the top of the ladder soon after sunrise. She was older, her face was gaunt, and dark shadows ringed her eyes. The Gilly she had known was always giggling behind her hand; this Gilly looked as if she hadn't smiled for a year. But she embraced Calwyn with the same generous warmth. "It's good to see you! We were so worried about what might have happened to you in the Outlands!"

"Surely you had enough to worry about here, without thinking about me," said Calwyn, and Gilly's face grew sober.

"It's been a terrible time." She moved to Marna's side and began to change the bedding. She wore gloves of white cotton and touched Marna gingerly. "Stay back, Calwyn. You don't have gloves."

Trout supported the sleeping woman with one arm. "It's all right, I'll help."

"Thank you." Gilly smiled at Trout, and Calwyn saw a flash of the merry, flirtatious girl she used to be. Gilly bent over the lantern and replaced the burnt-out candle. "I've brought you porridge and a little meat. There isn't much food for anyone, I couldn't take more than this."

"Don't you worry," said Mica stoutly. "We ain't big eaters." She grinned at Gilly, and after a moment Gilly smiled back.

"If Marna is in pain there's bitterthorn brew here," she said. "Not too much — a sip or two is enough."

"She woke in the night," said Calwyn. "She didn't know me at first."

"Her wits are wandering," said Gilly sadly. "And the bitterthorn makes it worse."

Calwyn's heart sank. She had not told Mica and Trout about her conversation in the night. The Tenth Power, the Wheel, whatever that was — perhaps it was only delirium after all.

She asked, "Gilly, how is Lia? Last night, in the kitchens, there was a fire —"

"Everyone's talking of your firestorm. Durtha was furious, but I haven't seen Lia today." Gilly rubbed her arm across her eyes in a weary gesture. "I can't stay. I'm supposed to be fetching hay for the goats."

The day passed slowly. Calwyn longed to ask Marna more about the secret lore, but the High Priestess slept without stirring.

Not long after sunset, they heard voices in the shell of the ruined barn below, and a lantern flickered, sending shadows swooping across the snow. At once Mica pinched out the candle-lamp and held the Clarion close. "Lucky we pulled up the ladder," breathed Trout, and Calwyn frowned at him to keep quiet. At last the voices and the lantern light went away.

Calwyn stood up. "I'm going to find Lia. I want to make sure she's all right."

"I'll come," offered Mica instantly. "I ain't stayin' cooped up here one breath longer!"

"No, Mica. It's safer if I go by myself."

"Calwyn's right," said Trout. "Remember what Gilly said. You don't want to end up in the Wall, do you — or worse?"

Mica opened her mouth, then closed it again. Something in her face told Calwyn what she'd been about to say: that if she went with Calwyn, she could protect her with chantment.

"I don't need you," said Calwyn, more brutally than she'd intended. "I know the Dwellings, I know places to hide. You'd only be in the way."

This was true, but Calwyn had another reason for wanting to see Lia alone: As one of the senior priestesses, she might know something about Marna's mysterious Wheel.

A hurt look crossed Mica's face, but all she said was, "Be careful, Cal. And take Trout's cloak. It's bitter cold out there."

* * *

Calwyn crept through the Dwellings, clutching Trout's cloak around her. The moons were hidden behind cloud, and Antaris was shrouded in shadow. All was quiet; the Daughters of Taris slept.

As Calwyn crossed the yard outside the bathhouse, she caught sight of another cloaked figure: It was too short to be Tamen. "Good night, Sister," murmured the priestess. It was Janyr, who tended the goats. Calwyn bowed her head and hurried past in silence, her heart thumping. Janyr might think it strange that she hadn't returned the greeting, but she couldn't risk having her voice recognized. Like most chanters, the Daughters of Taris had sharp ears. Calwyn glanced over her shoulder. Janyr had vanished into the Middle House.

Calwyn had decided to look for Lia in the House of Elders. It was near the center of the Dwellings, close to the kitchens, the bathhouse, and the old infirmary, so that the old women could be carried easily from one place to another. It made sense that Lia too would have a room there.

She skirted cautiously around to the rear of the House. No lights showed in the windows. Someone coughed fretfully. Calwyn pushed at the heavy back door and it swung open onto a deserted corridor. Again that restless cough sounded, and a rustle of bedclothes as someone turned over.

Calwyn crept forward. There was a faint edge of light under the last door in the corridor. Calwyn quickened her pace, tiptoeing on the stone flags. The door was ajar. Calwyn could just see a shadowy figure sitting up in bed with a shawl around her shoulders. "Lia?" whispered Calwyn, as loudly as she dared.

"Come in quickly, and close the door."

Calwyn obeyed. The room was very cold, and their breath made clouds in the icy air. Calwyn's cloak was draped over the end of Lia's bed; she seized it gratefully. She could just make out the pale oval of Lia's face and her blazing dark eyes. "Were you burned last night?"

Lia's face twisted. "A little. But I can't feel it. Ursca has put honey on the burns. I'm more concerned about you. Did you touch Athala's body?"

Calwyn looked down. "Don't worry," she said awkwardly. "I haven't caught the snow-sickness."

Lia let out a deep, fierce breath. "Thanks be to the Goddess!" She reached out and clutched Calwyn's hand. "The one who can set us free from this terrible evil must be someone with special gifts. Gifts like yours, Calwyn. We have prayed to Taris to send you back. Ursca and I, Gilly and Janyr, and Rina too . . ." Her voice caught, and she gave a bitter laugh. "Old women, and young girls, and a cripple. None of us is strong enough to defy Tamen. All too tired, and too hungry, to fight."

"But you are strong, you have defied her!" whispered Calwyn fiercely. "In the kitchens, you argued with her. And Ursca and Gilly are defying her every day that Marna lives."

"Marna, yes. She has kept herself alive. Waiting for you!" Lia's face was lit with a sudden, savage hope. "Marna believes you were born for a wonderful destiny. She has great faith in you."

Stricken, Calwyn stared at Lia. How could she tell her that she had no gifts anymore, that she was as broken and helpless as Lia herself?

"Marna told me something — some hidden lore?"

Lia held up a hand to silence her. "I know nothing of those matters. That is dangerous knowledge, revealed to only one priestess in each generation. You mustn't speak of it to me."

"So it is true — not Marna rambling? But what if she dies before she can tell me the secrets? All the knowledge will be lost!"

Lia shrugged. "If everything had gone as it should, the hidden lore would have passed to your mother, and then to you." Her expression softened. "Calida was not the most gifted chanter among us, but she had a light about her — when we were young, we would have followed her anywhere. Maybe even across the Wall, if she'd asked it. She was born to be a leader."

"So were you!" said Calwyn impulsively. "The novices, all of us looked up to you!"

Lia made an impatient gesture. "What's done is done. When Calida died, Tamen became the Guardian of the Wall. Marna made a mistake there; she knows it. That's why she has waited for you. You must learn it all before it's too late."

Close by a hinge creaked. Calwyn shot upright. The light of an approaching lantern showed under the door. Calwyn bolted to the window, pushed it open, and swung herself up and over the sill. When she'd dropped to the snow outside, she reached back cautiously and pushed the window closed. She caught a glimpse of yellow light and Tamen's forbidding figure looming over Lia's bed; she could just hear their conversation.

"Still awake, Lia?"

"You know I find it hard to sleep, Lady Mother." Lia's voice was taut with suppressed dislike.

"You should ask Ursca for a sleeping draft."

"Yes, Lady Mother. I will do so tomorrow."

The circle of light swung around the room as Tamen peered into every cranny. Calwyn ducked beneath the sill, heart pounding. Lia asked, "Have you found the girl?"

"Not yet." Tamen moved closer to the bed and laid her hand on Lia's. "Why, your hands are so cold, sister. Are your feet cold too?"

"Lady Mother, you know I cannot feel my feet."

"Yes, Lia. I know. Just think, if you were to catch the snow-sickness, you wouldn't know until it was too late." Tamen's voice was very soft, but her words were as menacing as if she held poison to Lia's lips.

Calwyn didn't wait to hear any more. Keeping to the darkest corners, she darted around the House of Elders, behind the bath-house and away. Snowflakes drifted down, filling in the marks that her feet left behind.

* * *

When she returned to the loft, she found Gilly, Trout, and Mica all seated on hay bales, talking. Famished, Calwyn fell on the food that Gilly had brought. The peppery herbs in the spiced mash helped to disguise the dull, dusty flavor of vegetables that had been stored too long. She wondered why Trout and Mica had stopped eating, and why Trout's face was so gray. Then she began to listen to Gilly, and her own appetite faded away.

"— and Rina was another," Gilly was saying. "She wasn't even ill. But she'd said things against Tamen. So Tamen poured bitterthorn down her throat and put her into the Wall."

Calwyn put down her bowl, remembering the catch in Lia's voice when she mentioned Rina's name.

Gilly looked directly at Calwyn. "They've been waiting for you, you know. Praying to the Goddess, to send you back in time."

"I don't — I don't know what I can do," faltered Calwyn.

She couldn't help feeling that it was all so unfair. She had traveled back to Antaris, hurt and tired and hoping to be cared for, but instead everyone expected her to take on these enormous problems, problems that she was totally unequipped to solve.

"Don't fret," said Mica, with a squeeze of Gilly's arm. "We'll help you somehow, won't we, Cal? P'raps Trout can build a machine, and we'll bundle that Tamen up like a bale of hay!"

Gilly giggled. "I would like to see that! And the goats, nibbling on her hair."

After Gilly had gone, Mica said decidedly, "Well, she's all right, anyhow."

Trout smiled. "It's your charm, Mica. You are irresistible, you know."

Mica snorted and threw a twist of straw at his head. "Any of that mash left? Reckon I could eat some now."

Calwyn was woken by someone whispering her name. She started up. By the golden glow of the Clarion, she saw Marna staring at her, flushed and wild-eyed.

Calwyn hurried to her side. "Lady Mother, are you all right, are you in pain?"

Marna shook her head. "There's no time to waste. I must teach you" — she paused to draw breath — "the shadow chantments."

"Is that the Tenth Power, Lady Mother?"

"No, no. This must come first . . . the hidden face of the Goddess. Taris is the Mother of death and pain, as well as ice and cold. This is dark magic, child. But no High Priestess can leave this knowledge unlearned. You must be armed against — against evil." Marna closed her eyes, and for a moment Calwyn saw the bones of her skull just beneath her skin. "You must learn the dark chantments that can kill in a dozen different ways, chantments to cause illness . . . to paralyze, and to bring pain . . . put someone into a sleep so deep that only another chantment will wake them."

"Lady Mother, I can't — I can't learn these chantments," stammered Calwyn.

"I understand, child. I felt the same, when my turn came. But without the dark, there can be no light. And dark defeats dark — there are no shadows at moondark." Marna looked directly at her, and said clearly, "I let the sorcerer live. I lacked the courage to act. Do not make the same mistake."

"Lady Mother," whispered Calwyn, her eyes downcast.

"Listen. I must teach you these chantments piece by piece, so their power is not released."

Calwyn was filled with misgivings. This was knowledge that should only be passed from the High Priestess to her successor; without the power of chantment, Calwyn could never fill that role. In any case, it was knowledge that Calwyn did not want, a dark and dangerous power. But she listened as Marna sang the secret chantments, in a soft and quavering voice, section by section, never singing one complete chantment. Calwyn was used to learning things by heart, and she was able to repeat the fragments back to Marna after a single hearing.

It was almost dawn before they finished their strange, murmuring duet. At last Marna leaned back against the wall of the loft. "It is done," she whispered. "I know you will remember. Don't speak of this . . . to anyone."

"Yes, Lady Mother." Calwyn wished with all her heart that she could forget what she had just learned. The malevolent songs writhed and spiraled in her mind like a nest of snakes. The dark chantments were like and unlike the other chantments of ice-call; there was no joy in them. Even hearing them in fragments had sent chills down Calwyn's spine, and when she sang what she had heard, her lips felt numb, as if she'd rubbed them with ice. She would never feel the magic rise as she sang the chantments complete, and for the first time since she'd lost her powers, Calwyn was almost glad of it. She whispered, "And the Tenth Power?"

"Later," murmured Marna. Her eyes closed. "I must . . . rest."

Calwyn too was exhausted. She pulled a sleeping-fur over herself and fell asleep where she sat, close enough to Marna to feel the old woman's breath on her cheek.

Gilly did not come the next morning. The freeze had broken and it was snowing hard; it would be difficult to find an excuse to go outside. With three of them in the barn to see to Marna, it would be an unnecessary risk.

Calwyn rested her aching head on her knees. The shadow chantments whispered in her mind, and so did other voices. *Marna has always had great faith in you.* Lia had faith in her too, and Gilly and Ursca, but she didn't have the courage to tell them there was nothing she could do to help.

Darrow had thought she might be healed in Antaris. He remembered Antaris as a peaceful place, filled with song and light and healing. But there would be none of that for her.

"Cal!" Mica called softly. "She's awake."

Calwyn threw herself down by Marna's side and clasped her soft, wrinkled hand between her own. "Lady Mother?"

Marna murmured something, so faintly that Calwyn could only catch a few words here and there. "No time . . . the secrets . . . this is my punishment."

"No, Lady Mother!" Calwyn spoke in a fierce whisper. "You always taught us that the Goddess doesn't punish —" She stopped. Hadn't she, in despair, wondered if her own loss was a punishment from Taris? But it was true: Marna had always taught them to know a loving Goddess, whose ways might be mysterious but never cruel. Calwyn smoothed the thin, silky hair.

Very slowly and shakily, Marna raised her other hand and touched the end of Calwyn's long plait. "Don't grieve, child . . . for what you have lost."

Calwyn blinked back tears. So Marna knew. How long had she known?

The High Priestess's lips moved. "You live in darkness now, but the darkness will end, as the night ends . . . and the winter turns to spring. What is broken . . . will be whole again."

Calwyn could not speak. Marna's cool fingers rested in her own, reminding her of Halasaa's healing touch. But not all hurts could be healed, and not all winters end in spring, Calwyn thought. Perhaps this winter would never end.

"Lady Mother, please, tell me!" she whispered. "What is the Tenth Power?"

"Find the Wheel." Marna's voice was so faint that Calwyn had to put her ear almost to her lips. "Time for song . . . and time for silence. You must learn . . . to *listen*."

"Yes, Lady Mother."

"We sing, but we are also sung," whispered Marna. "Little daughter, the Goddess sings for me." Her blue eyes closed, and she sighed, as if she had laid down a heavy burden after a long journey.

Calwyn rubbed Marna's cool hand between her own. "Lady Mother? Please, tell me —"

"Calwyn!" Ursca's voice was sharp. "Stand back! It won't help anyone if you catch the sickness too."

Calwyn dropped Marna's hand abruptly. Ursca's cloak and hair were crusted with snow, and her face was pink with cold. She knelt on the floor and gently touched Marna's face with her gloved hand. "Taris whispered it to me, that it would be today! The Goddess has taken her daughter."

Ursca folded Marna's hands on her breast and reverently touched her forehead, her throat, her heart. Even when Ursca unpinned her hair and began to croon the lament for the dead, Calwyn did not believe it.

Mica touched her shoulder; her face was frightened. "Is she dead, Cal?"

"She — she has gone to —" Calwyn's voice choked in her throat. Wordlessly she turned, and Mica's arms went around her. Calwyn clutched her tight and let her tears soak into Mica's tunic, wishing that Darrow were there to hold her. Trout patted her awkwardly on the back.

"No, no!" Calwyn struggled free. "I must help sing."

With shaking hands, Calwyn unbound her own hair and shook it out so that it fell loose around her face. The low, mournful swell of the lament to the Goddess mingled with the doleful howling of the blizzard outside as Ursca and Calwyn did honor to Marna. Then Ursca recited the prayer for the dead, her hands cupped before her. A troubled frown puckered her face, as if to say, *This is not my task, this is one more thing that should not be.*

When the prayer was complete, Ursca covered Marna's peaceful face with the sheet. "She was waiting for you, Calwyn. She held herself here until you returned, and she had said what must be said."

Calwyn dashed the tears from her eyes, and her voice wobbled in childish protest. "But she didn't tell me everything! There wasn't time. She was going to tell me about the Tenth Power, about the Wheel —"

Ursca held up a hand. "Shh! I am not learned in the secret lore, these are not matters for my ears," she said severely. "Whatever our dear Lady Mother left unsaid, you must find out for yourself." The lines of exhaustion on her face were more deeply etched than ever. "Stand aside, dear," she said more gently. "I must wrap the body." She clucked her tongue. "Nothing done properly, no oils, no shrouds! Our High Priestess to be laid to rest in a bedsheet! What has become of us?"

"Let me help," begged Calwyn. "Please!" She took a deep breath. If Marna had known, then Ursca should know too. "No harm can come to me. I — I am not a chanter anymore. I lost my powers of magic half a year ago, in Merithuros."

Ursca stared at her, and put out a hand to steady herself. "Oh, my dear child," she said softly. "My poor dear child. The snow-sickness?"

"No. Not that."

"That Merithuran's work then, no doubt!"

Calwyn smiled weakly. "No, Ursca. I tried a chantment that was greater than my strength. It wasn't Samis's fault. It was my own." As she spoke the words, she knew that they were true, and a small part of the bitter weight she carried lifted from her. "Please, Ursca. I'm not a priestess or even a novice anymore, but I loved Marna. Let me help you."

Ursca hesitated. Then she said, almost to herself, "Yes, it's fitting you should tend her. If you'd stayed, you would have been the one to light her pyre and scatter the ashes beneath the blazetree."

Calwyn felt sick with fresh grief. Traditionally, it was the successor to a dead priestess who lit her pyre. Lia had said the same: that Marna had intended Calwyn to follow her as High Priestess. If Calwyn had stayed in Antaris, everything would have been different. After her initiation, Calwyn would have replaced Tamen as Guardian of the Wall; Calwyn would have been governing Antaris now, not Tamen. If Calwyn hadn't run away with Darrow, there would have been no sacrifices to the Goddess, and Marna would have died in her own bed, surrounded by those who loved her.

Perhaps she would never have caught the snow-sickness. Perhaps there would be no snow-sickness, if Darrow had not come.

Calwyn put the thought from her mind. It was too late now for regrets. Tenderly, she and Ursca washed and dried the High Priestess's body. Trout and Mica sat quietly in a corner of the loft, sensing that this moment was not for them to share.

While Ursca dressed Marna's body in the dark blue robes of the High Priestess, Calwyn combed out the thin, tangled hair and plaited it smooth. Then she fixed it with pins from her own hair, so that Marna looked regal again, as Calwyn remembered her. As she slid the last pin into place, she had never felt so lonely. Ursca wept as she worked, but Calwyn was too numb to cry.

They wrapped the old woman's shrunken body in a sheet, leaving only her peaceful, serene face exposed. After dark, Gilly would drag the body on her sturdy sledge to the village of Anary, where there were people who would help them. Marna would be buried with the common folk in the Anary graveyard.

"That our High Priestess should lie there, not in the sacred valley where she belongs," mourned Ursca, then shook herself. "The Goddess's light shines there as much as anywhere else within the Wall, I suppose. And there are worse things to cry over, these days." She darted a look at Calwyn, who turned away.

Ursca and Lia and the others who had hoped so much from her return would surely feel betrayed, now that her secret was revealed. With a heavy heart and aching eyes, Calwyn bid Ursca farewell and went to sit with Trout and Mica.

"You all right, Cal?" Mica slipped an arm around her friend's waist. "When my grandma died, I felt like someone ripped my heart out." Mica's grandmother had been murdered by slave traders; Calwyn was touched that the younger girl regarded her loss as equal to her own.

"I'm sorry, Calwyn," said Trout awkwardly. "At least you spoke to her before she died."

"Yes." Calwyn hugged her knees and stared across the loft to where the white-wrapped body lay. "A little. But there was so much left unsaid, so much knowledge lost forever. She told me there's a Tenth Power — can you imagine that? But now we'll never learn its songs. I don't even know what sort of magic it is, what it controls. We'll never find out now."

"P'raps we'll find out some other way," said Mica stoutly. "Can't be a whole other power of chantment just *gone*. Everyone thought the Power of Beasts was lost, but you still knew it. And the Power of Fire was lost, only you found the Clarion and saved it."

Trout coughed indignantly. "*I* found the Clarion!"

Mica waved her hand. "*Someone* found it, that's what I'm sayin'. It weren't really lost. And this power won't be neither, you'll see."

Calwyn frowned. "There was something else: a Wheel. Marna said it's an object of power, like the Clarion; she said it holds the answer to ending the long winter and this sickness. We have to find it."

"An object of power. That isn't much to go on," said Trout gloomily.

"Wait. Marna did say — she said, 'The Wheel is safe with your friends.'"

"*Us?*" squeaked Mica. "We ain't got it! If we had somethin' else magic like the Clarion, we'd know it. You could feel the Clarion buzzin' from the bottom of the sea!"

"Darrow then?" suggested Trout. "Could Marna have given it to Darrow before you left Antaris?"

"Don't be a goose!" exclaimed Mica. "He couldn't have carried somethin' magic around for two years without knowin' it, any-more'n we could!"

"Then Marna must've been talking about your friends here in Antaris," said Trout.

Calwyn was silent. She had never had many friends among the sisters. The older priestesses had kept their distance, and so had the other novices. Darrow was the first person she called a true friend; a lump came into her throat at the thought of him. She had spent her time at the top of the western tower, gazing across the forests, or else down in the orchard, with the bees.

Marna had smiled, and her breath went *zzzz.*

With a cry, Calwyn scrambled to her feet. "That's it! That's what she meant! Mica, I need you to come with me. I know where we'll find the Wheel."

The Treasure of the Bees

At nightfall, the snowstorm was raging as fiercely as ever. Mica peered through a chink in the wall. "Gilly ain't comin' through all this. There's bits of ice big as your hand flyin' round out there!"

"Gilly is a priestess of ice-call," said Calwyn. "She'll be able to sing a clear path."

"Here she comes!" Trout ran to let down the ladder, and Gilly's head emerged into the hayloft. She was out of breath and red-eyed; she stole one glance at Marna's white-wrapped body, then turned quickly away, saying, "It's wild out there! I cleared the snow, but the wind nearly blew me down!"

"I could've kept the winds off," said Mica almost shyly.

"That's right, you're a chanter of the winds." Gilly pushed back her hood and the two girls looked at each other for a moment. "We'd make a good team! Could you — would you come with me to Anary tonight?"

"I need Mica tonight," said Calwyn abruptly. "She and I are going to the orchard."

"To the *orchard*? Whatever for?"

"I can't tell you," snapped Calwyn. "It's secret lore Marna told me before she died."

"Oh." Gilly's eyes dropped. "Then I suppose you have to go. But be careful, Calwyn. If Tamen finds you, she'll put you in the Wall with the others. She wants to make an example of you. It was your disobedience that started everything going wrong, she says, and all this is the punishment of the Goddess."

"You don't believe that, surely," said Trout.

"It's what Tamen believes that counts," said Gilly. "Even if she knew Calwyn couldn't sing anymore, it wouldn't make any difference —" She stopped, and bit her lip. "Ursca told me. I'm so sorry, Calwyn. You were the strongest chanter of all of us."

Calwyn could not bear Gilly's pitying look. She felt herself flush. "We must go." She turned away to fasten her cloak and hide the Clarion safely under a pile of straw. "We've wasted too much time already."

"I'll help Gilly with the sled," said Trout. "I can't sing the winds away, but I can help pull."

Gilly gave him a quick, grateful smile. "Thank you." She hesitated over the High Priestess's silver-topped staff. "What should we do with this? It doesn't seem right to leave it here, in the hay."

"I'm sure Tamen would like to have it," said Calwyn bitterly, but Gilly shook her head.

"She's afraid to touch anything that belonged to Marna in case she catches the snow-sickness."

"Well, leave it there," said Calwyn. "It's safe enough for now."

They helped Gilly carry Marna's body down the ladder from the loft. Calwyn felt a pang of distress that they had to drag their beloved High Priestess about like a sack of apples. But, she reminded herself, this was not really Marna. Their Lady Mother had joined the great river that Halasaa spoke of, the First and greatest of the powers, the joyous flow of being that included the Goddess herself and the spirit that animated every living thing. Marna was among the stars, and the whispering leaves, and in the sleeping soil that waited for the touch of spring.

Mica and Calwyn lifted Marna's body onto the sledge and watched as Gilly and Trout disappeared into the whirling snow.

"Ready?" shouted Calwyn. Mica nodded and sang a chantment of the winds to make a tunnel of clear air through the heart of the blizzard, so she and Calwyn could run to the orchard and the river and the beehives.

Before they reached the orchard the wind dropped. Snowflakes swirled around their heads and floated silently to rest. "You can stop singing," panted Calwyn, but Mica shook her head.

"Gotta fill our footprints in."

Before long, the gnarled, dark skeletons of the apple trees loomed from the stark white snow. Clouds scudded across the sky, and the moonlight was fitful; from moment to moment, the landscape was illuminated with silver, then plunged into darkness again.

A faint murmur rose from the dark mound that was the first of the domed hives. Mica hung back. "Is it full of bees? Ain't they sleepin'?"

"Bees don't sleep in winter. But they won't harm us if we treat them with respect," said Calwyn.

Mica screwed up her face. "They'll sting me!"

"They won't sting you, I promise! Come on, Mica. There are twenty hives, we must hurry. All you have to do is tell me if you can sense something inside the hive, an object with power, like the Clarion."

Mica sidled gingerly up to the hive. "Do I have to touch it?"

"Here!" In exasperation, Calwyn grabbed Mica's hands and pressed them to the wall of the hive. Mica yelped.

"Shh! Don't startle them!"

"I'm scared of them bees, Cal!" hissed Mica reproachfully.

Calwyn let go of her hands. What had Marna said to her that very day? *You must learn to listen.* Even Darrow had been wary of the bees at first.

"All right," she said. "You don't have to touch the hives. Just get close enough to tell. I'll listen to the bees, I'll warn you if they stir."

Mica nodded, somewhat mollified. She edged forward, hands outstretched, still expecting the bees to swarm out and attack her. She shook her head. "There ain't nothin' here."

Calwyn tugged her. "Let's try the next one."

Each hive had a name and a history. This one was colonized in the summer Darrow had come to Antaris. This one had a temperamental queen; it had done poorly two years in a row. This one by the bend in the river was a happy hive, Calwyn's favorite; she could distinguish the taste of its honey from any other. And this one, in summer, was always surrounded by clover. It was the oldest of the hives, and a crack ran all the way down its side. But Mica couldn't sense a hint of magic anywhere.

"You sure it's here, Cal?"

"There's still Timarel hive. It must be in there." Calwyn clutched the folds of her cloak tightly under her chin. What would they do, if she had misunderstood Marna after all?

"Cal!" Mica clutched her arm. "Over there!"

Lanterns were swinging down the snow-covered slope between the Dwellings and the orchard.

"Quick! Follow me!" Calwyn dodged past the squat dome of Timarel hive and pulled Mica after her. They darted from one tree's shadow to the next, heading for the wooden shack of the Bee House. No one had entered it for a long time; snow was heaped waist-high all around, even in front of the door. Calwyn felt a twinge of protective fury. Hadn't anyone bothered to tend the bees since she'd left Antaris, given them water, or checked them for parasites? There was more to keeping the bees than collecting wax and honey.

Mica was already singing a high, clear chantment of the winds to blow the snow from the doorway. Calwyn was struck by an idea. "Mica! Bees hate the wind. Could you sing a storm around the hives and stir them up a little?"

Mica nodded, her golden eyes alight, and as soon as the door was clear she launched into a second chantment. A moaning wind threaded between the hives, stirring up a flurry of loose snow that would also hide their footprints. Calwyn heard a distant grumble of anger from the bees. She pulled Mica into the Bee House and fastened the door behind them.

They crouched below the windows, shivering with cold. They could hear the swelling murmur of the bees, roused a second time from their rest, and then shrieks and yells as the sisters stumbled into the maddened guard bees. Mica winced. "Poor things," she whispered, though Calwyn wasn't sure if she meant the bees or the priestesses.

After a time the shouts and yells died away; the searchers turned back to the safety of the Dwellings. But angry words carried through the still air.

"— bees are cursed! Outlander sorcery —"

"— since *Calwyn* ran off."

Calwyn shivered at the hostility in their voices.

Mica whispered, "What now?"

Calwyn glanced through the window, laced with frost. "The Wheel must be in Timarel hive, it's the last one. But the bees are too upset now." Mica's teeth were chattering. "Go back to the barn, there's no need for both of us to stay. Can you find your way without me?"

Mica nodded, then clutched at Calwyn's sleeve. "I know, Cal!

You go fishin' in that hive at sunrise. Me and Trout and the Clarion'll make sure no one's lookin' this way!"

"I don't think that's a good idea, Mica. You and Trout stay hidden. I'll manage by myself."

Suddenly Mica's temper flashed. She stamped her foot. "I'm only tryin' to help you! Ever since Merithuros, you been cross as a shark with no dinner. It ain't our fault what happened. You reckon you can do everythin' by yourself — it ain't true! You ain't such a great chanter no more, you can't do *nothin'*!"

There was a stricken silence as the two girls stared at each other. Then, with a stifled sob, Mica yanked open the door to the Bee House and stumbled away through the snow. Calwyn sank back numbly onto a pile of sacks. She didn't care what Mica said; if she was as cross as a shark, she had every reason to be. And Mica hadn't meant it. She would never have said anything so hurtful if she hadn't been cold, and tired, and scared.

Calwyn pulled her cloak around her. The Bee House was sturdy, but it was never intended to shelter anyone overnight, especially not during a freezing winter. Calwyn forced herself to pace up and down the cramped hut to keep the blood moving in her limbs. Without the Clarion to warm her, this was the first night she had felt the true bite of winter. It would be easy to lie on the floor and drift into a deadly sleep, but she knew she mustn't give in to tiredness.

In the cold and the silence, the shadow chantments squirmed

like a nest of spiders in her mind. Dark, disturbing snatches of song repeated themselves, over and over. Even in fragments, the power of the chantments repelled her. She couldn't imagine using them to kill, or maim, or inflict agony, even if she were capable. And what if it was the only way to save Tremaris? She was glad she would never have to make that choice.

She wished she could talk it over with Darrow, despite the vow of secrecy she'd made to Marna. And with Mica's outburst ringing in her ears, she was engulfed by a wave of loneliness. She missed Marna's wisdom, and Halasaa, who understood her so well, and Tonno's gruff reassurance. Most of all, she missed Darrow. Where was he now? She had never been to Gellan, and she found it difficult to imagine him there. As she shivered in the cold shed, she yearned for the warm shelter of his arms, his quizzical smile, and the humor in his gray-green eyes.

As she fingered the wooden hawk at her throat, she remembered their last embrace on the docks in Kalysons, before *Fledgewing* sailed north, and how he'd crushed her against him, so fiercely that she could hardly breathe. When at last he'd let her go, he strode off without looking back, his fair hair shining in the watery sunlight. But the memory was too painful, and she pushed it away.

The small windows had steamed up with the warmth of her breath. Calwyn rubbed a hole to peer out at the night, unsure if she'd imagined a faint light in the east. The bones of the trees seemed more distinct than before, and she could definitely make out the silhouette of the mountains against the sky. There was the

Falcon, the proud bird's head. Day after day she and Darrow had walked toward that peak, on their long journey through the mountains. She only glimpsed it for a few moments before the dawn mists rolled down into the valley. The bees would be calm now.

As Calwyn crept out of the Bee House, she heard a loud bang, then a distant fizzing sound, then three more explosions in rapid succession. For the space of several breaths there was silence. Then the bells began to clang in a discordant frenzy, very different from their usual calm, measured tolling, and shouts came from the Dwellings. "Fetch the High Priestess! The barns are on fire!"

Mica and the Clarion had made their diversion after all. The sky was streaked with soaring arrows of flame, and Calwyn ran.

She had dreaded this moment all through the long night of waiting. She knew she couldn't rely on chantment to help her, but as she ran through the crisp snow to Timarel hive, she found herself mouthing the words of the old song. Would the bees remember her? Would they blame her for disturbing them in the night? Perhaps they'd always resented her for stealing their honeycomb and scraping up their wax, interfering in their peaceful community; perhaps only the power of chantment had prevented them from expressing their fury.

Timarel hive loomed before her. It was the largest of the hives, guarded by the fiercest bees in the valley. Calwyn hesitated. Once she would have been able to plunge her hand into a hive without anything to protect her but the songs she'd learned from Damyr. But now she knew that those songs were really chantments, spells of the Power of Beasts. She had believed the bees left her alone because they loved and knew her, but now she understood that the chantments had compelled them to obey.

Calwyn sang under her breath, praying to the bees. *Please don't hurt me, please forgive me!* For the first time in her life she trembled before the humming mystery of the hive. Tall as she was, the top of the dome was as high as her head. Moving slowly so as not to antagonize the bees further, she lifted the heavy lid aside as she murmured the song Damyr had taught her. Too late, she realized that she should have brought gloves and a veil from the Bee House.

The bees were stirring. A few guard bees buzzed around Calwyn's face, studying her. First one, then another, landed on her hand. Calwyn forced herself to breathe steadily, not to brush them away. "Bees of Timarel, I mean you no harm," she whispered. "You have been watching over something very precious. But it is time to surrender it. Please, trust me."

Behind her, from the Dwellings, came the sound of shrieks and running feet; the bells still jangled their alarm. "Fire! Fire! Where is Tamen?"

"The kitchens are ablaze!"

"The barns — "

Standing on tiptoe, heart thumping, Calwyn peered down into the hive. The honey-frames hung in a row, patched with honey-comb and crawling with worker bees. One flew up into her face, startling her, but she didn't make a sound. There were bees in her hair, all over her hands, creeping up her arms and her face.

"Bees of Timarel," murmured Calwyn. The bees were crawling all over her face, around her lips and nose. It was like the terrifying illusion that Samis had created, the night he came to Antaris, except that this was real — and this was not terrifying. These were her own bees. Marna had called them her friends, and suddenly she knew that it was true. Their murmuring hum was a song of welcome; she had nothing to fear.

Calwyn plunged her hand carefully into the very heart of the bees' citadel. The tips of her fingers brushed a silk-wrapped object, smeared with honey and wax. As she drew it out, the bees rose from her skin and formed a golden, singing halo that spun around her head.

Calwyn held out the precious thing in both hands and bowed to the hive. "Thank you, bees of Timarel. Thank you, queen and workers, for your vigilance."

Hardly daring to breathe, she unwrapped the faded silk from the small, heavy object in the palm of her hand. The silk itself was old and delicate, shimmering green and purple like a peacock's feather. Calwyn pulled the cloth aside with trembling hands. She held a solid half-circle, a broken disc, made from dark, dense stone, its surface marked with faint, very ancient dents and scratches. One edge was jagged where the Wheel had been snapped in two. Whole, it would have been the size of the circle of her thumbs and forefingers.

Unconsciously Calwyn sank to her knees in the snow. Marna's words came back to her: *Broken . . . but it can be mended.*

Where was the other half?

Calwyn pressed the half-Wheel between her hands, feeling its cold weight. Suddenly she became aware of a growing commotion from the buildings behind her. She thrust the half-Wheel inside her tunic and set off up the slope.

As she went, knowledge came to her, hard and clear and certain. Her task was not complete. She must find the other piece of the Wheel; she must join the two halves together. *It can be mended.* That was the answer that would undo the evil that had befallen the world. Marna had said so. She would need Darrow's help . . .

Calwyn ran toward the Dwellings.

The courtyard teemed with women, all bundled in winter cloaks. No one noticed Calwyn dart upstairs and hide herself behind a pillar where she could see everything below. A knot of priestesses clustered on the far side of the courtyard, and the rest of the sisters craned toward them. "Let me go!" came Trout's desperate cry. A confused murmur ran through the crowd of women.

Calwyn scanned the courtyard. At last she glimpsed Mica peering from the shelter of a dark archway. Mica saw Calwyn too; she stared up with a look that was half defiant, half pleading. She pulled aside her cloak to show that she had the Clarion ready. Emphatically Calwyn shook her head. Mica's mouth had set in a stubborn line, and Calwyn thought that Mica would defy her. But then the younger girl let her cloak fall over the Clarion.

"This boy is an Outlander!" Tamen's deep voice rang out. A space formed around her and Trout and the two strong sisters who held him pinned by the arms. "What shall we do with him?"

There was a moment's uncertain silence. At last someone hazarded, "Put him into the Wall?"

"No!" rapped Tamen sternly. "We cannot sully the Wall with the body of an Outlander! We must take him to the blazetree!"

The crowd buzzed in bewilderment. Calwyn's mouth twisted grimly. The sisters of Antaris might have consented to dreadful deeds, but they had done so reluctantly, and for the preservation of all they held dear. Tamen would have to work hard to persuade them to commit cold-blooded murder.

A thin voice rose from the center of the courtyard. "Lady Mother, the fires burned nothing. The boy has done no harm."

"No harm!" cried Tamen, and her arm shot skyward. "Look at the moons! Now is the time of the Weaver and the Shuttle. The trees should be in blossom, the spring meadows in flower, yet the thaws have not even begun, and snow still falls! Our cellars and storehouses will soon be empty, and every few days another of our sisters is stricken with the snow-sickness. You all know that this evil came to us from the sorcery of the Outlands! And yet you would spare him?"

The sisters swayed and muttered uncertainly. Trout gave a whimper of fear.

Calwyn could contain herself no longer. She braced herself with both hands on the gallery railing and cried out, "The long winter and the snow-sickness are an Outlander's doing! But not *this* Outlander!"

A sea of faces turned up to Calwyn, framed with hoods and shawls, and a shiver of recognition, of horror, of hope and excitement rippled through the priestesses.

"Be silent!" commanded Tamen. "The girl is no better than an Outlander herself. It is she who opened the door to our troubles."

"I'm a Daughter of Taris!" cried Calwyn, her eyes blazing. "You have no right to silence me!"

"I have the right to condemn the enemies of the Goddess."

"I'm no enemy, but a sworn novice of the Dwellings!"

"And I have the right of the High Priestess to reprimand a novice," hissed Tamen. The heads of the sisters swiveled back and forth as if they watched a pair of village boys at pat-ball.

Calwyn said, "By what right do you call yourself High Priestess, Tamen? Did Marna tell you the secrets that belong to the office of High Priestess? Did she give you her staff?"

All the sisters gasped, and a loud hum ran through the courtyard. Tamen said loudly, "There was no time! The Outlander —"

"There was time!" Lia's strong, clear voice rang out from the edge of the courtyard. She had been carried there in her chair, and now she glared at Tamen with open scorn and loathing. "You all know that Marna was not ill with the snow-sickness at first. How did she catch it, with Ursca tending her so carefully? Tamen was her only regular visitor. Perhaps she has the answer to this riddle!"

Tamen's eyes narrowed. "What you suggest is preposterous and unspeakable."

"Not preposterous, only unprovable. Because the poor girl you used to infect our Lady Mother lies cold and silent within the Wall!"

A storm of exclamation broke out among the assembled sisters. Lia spoke clearly through the din. "Marna was alert for a long time before her illness overtook her. But she chose not to tell Tamen the most secret lore. She did not give Tamen her staff. She did not proclaim Tamen as her successor." Lia turned her head and gazed up at Calwyn. "She was waiting for Calwyn to return."

Calwyn flushed. She had not expected this when she challenged Tamen; she had only thought about saving Trout. She took a breath to steel herself.

Tamen shouted, "I was the Guardian of the Wall! The Guardian is always successor to the High Priestess!"

"Not always." Lia's voice was still steady. "Not always."

Tamen threw back her head. "If not for me, you would all have perished long ago. Marna was a weak old woman, too weak to do what had to be done. Antaris must have a leader. None of you had the courage to deal with the evil that has come to us!"

Lia gripped the arms of her chair. "You call it courage, to murder the sick and defenseless? Every one of us in this courtyard has shown more courage than you, living each day in hunger and fear!"

Calwyn found her voice. "Tamen is right. Antaris must have a leader. But there is another way." The faces turned back to her like a field of starflowers turning to the sun. "You, my sisters, may choose for yourselves who is to be High Priestess now that Marna is gone."

Tamen's eyes glittered. "Let them choose!" she cried at once. "Foolish girl! You think they'll choose *you*, a mere novice, not even initiated? A traitor to Antaris, and Outlander-born?" She threw back her head. "Very well, then! Who is it to be? Myself or Calwyn?"

"I do not offer myself!" cried Calwyn quickly. "I offer Lia!"

The clamor of the sisters swelled to a roar. Tamen stood as still as stone. The two priestesses who had gripped Trout's arms let him go and gazed about uncertainly. Calwyn clapped her hands for attention. "My sisters, be quiet! All of you who choose Tamen, move to her side. Those who choose Lia, go to her."

For a few moments there was confusion. The women milled about, talking eagerly; they seized each other's hands, shook their heads, darted this way and that. Ursca and Gilly were beckoning others to Lia's side. Tamen stood with her head held high, proud and unmoving. Lia sat very straight in her chair; just once she glanced up at Calwyn with a steady look.

Suddenly a single impulse seemed to grip the whole assembly. Like a flock of swallows in flight, almost all the sisters wheeled toward Lia. Only a handful of priestesses gathered near Tamen. A hush fell as the sisters, shocked by their own daring, held their breath.

Up on the gallery, Calwyn began to sing. It was not a chantment; she sang the song of thanksgiving that was sung after the
initiation ceremony, when the novices had crossed the black ice and
stepped ashore as new-made priestesses. One after another the
Daughters of Taris joined in, and the song rang through all
the Dwellings. The voices of the sisters swelled with joy and triumph, but Calwyn could not feel it.

Mica seized Trout's hand and skipped round the courtyard in
celebration, waving the Clarion like a victory trumpet. She grinned
up at Calwyn in wholehearted delight. Calwyn nodded to her. Mica
had been wrong: There were some things she could do. It was true,
she wasn't a chanter anymore, but this battle had been fought
without chantment; the only weapons they'd used were words.

Tamen alone did not join the thanksgiving song. She stood
with her head bowed and her fists tightly clenched by her sides.
The sisters who had joined her stepped quietly away. A few glanced
at her apologetically; others would not look at her at all. Only
Calwyn was watching when Tamen reached up and let down her hair,
so that it hung loose around her face, in the gesture of mourning.

Calwyn walked more and more slowly as she approached the room
where Tamen was kept under guard. Half a turn of the moons had
passed since the scene in the courtyard. Winter was no closer to
lifting. Calwyn, Trout, and Mica would leave for Gellan the next
day to find their friends and begin the search for the other half

of the Wheel. Calwyn had been surprised by the message from Tamen, asking to speak with her; she wasn't sure what to expect. Did the older woman want another chance to accuse her of treachery?

Janyr nodded to Calwyn and unbolted the stout door to let her in. "Knock when you're ready, my Sister."

Calwyn stepped into the shadowed room; she couldn't suppress a shiver as the bolt thudded back into place. Outside, the day was clear and crisp, but Tamen had closed the shutters and the room was dark. A single candle-lamp cast a pool of light onto the table. Only Tamen's folded hands were visible, resting inside the circle of light; her face was in darkness. But when Tamen spoke, her voice was as deep and compelling as ever.

"Thank you for coming." She did not invite Calwyn to sit.

Calwyn cleared her throat. "You wanted to speak to me?"

"Yes." There was a silence; Calwyn could hear Tamen's slow, steady breathing. At last the priestess said, with an effort, "Marna — I know that Marna was not dead. She told you — some secrets."

"Yes."

"She told you about the Wheel."

Calwyn hesitated. She did not want to speak of anything that Tamen did not already know. She must not mention the Tenth Power unless Tamen did so first. She said cautiously, "Marna told me that the Wheel held the answer."

"Did she tell you where it is hidden?"

Calwyn said, "I've found it."

Tamen laughed mockingly. "Of course you have. Bravo to you, Calwyn the prodigy!"

Calwyn said slowly, "I must ask for your help, Tamen. Marna said that the Wheel is an object of power. But I found only half of it. Do you know what became of the rest?"

Tamen let out a long breath. "So it has come to this. Calida's daughter, begging for my help. Where is your pride?"

Calwyn swallowed. "If it is a choice between saving Tremaris and saving my pride, then I give up my pride willingly."

"That is the difference between you and me," said Tamen. Her chair scraped back and her hands disappeared abruptly from the circle of light. Calwyn heard the whisper of long robes against the stone floor. When the priestess spoke, her voice came from the other side of the darkened room. "Yes. I know what happened to the other half of the Wheel."

Calwyn drew in a sharp breath. "Tell me!"

"When the Merithuran came, Marna told me to hide the Wheel — to keep it safe, in the hive. But I was not afraid to make the sacrifice — to keep us all safe."

"What did you do?" whispered Calwyn.

"I broke the Wheel. And I gave one part to the sorcerer."

"*You* broke the Wheel? You *gave* it to Samis?"

Tamen's voice in the darkness was hard and clear as ice. "I made a choice. The sorcerer came to steal our chantments of ice-call. I gave him the half-Wheel; I told him that was all we had, and he believed me in the end. It was not easy to convince him, but at last he went away. He could have killed us all. I did not know what would happen when the Wheel was broken. How could I know, when Marna refused to trust me with the secret?"

Calwyn realized she was twisting her hands together. She whispered, "I don't understand — "

"Isn't it obvious? There were dark chantments, secret powers, locked inside the Wheel. When it was broken, those chantments were released. The long winter, the snow-sickness, perhaps worse to come."

The Tenth Power, thought Calwyn. *The darkest chantments of all.* She put her hand to her head. "Worse to come?"

"Chantments to alter the seasons, chantments to strike down every chanter in Tremaris. If the Wheel is broken again, more dark magic will be released." There was a brief silence. "I did not know what would happen. I was told nothing. I begged Marna to trust me with the hidden lore. *She* is the one to blame! Time and again I told her, she must do her duty to the Goddess and pass on the secret knowledge. But even when she knew she was dying of the snow-sickness, when I thought she would have no choice, she refused to tell me —" There was a harsh sound that might have been a sob. "She waited for you. You — you were always Marna's darling. Marna's darling," she repeated bitterly. "And now you have no more chantment in you than a common village girl. Marna was weak. You ran off with your precious Outlander. I was the one who saved us! Yet here I am, trapped like a rabbit in a snare."

Stricken, Calwyn was torn between wanting to argue with Tamen and wishing she could offer her comfort. She faltered. "Tamen, if we could repair the Wheel, would that undo the dark chantments? End the winter, cure the snow-sickness?"

"I cannot answer your questions. I did what was necessary. I could not know that the cost would be — would be so high." Then, in a voice so low that Calwyn could barely hear, Tamen murmured, "The Goddess will forgive me, if you do not."

Calwyn whispered, "My sister . . ."

Without warning, Tamen's pale face loomed out of the shadows, and her bony hand thrust Calwyn away. "Leave me!" she hissed. "Leave me alone."

Calwyn backed away and rapped on the door for Janyr. The bolt rattled free, and she stumbled out into the dazzling light of the corridor. Janyr slammed the door and locked it; seeing Calwyn's face, she laid her big square hand on the younger woman's shoulder.

"She asked for two things this morning," said Janyr quietly. "One was to talk to you. The other was a vial of bitterthorn."

Calwyn gazed at her, not understanding at first. Then she put a hand to her mouth.

Janyr nodded. "She will find her own way to the Goddess."

Calwyn made her way slowly to the big workshop that Trout had taken over. She had never loved Tamen, but the harshness of the older priestess had been as much a part of her childhood as the kindness of Marna, and the thought of Tamen's death held its own grief. At least she knew now what must be done. If the Wheel had unleashed dark chantments, they must find the other half before Samis could use it to release more evil — if it was not already too late. And surely, if the Wheel could be mended, the dark magic would be undone. Calwyn stood for a moment before the workshop door, collecting herself, before she slipped inside.

Mica perched on a bench, watching Trout closely as he bent over his latest contraption, a wheeled chair for Lia. The High Priestess herself sat nearby, resting her hands on the silver-topped staff. Shining steel skate-runners lay waiting on a benchtop, and a long, sturdy sled, also equipped with steel runners, was propped against one wall.

"— the idea from Darrow," Mica was saying. "He made the Grand Council in Merithuros choose if Fenn or Heben would be leader while he was away. Only them two always said they'd help each other, whoever got picked, and you wouldn't want no help from Tamen."

"What'll happen to her?" asked Trout, tightening a bolt.

"She'll be judged, when the time comes," replied Lia. She caught Calwyn's gaze, and Calwyn realized that she knew about the vial of bitterthorn. "Those who helped Tamen did so mostly from fear. Their own remorse will be the harshest punishment."

Mica sniffed. "I'd put 'em all in the Wall if it was up to me!"

Lia said firmly, "No one will be put into the Wall. Those days are past."

The bodies of Athala and all the others had been recovered and given proper funeral rites in the sacred valley. Only Marna's body would remain undisturbed in the Anary graveyard. Those who feared they might have the snow-sickness came openly to Ursca and were housed in an airy dormitory in the House of Elders. There was still no way to cure them, but at least they need not fear they would be sacrificed to the Goddess.

Lia had begun the work of bringing order to the Dwellings, where so much had been neglected during Tamen's rule. The new High Priestess had appointed Gilly as beekeeper. Only the day before, Calwyn had been almost bowled over by Gilly and Mica running helter-skelter to the orchard. "Mica and I are teaching each other not to be scared of the bees!" laughed Gilly, then added uncertainly, "It's only till you come back, Calwyn."

Calwyn nodded, though she was far from sure that she'd ever return to Antaris, and she watched the two girls run off together.

Now Lia offered a hand from across the workshop, and silently Calwyn came forward to clasp it. She didn't want to answer any questions about Tamen, and the High Priestess seemed to understand that without words.

"Lia," Calwyn said in a low voice, out of Trout and Mica's hearing. "I want to pass on the secret knowledge to you, the things Marna told me before she died."

But to her surprise, Lia shook her head. "Only one priestess is permitted to hold that knowledge. Marna entrusted you with those secrets, not me. We must respect her wishes. Don't break your vow."

"But, Lia, I'm no priestess; I have no gift of chantment. I'll never be able to sing the songs Marna taught me."

"*Never* is a word that only the Goddess should use. I'll make a bargain with you, Calwyn. If, when you return to Antaris, you are still without your powers, then you may teach me the secrets you've learned."

Calwyn looked down. She did not want to carry the burden of those malevolent, dangerous chantments alone. "What if I don't return?"

"You will," said Lia simply. In a louder tone, which included Mica and Trout, she asked, "When do you leave?"

"Tomorrow morning, if Trout finishes in time."

Without looking up, Trout said, "I'll finish it. Pass me that small clamp, Mica."

Calwyn slipped her hand from Lia's and paced up and down the room. "We must reach Gellan as quickly as we can. Samis has the other half of the Wheel." She told them what she had learned from Tamen, though not that Tamen had given the Wheel to Samis. She thought, *Tamen will soon be dead. Why should she be hated even more than she is already?* She said, "We must find him, and the Wheel. If it's broken again, more dark magic will be released. Perhaps he doesn't even realize its power, but what if he does? It might be too late already. But if we can mend the Wheel, it will undo all the harm."

"Calwyn!" Lia shot a warning glance at Trout and Mica. "These are matters that should not be spoken openly."

Calwyn shook her head. "I'm sorry, Lia. But I trust Mica and Trout with my life. I must be able to trust them with other knowledge too."

"Too many secrets." Trout wrenched at a stubborn bolt. "Half the trouble in the world's from secrets. Knowledge should be shared freely."

"Some secrets are dangerous," said Lia with a frown. "That is why they are secrets."

"Cal and Darrow's always sayin' we should share the chantments round, not hang onto 'em," said Mica.

She looked fleetingly at Calwyn, who said nothing. Calwyn had dreamed of a college of chantment, where the songs of magic could be learned and shared. But if the snow-sickness spread all over Tremaris, there would be no more chantment. All the songs would be lost, all the chanters dead and forgotten.

Mica was saying, "Then we wouldn't forget 'em neither. My grandma said there's a chantment lost every generation, just from someone forgettin' how to sing it right."

"We guard our magic carefully here," said Lia. "None of the chantments of ice-call has been lost since Antaris was first built."

"How do you know?" crowed Mica. "If you can't remember the chantment, how'd you know you'd forgot it?"

Lia smiled. "We'll miss you, Mica. You keep us from becoming too serious."

To Calwyn's surprise, not only Gilly but all the priestesses had made a pet of Mica. They were fascinated by her exotic looks and chantments, and took delight in her cheeky remarks. If Calwyn had said those things when she was a novice, she would have earned endless scoldings and extra chores, but when Mica said them, everyone shook with laughter.

"Ready!" Trout's tools clattered to the floor as he stood up. "Help me turn it over, Calwyn."

Mica and Calwyn lifted Lia into the wheeled chair. Trout had fixed a pair of small wheels to the front and a large pair to the back. "Someone can push you with these handles. But when you're on flat ground you can push yourself along with your hands. And there's a brake here, see?"

Lia's broad, calm face broke into a rare smile as she wheeled herself across the room. "This is wonderful, Trout!"

Trout blushed. "It's nothing, really. I made a wheeled chair for one of the Masters in Mithates once."

Mica sniffed. "How're you goin' to get that thing up stairs, if you're so clever?"

"Put a ramp over the steps —" Trout broke off. "What's that noise?"

Calwyn and Lia stared at each other. "The traders' gong?" said Lia. "In the depths of winter?"

Calwyn's eyes went wide, and her fingers flew to her temples.

Mica gasped. "Is it Halasaa? Can you hear Halasaa? Is he talkin' in your head?"

Calwyn nodded. Mercifully, her loss of chantment had not affected her ability to communicate with silent Halasaa in mind-speech. "They're here, they're all here! Darrow and Halasaa and Tonno, they're by the Wall, waiting for us to let them in!" She was halfway to the door when she faltered and turned back. "Forgive me, Lia," she said formally. "I forgot to ask. Do you permit them to enter?"

"Darrow? The sorcerer?" Lia hesitated, then nodded her head. "Take a party of the sisters to the Traders' Path, and let the song of unmaking be sung. Your friends are welcome here."

Mica clapped her hands. "Halasaa's a healer! He can mend your back, you'll see! You won't need Trout's chair!"

"Oh!" Trout's face fell.

"Thank you, Lady Mother!" Impulsively, Calwyn bent and kissed Lia's cheek, then flew out of the room, with Trout and Mica close behind.

"May the Goddess go with you, daughter," said Lia quietly. She put her hands to the wheels and pushed herself toward the door.

The Red City

While Calwyn, Trout, and Mica were still skating toward Antaris, their friends Tonno and Halasaa were far away in the north, shivering in a narrow Gellanese street. The overhanging buildings and the faded banners strung between them gave little shelter from the wind, and every few moments the two men were jostled by passersby, heads bent against the cold, hurrying home before dark.

From Kalysons, Darrow, Tonno, and Halasaa had sailed north as far as Nesca, the last port whose harbor was not yet ice-bound. They had left *Fledgewing* there and made the rest of their journey over the sea ice. They'd arrived in Gellan twelve days ago and begun their search for Samis.

They found the Red City in the grip of famine and a plague that afflicted only chanters. Both problems were worsened by the oppressive actions of the Guild that governed Gellan. The Guildmasters took most of the available food for themselves. The Guild's soldiers, known as the Protectors, who were normally charged with keeping the peace, now roamed the streets searching for the sick and hauling them away to the Lazar-House, a forbidding building that had become part prison, part infirmary for the lazars and plague-stricken chanters.

"Nearly curfew," grunted Tonno, and the burly fisherman thrust his hands deeper into his pockets. "Tell Darrow to get a wriggle on."

Thin, copper-skinned Halasaa was calm and untroubled as he replied in silent mind-speech. *There is time before sunset. See, he is coming now.*

For some time, Darrow had been talking with an elderly woman who peered from the doorway of a pinched little house built from the crumbling brick that gave the Red City its nickname. Now at last he raised his hand in farewell and strode back to his friends. His face was grim, and the scar that cut across his eyebrow was matched by a deep frown.

"Samis was here," he said. "No doubt of it. The old woman recognized his description at once. He moved into this lodging house at the beginning of autumn and filled three rooms with his baggage."

"Then we got him!" cried Tonno.

But Darrow shook his head, his face grimmer than ever. "He's gone, and all his boxes with him. The housekeeper didn't know where, or said she didn't. But he'd made preparations for a long journey. He had a sled and enough supplies for three turns of the moons."

When did he leave? asked Halasaa.

Darrow's mouth twisted. "Four days ago."

Tonno cursed and spat into the gutter. Even Halasaa bowed his head in frustration that they'd come so close to their quarry, only to have him slip through their fingers. Four days! It was such a short time, but with Samis's gifts of chantment to speed his sled, there was no knowing how far he could have traveled.

He could not have left this crowded city unseen.

"Halasaa's right." Tonno looked up. "The Guild mans the watchtowers night and day, even now the harbor's frozen over. *Someone* must've seen where he was headed. A few coins in the right pockets —"

"Spoken like a Gellanese," said Darrow wryly. "But there is something else." He glanced over his shoulder and lowered his voice. "Samis shared the house with another man, a chanter called Tragg. The two of them were as close as two coins in a purse, according to the old woman. The day Samis left Gellan, she went up to clean Tragg's room as usual and found him —"

Dead. Halasaa finished the sentence.

"Murdered," said Tonno. "So, Samis had secrets, did he? Did the old one know what they were up to?"

Darrow took his companions by the elbows. "People are staring. Let's walk on. She was too frightened to tell me much. But she did say that she overheard Samis and Tragg arguing about the lazar-sickness, and something about a wheel."

Tonno snorted.

"They were excited, speaking loudly." Darrow hunched his

shoulders inside his jacket. "It's not much," he admitted. "But it's all we have —"

Without warning, a group of half a dozen uniformed men burst from an alleyway. All were dressed in skirt-coats of muddy green and brown, and brandished long whips. Before the three friends realized what was happening, the Protectors had surrounded Darrow, separating him from the others, and two whips were twined around his arms to hold him fast. Passersby drew back. In a city filled with chanters, no one but the Protectors would touch a lazar.

"Hey! *Hey!*" shouted Tonno. "Let him go!"

The captain shrugged. "Darrow the ironchanter? You're under arrest."

"You've made a mistake." Darrow's voice was calm. He could have used a chantment of iron to free himself from his bonds, but the Protectors were clustered close around him and could soon overpower him. "You have no authority to detain me. I've broken no law, and I am no lazar."

"Look at his skin, you fools, you can see he's not sick!" cried Tonno.

"Guild orders," said the captain impassively. "He's going to the Lazar-House."

At that, Darrow did open his mouth. But before he could begin to sing, one of the Protectors viciously jerked his head back and stuffed a gag between his jaws. With a cry, Tonno drew out his short, sturdy fishing knife and launched himself at the soldiers. But the tip of one whip flicked the knife from his hand, and a second curled around his legs and brought him down. The crack of another whip knocked Halasaa to the ground. No one moved to help them; people hurried on as Darrow was half-dragged, half-shoved away.

Tonno struggled painfully to his knees. "Got to follow 'em," he panted, groping for his fallen knife.

"Not tonight, my friends," came a musical voice beside them.

Halasaa looked up at a woman with emerald-green eyes, her face thickly painted and powdered in the Gellanese fashion. She wore a brightly colored turban, and her dangling earrings clashed and jingled as she held out her hands to help the two men to their feet. "My name is Matifa. Come, I live across the way. It's almost curfew, and I can help you."

"Help us how?" growled Tonno, rubbing his head. Twelve days among the tricksters and liars of Gellan had made him suspicious of any friendly advances.

"Come *on*, come inside!" Matifa's wide-striped skirts rustled as she ushered them along the empty street. "This is my house. Your friend gave someone cheek, did he?"

"He's done nothing."

Matifa clucked her tongue as she propelled them into the narrow house. "The Protectors think they rule the streets these days, it's a public disgrace! Look at someone sideways and they clap you in the Lazar-House. That's what happened to my cousin's husband's sister's boy — I was too late to help him, but I can help you! Not tonight, it's too late tonight, but tomorrow. Tomorrow, we'll have your friend out of the Lazar-House, easy as winking!"

"Why should we trust you?" Tonno scowled.

"Why should I trick you?" countered Matifa, stretching her green eyes wide. "What profit would there be for me? Only trouble if I'm caught. You know what they say: no profit, safe promise!"

"They don't say that where I come from," said Tonno sourly. He and Halasaa exchanged a glance.

Halasaa's voice sounded in Tonno's mind. *We must trust her, my brother. At least for now.*

"If you say so," grunted Tonno, and gave the beaming Matifa the grimace that, for him, passed for a smile.

The next morning Tonno and Halasaa were in the dark cellar of Matifa's lodging house, tugging at a trapdoor in the floor, while their new friend held up a lantern. Tonno couldn't help thinking that, with her powdered face, she looked like a little girl who'd fallen into her mother's flour bin.

All three stepped back as the trapdoor flew open and the putrid odor of the sewers erupted into the cellar. Tonno gagged, Matifa covered her face with an embroidered handkerchief, and Halasaa's face paled beneath his spiraling tattoos.

"Sure you won't come with us?" asked Tonno wryly.

Matifa blinked above the mask of her handkerchief, and her turban shook vehemently. "No, I'll stay," she said in a muffled voice. "But I wish you all speed and profit! You remember the directions?"

Halasaa nodded, and replied in his silent mind-speech. *We should reach the Lazar-House by midday.*

"And you're sure this is the only way in?" muttered Tonno.

"Poor man!" sighed Matifa, and her bright skirts rustled as she handed the lantern to Tonno. "Locked up in *that place!* Off you go now, and fortune go with you!"

Thank you for all your help. Halasaa could never remember that the Gellanese did not thank each other. It was considered a shameful loss of status, an admission that you had not paid a fair price for something.

"Good-bye, good-bye!" muttered Tonno as they descended the slimy ladder into the knee-deep stream of filth that ran through the tunnels. "I won't deny she's helped us, but that woman can't keep her mouth shut long enough to take a breath."

The sewers of Gellan were almost as old as the city itself, and they were in an even worse state of repair than the crumbling red buildings above. For hundreds of summers and hundreds of winters, the waste and filth of the city had slopped through the ancient tunnels. The contents of chamber pots, blood and entrails from the slaughterhouses, murk from the famous Gellanese dye pans and paint shops, vomit, rancid food scraps, animal droppings, all washed into the gutters with every fall of rain.

The sewers followed the line of the most ancient streets above, more or less, and Matifa had given Halasaa and Tonno detailed directions to the Lazar-House. Occasionally a faint splash echoed through the tunnels, or a steady trickling sound marked the place where a gutter flowed in. Always, they heard the squeak and skitter of rats. Far above their heads came a distant rumble of carts and tramping shoes, while their own feet sloshed through the sludge below.

"Glad I didn't wear my best boots," muttered Tonno. "How does Matifa know so much about the sewers, anyway?"

She said her husband was an engineer before he died.

"Lucky for us."

The Gellanese do not believe in luck. Halasaa's voice was serious. *Everything must be paid for.*

"I've paid plenty, listening to her yabber on till my ears ache," growled Tonno.

Take the next right turn. Halasaa's words sounded serenely in Tonno's mind.

"Can't be far now, thank the gods." Tonno's lantern threw grotesque shadows up the curved walls of the tunnel, which was partly carved from sheer rock and partly built from reddish bricks. Something large and sodden swirled past them on the stream, and Tonno's lantern dipped suddenly as he jumped out of the way.

Peace, my brother. It is only a dead dog.

Tonno grimaced. "Hope Darrow's grateful for this."

Left here. This is the last turn.

This tunnel was the narrowest yet; both men had to bend their heads, and the river of filth rose until it almost reached their thighs. The floor of the tunnel was very slippery, and only Tonno's quick hand prevented Halasaa from plunging under.

Look there. Halasaa pointed to a set of steps cut into the wall ahead. *They must lead to the Lazar-House.*

"I hope so," Tonno grunted. "I'm a seaman. I wasn't meant to creep around underground like a rat."

Halasaa smiled. *We won't return this way. Darrow can open the locks with chantment, and you and I will shield him from the touch of the lazars. We are not chanters, the sickness cannot harm us. We will all walk out together.*

Tonno looked down at himself. He was spattered with muck, and his legs were caked with foul slime. Halasaa was even filthier. "I never walked the streets of any town, looking like this. And even after a turn of the moons at sea, I never smelled so bad."

Steadying themselves against the slick, mossy wall, they scraped off as much dirt as they could, then squelched up the steps. The door had been installed for the use of the sewer engineers; it was bolted on the inside and obviously had not been opened for many years. With a mighty effort, Tonno forced the bolt and peered out into the Lazar-House.

As soon as the door swung open, they realized there was no need to be quiet nor to worry what they smelled like. The place stank almost as much as the sewers, though the smell was different, a fetid waft of stale bed linen and urine and musty air. Trouble-makers and sick chanters alike were dragged to the Lazar-House by the Protectors, and once imprisoned, the lazars could earn greater comforts by acting as guards. There was no one to care for the ill, to change their sheets or strew sweet herbs.

Halasaa and Tonno had been expecting the hush of the sick-room or the grim silence of the dungeon, but the Lazar-House rang with shouts and groans. Somewhere nearby, a tin cup scraped against stone, while someone screamed, *"Shut up!"* A tuneless song echoed through the corridors. There was a tramp of boots and a clatter of plates, and a handbell clanged while one of the guards bawled, *"Dinner!* You miserable worms, wriggle out and get yer dinner!"

Tonno touched the hilt of his knife. "Ready?"

Halasaa nodded, and they moved off down the corridor, leaving the door slightly ajar.

The Lazar-House was heavily fortified on the outside; the walls were made of thick stone, and the high windows were all barred. But every internal door gaped open, and the inmates wandered freely about the place. Listless men and women shambled down the corridors and slumped in doorways.

Halasaa spoke into Tonno's mind. *Do not walk so straight, my brother. You must try to look ill.*

"That's not hard," muttered Tonno, queasy from the stench that clung to them.

Anyone who looked closely would have seen that their faces were not pale enough for lazars, especially Halasaa with his coppery skin, but they were filthy and bedraggled enough to blend in with the other inmates, and no one gave the pair more than a casual glance as they shuffled through the Lazar-House. The green-and-brown uniforms of the Protectors were nowhere to be seen.

"Where's Darrow, I wonder?" muttered Tonno.

Halasaa grinned. *Why not ask?*

Tonno snorted, then shrugged. "Why not?" And he thrust his head around the nearest doorway.

A group of four men, wrapped in striped blankets, sat on dirty straw, playing clumsily at knucklebones. They glared at Tonno. "You want something?"

"Prisoner called Darrow," growled Tonno, just as surly. "Know where we could find him?"

A man with thinning hair and a sly face like a weasel looked up with a faint spark of interest. "Darrow, the ironcrafter? What's it worth?"

Tonno grimaced. Nothing in Gellan came without a price; they were prepared for this. "Two silver bits."

"Make it six, that might jog my memory."

"Four."

The weaselly man shrugged, and Tonno handed over the silver pieces.

"They got him gagged and guarded, up in Traitors' Tower. That way — the tower in the south, overlooks the grave pits. Where they keep the dangerous ones. You won't get in *there* just by asking."

Tonno began to thank him, then stopped. Instead he said, "If you want your freedom, there's an open door to the sewers."

The four men looked at one another. One of them chortled. "Freedom? What's that worth? There ain't nothing for the likes of us out there. In here they feed us and give us a dry place to die."

"Your friend know you're coming for him?" The weaselly man gave a ghoulish grin. "Maybe he'd rather stay here."

"He's not sick," Tonno said through clenched teeth.

A sour-faced man chuckled. "Maybe he weren't sick before. But I'll bet you a gold bit he's sick now."

With one swift movement, Tonno jerked him to his feet. "Liar!" he snarled.

Halasaa laid a hand on Tonno's arm. *Peace, my brother! The man is ill.*

Tonno gave the sour-faced man a shake, like a dog with a rat, then threw him aside. As he and Halasaa made their way down the stinking corridor, he said fiercely, "Darrow wouldn't *let* himself get sick."

Darrow is strong and quick-minded. Do not fear for him.

Tonno grunted and they walked on. But both were more anxious for their friend than they were prepared to admit. "All these Gellanese are liars, curse them. Can't trust a single one of 'em."

There is good and bad inside every Gellanese, my brother, just as there is inside every other person.

"Every person? So there's good inside Samis, is there, may his bones rot?"

Even Samis is not wholly evil. He wishes to unite Tremaris and for the lands to help each other. That is a wish we all share.

Tonno snorted.

A group of lazars were shuffling into a cramped dining hall where some kind of slop was being ladled out of vast cauldrons. Half a dozen Protectors in their green-and-brown skirt-coats, and some lazar-guards with checkered armbands, lounged against the walls, looking bored and yelling abuse. One of them glanced up as Tonno and Halasaa passed the doorway. His eyes met Halasaa's. The man stared at him, unblinking, then his eyes flickered away, as though he was willing them to disappear.

Strange, mused Halasaa, as he hurried after Tonno. *He seemed to know us, and yet he let us pass by.*

Tonno walked faster. "Mebbe they don't care if anyone breaks in. Everyone inside these walls is going to die, no matter what."

We will not die, my brother. And nor will Darrow.

They made their way cautiously through the Lazar-House, until they emerged onto a bare, windswept terrace. The dull red flagstones underfoot were slippery with snow, and the edge of the terrace dropped away steeply, with no wall or guardrail. Far below spread a bleak field, dotted with stones and ringed by a high wall. The sky was a leaden canopy above the city, almost low enough to touch.

Fighting the wind, Tonno peered over the edge of the precipice, then recoiled. At the foot of the cliff were dozens of bodies, sprawled where they had fallen. The deep cold had preserved their flesh; no one had collected the corpses for burial or burning. "These Gellanese don't respect the living nor the dead. Look at that! Just throw the bodies over and leave them there to rot!"

Halasaa looked somber. *I wonder how many throw themselves down, rather than wait for death.*

Tonno turned away with a shudder and stared up at the round tower that reared above the terrace. It was a grimy reddish-brown, the color of dried blood. "This must be Traitors' Tower."

They found a blackened door; it was locked, but Tonno's sturdy fisherman's boot made short work of the rotting timbers. The two lazar-guards inside were taken by surprise. Tonno felled one with a well-aimed blow to the jaw, and Halasaa wrestled the second to the ground. With Tonno's help, he deftly bound both guards with the lashes of their own whips and used their gloves to gag them.

"That was easy," panted Tonno. "Thought there'd be more guards."

Yes. Halasaa frowned. *Very easy.*

Tonno was already thudding up the stairs. Dozens of tiny cells honeycombed the tower. The knucklebone players were right: Every door was bolted shut. One after another, Tonno and Halasaa flung open the doors and pale, wretched figures stumbled out. These were true prisoners, the enemies of the Guild, and they didn't wait for explanations. Those who could walk staggered down the stairs, barely glancing at their rescuers in their haste to be gone. Those who were too weak to move cried out feebly, but the stronger ones ignored their pleas for help.

"Darrow? Where's Darrow?" shouted Tonno.

"At the top!" came the reply, and Halasaa and Tonno sprinted up the winding stairs.

Tonno yanked back the last bolt and threw open the door. Darrow was sitting upright on a bench beneath a high window, unbowed and seemingly unharmed. Chains bound his wrists and ankles, and he was gagged with a grubby strip of cloth. Darrow's gray-green eyes came alive with a mixture of delight and anxiety. Tonno's knife flashed from his sheath, and with a single cut the gag was gone. Darrow rasped out a chantment, the chains fell away, and Tonno pulled him into a glad embrace.

"Thank the gods! You all right?"

"I'm not infected." Darrow stepped back. "But my luck could not have held much longer. Come on!" He led the way, pelting down the steps, stumbling slightly on legs stiffened by the cold.

They were quick, but not quick enough. At the foot of the stairs a group of Protectors was waiting. The tip of a whip flickered through the air. Tonno cried out; his hand flew to his cheek and came away stained with blood. Darrow threw back his head and with fierce energy growled out a song of ironcraft. Instantly the whips twined in the air like searching snakes, tangling the arms and legs of the Protectors, writhing into knots. The guards yelled and swarmed up the steps. Tonno unsheathed his knife with a roar and strode down to meet them. Halasaa kicked out and sent the nearest Protector sprawling back on top of his fellows.

Step-by-step, the three friends fought their way forward, down the stairs, then out onto the terrace. It was sleeting hard. Darrow sang fiercely; his chantments tripped the Protectors' boots beneath them, made gloves fly up to hit their owners in the face, and twisted whip handles from the grip of those who held them. An icy wind blasted across the terrace, driving everyone back against the wall.

Slowly, slowly, Darrow and the others struggled across the slippery flagstones. Sleet stung their faces. One by one the Protectors fell, tangled in the lashes of their own whips or slumped on the stones. "This way!" cried Darrow. The wind tore the words from his lips as he beckoned his companions toward the edge of the terrace.

Tonno gripped Darrow's arm. "Have you lost your wits?" he yelled, his thick black eyebrows crusted with ice. Darrow shrugged off his hand and bent forward into the wind.

Look out! Halasaa called a warning. Another group of guards had burst from the building behind them, a mixture of Protectors and lazar-guards with their checkered armbands. Darrow glanced over his shoulder. He mouthed to the others, *Come on!* and fought against the wind toward the precipice. Tonno and Halasaa followed through the driving sleet.

The yells of the guards and their drumming footsteps were lost in the screaming wind. Darrow was close to the cliff; he launched himself forward and slid on his stomach to the edge. With a howl, one of the lazar-guards leapt after him and gripped his ankle just above the boot. Darrow kicked wildly, but couldn't shake him off; his trousers ripped, exposing bare skin, and the lazar-guard wrapped both hands around Darrow's shin.

A big, dim shape loomed like a bear out of the sleet. Tonno grabbed the lazar by the shoulders and wrenched him aside. Darrow wriggled forward and disappeared over the precipice.

Come, my brother, come! Halasaa was at Tonno's side, tugging him onward. Tonno screwed up his face, then plunged.

An arm's length below the edge, the cliff angled back steeply into the red rock; somehow the three managed to cling with fingers and toes to clefts and crevices, their cheeks pressed against the icy stone. For a few moments they hung there; above their heads the guards scanned the drop, shook their heads, and, unable to see the fugitives, let themselves be driven back, whipped by the wind, into the shelter of the Lazar-House.

Stiffly, Darrow moved one limb, then another, groping for handholds. Where he could, he used chantment to deepen the cracks in the rock where the others clung, or carved out new ones. Little by little they eased their way down, until they came to a narrow ledge where they could rest for a time, buffeted by the freezing wind. After that, the going was easier, and they crawled down, aching all over, but alive, to the foot of the cliff where the frozen bodies of the lazars lay tumbled.

Tonno hammered on the door of Matifa's house. Behind him, Darrow and Halasaa stamped and shivered, their hair dusted with snow. The afternoon's storm had helped to conceal them; the streets were almost deserted, with people forced inside by the driving snow and sleet.

"Open up, for pity's sake!" Tonno roared, and his fist was raised to strike again when the door opened a crack and Matifa's emerald eye peered out. At once Tonno shouldered his way inside. "We need blankets — hot soup — a fire!"

He shoved past her and up the stairs into the stuffy, overcrowded parlor, with its garish wall-paintings and fat-bellied stove. Halasaa whisked the striped blankets off the couches and threw one to Darrow. Matifa stood in the doorway, her hands pressed to her mouth, her cheeks flushed beneath their rouge. "Didn't you hear me?" barked Tonno, tugging off his grime-caked boots and throwing them into a corner. "We need hot soup, something to warm us. We're frozen through!"

"I'll fetch some tea," said Matifa, her bright eyes gleaming with excitement. "And something better: a surprise!" She winked mysteriously and whisked from the room, with a busy rustle of her layered skirts.

"Just the tea will do!" growled Tonno, then, turning to Darrow, "Come on, man. Take off your coat before it freezes to your back."

Darrow had let the blanket fall unheeded from his shoulders. In a low voice, he said, "The fellow who grabbed me on the terrace. Was he a Protector? Or —"

Tonno shook his head. "A lazar."

"I see." Darrow's face was expressionless. "Halasaa, can you tell if I — if he's given me the sickness?"

Silently Halasaa stood and laid his hands on his friend's head. Darrow's hair was plastered to his skull, dark as wet straw. *I am sorry, my brother.* Halasaa's words were infinitely gentle.

Darrow let out a harsh breath and dropped his face into his hands.

Halasaa gripped his shoulder. *I can help to ease the outward pains, the cold in the hands and feet. And I can slow the disease. Your powers will not fade for a long time.*

"But you can't heal him!" said Tonno bitterly. Halasaa had helped several afflicted chanters since their arrival in Gellan, but he had not succeeded in curing anyone.

Halasaa looked troubled. *I have never known a disease that the Power of Becoming could not heal. And I thought, because I am no chanter, that the illness could not touch me. But perhaps my own gifts have been weakened by this plague.*

"You think so?" Tonno snorted. "Come and test your powers on this." He indicated the slash on his cheek from the Protector's whip. Halasaa touched it with his lithe brown fingers and began the swift complex movements that made up the dance of healing, tapping and soothing the hurt skin. When he lifted his hands away, the cut had vanished as if it had never been. "You see?" grunted Tonno. "Nothing wrong with *you.*"

Darrow turned away and pushed some sticks into the crackling stove.

The door creaked open, cups rattled on a tray, and there was a self-important rustle of skirts and draperies as Matifa came in. "Here I am!"

There was a brief, stunned silence, then Tonno choked out, "*You* —!"

Darrow was so astonished that for a moment he forgot what he had just learned; he could only gape.

There stood Keela, once the Third Princess of the Merithuran Empire, half sister of Samis. The year before, Darrow and Calwyn and their friends had thwarted her attempt to seize the throne of the Empire for herself and her half brother. But even before the Republic had been properly established, she'd escaped. They had guessed that she'd fled to Gellan to join Samis, but there had been no news of her since her disappearance.

She was dressed in Matifa's colorful clothes, but the huge turban had vanished, revealing smooth golden hair scooped back into a simple bun. She had scrubbed away the mask of thick Gellanese face-paint, and her own large, ice-blue eyes gazed out with an expression of cool, arrogant triumph.

"Gellanese sorcery!" muttered Tonno.

Keela gave a trilling laugh. "Not at all, darling! Let me show you." She bent over her cupped hand. When she straightened up, her eyes were a brilliant emerald-green: Matifa's eyes. "Simply paint and a turban and chips of colored glass, and behold! Your sympathetic friend! Isn't it *delicious?*"

Keela clapped her hands together. She was so beautiful, and so childishly delighted, that for a moment even Tonno was tempted to indulge her. He could scarcely believe that they'd been fooled so easily, by eye-color and costume and paint. Admittedly all their contact with Matifa had taken place in darkened streets, or windowless rooms shrouded with draperies, but that was usual in Gellan. He stepped toward her, fists clenched as if he could only just restrain himself from strangling her.

"In the name of all the gods, what game are you playing?"

Keela pouted. "Aren't you pleased that we're all together again? Tonno, Halasaa, and of course Darrow. Such an *extraordinary* man! If only dear little Calwyn were here! But I must content myself with having the Lord of the Black Palace in my parlor. What an honor!"

"That's enough," said Darrow coldly.

Halasaa shook his head. *You cannot expect us to be happy to see you.*

"But I've been *terribly* helpful! Didn't I tell you how to rescue dear Darrow? Didn't I lend you my lamp? Where is my lamp, by the way? You don't mean to say you've *lost* it?"

"Was that your idea of a joke? You sent us crawling through the sewers like rats!" roared Tonno.

Keela tossed her head, and her frivolous manner vanished. Her face hardened. "Half the Guild is — how do the Gellanese put it? — in my coin-pocket. Luckily I was able to bring a few jewels with me when I was forced into exile after your *little rebellion* in Merithuros, enough to buy some favors. My spies have been watching you since you arrived."

"I don't believe you," snarled Tonno.

"Wasn't Darrow arrested as soon as I gave the signal?" said Keela smugly. She snapped her fingers. "And then, of course, *helpful* Matifa was able to tell you the way into the Lazar-House. How could I resist such a delicious charade? I haven't had so much fun since the Palace of Cobwebs!"

Halasaa spoke quietly into Tonno's mind. *It is like Keela to send us through the sewers for her own amusement. And the guard in the dining hall pretended he did not see us, and those at the foot of the stairs did not fight back.*

"And all the time she was sitting here, like a spider in a web," growled Tonno. "Pity she didn't tell *all* the guards about her little scheme. Then Darrow could have been spared the lazar-sickness —"

"Oh, dear!" Keela clasped her hands together. "What a shame!"

"You!" Tonno thumped his fist into the wall. "You did it on purpose — you *planned* it, you ordered them!"

"No, no!" protested Keela. "I swear it, on my father's life."

Your father is dead. Halasaa was expressionless.

"It doesn't matter," said Darrow dully. "No chanter can enter the Lazar-House without expecting to become infected." Automatically his hand moved to the place on his finger where the Ring of Lyonssar had been; but he had left that behind in Merithuros, so it could offer him no comfort. He held his hands to the fire, staring at them, front and back, as if he had never seen them before.

Keela pulled a sympathetic face. "I'm *so* sorry. But your clever friend here can heal you."

"Your spies are not as well-informed as you think, Keela," said Darrow. "This is a sickness Halasaa cannot heal."

Keela flashed him a look, then lowered her eyelashes and toyed with the teacups. She might have been pretending to be surprised by this news, or pretending *not* to be surprised: It was impossible to tell.

Tonno glowered at her. "And where is your brother? Or is he your lover? I never was sure about that."

Keela tossed back her head. "We of the royal blood do not live as you petty commoners do. Samis and I have a unique bond. You could never understand."

"Is that so?" sneered Tonno. "If you're so close, why didn't he take you with him?"

"He — he wanted to protect me from the rigors of the journey."

"What journey? Where's he gone?"

Keela's eyes were cool and defiant, calculating. "I'll tell you everything I know, on one condition. When you go after him — and I know you *will* go after him — you must take me with you."

"I'd rather take one of the rabid dogs from the market square," snarled Tonno.

"Darrow? What do you say?" Keela swung around with a swish of her skirts.

Darrow did not look up. "Did Samis ever speak of a wheel? What do you know of the chanter Tragg?"

Keela sniffed. "That boring old man? Day after day, the two of them were shut up together, they never let me hear what they were talking about. But no, let me think, there was something about a wheel," she added hastily. "Yes, I remember, of course, there was a missing piece. It's a magical thing, isn't it?"

"Don't listen to her, Darrow." Tonno turned away in disgust. "She's saying whatever she thinks you want to hear. I don't believe a single word that comes out of that pretty mouth!"

"Let Darrow make his decision." Keela pouted. "Will you let me help you? Will you take me with you?"

Darrow stared into the fire. "It's a ridiculous idea. Keela, your brother and I are sworn enemies. If we meet again, it must end in death for one of us."

"Oh, yes, I know." Keela brushed this detail aside. "And no doubt you believe *you'll* be the one to kill *him*. But I know that he'll never be defeated, certainly not by *you*, especially if you're ill. So let's agree to disagree on that point, and meanwhile, we can help each other. I'll pay for supplies, for everything we need, if you'll take me with you."

Darrow crossed to the window. Pushing aside the heavy curtain, he leaned his forehead against the cold stone. The sprawling warren of Gellan was laid out below: the narrow, winding streets with their overhanging buildings; the red-tiled roofs, wet with grimy snow; the blunt fingers of the watch-towers by the frozen harbor, and the tiny ships trapped there. With his back to the room, he said, "There is no reason for us to agree and every reason to refuse."

"Pardon me," said Keela silkily. "I'm afraid, if you don't agree, I will have you all killed. You can buy anything in Gellan, including assassins. You couldn't hope to leave the city alive."

"And what makes you think you'll be safe with us, Princess?" asked Tonno. He drew his knife and pointed the blade at her. "What's to stop us slitting your throat, right here and now?"

Keela smoothed her wide, garish skirts. "I know what manner of men you are. Put the knife away. You will not use it."

Tonno glared at her. There was silence in the room. Then Tonno swore under his breath and slid the knife back in its sheath.

Suddenly Keela launched herself across the room to clutch at Darrow's sleeve. "You must take me, you *must!* No one else will do it, no matter how much I offer. Not in this winter. I could buy galley slaves, but what use would they be? You are experienced travelers, by land and sea. You've traveled the Wildlands before. I'm stronger than Samis thinks, I'm not afraid. But I can't go after him alone!"

"The Wildlands," said Darrow in a tired voice.

You think he is returning to the Lost City, to Spareth? asked Halasaa.

Tonno said, "If he did have some *thing* — not that I believe her — that'd be the place to use it."

"If he goes to Spareth overland, he will pass close to Antaris," said Darrow.

"Is *that* where little Calwyn is? I did wonder — you haven't quarreled, have you, darling? Well, she'll be quite safe there. No need to involve *her* in all this."

"That's for us to decide!" growled Tonno.

Darrow said, almost to himself, "I would like to be sure that he hasn't harmed her."

Keela smoothed her hair with a sly look. "Well, isn't it time for one of your famous *votings*?"

"Your wits must be as scrambled as the egg I ate for breakfast," said Tonno. "I suppose you'll want us to warm your boots and curl your hair and wait on you every step of the way! I'm not scared of your hired assassins. You're not coming with us, and that's flat."

Wait. Unexpectedly, Halasaa held up his slim brown hand. *We should listen to her.*

Tonno rounded on him. "Did the fumes in the sewers turn your wits?"

Halasaa's dark eyes had a faraway look. *The fate of Tremaris lies in the balance. And Keela . . . Keela is a part of the unfolding.*

Tonno shook his head. "So you can foretell the future now, as well as mending broken bones?"

No, my brother. I do not have that gift. I see shadows and dreams, that is all. But part of what she has told us is the truth.

Tonno snorted. "Which part?"

Halasaa spread his hands apologetically. *I do not know.*

"It seems the vote is yours, Darrow," purred Keela.

Slowly Darrow turned around. He stared searchingly at Halasaa. "You are sure of what you say, my brother?"

As sure as I can be.

Darrow nodded. Abruptly he turned to Keela. "There is much

to be done, and no time to waste. We are going to Spareth. We will stop at Antaris and collect Calwyn and the others. You and Tonno and Halasaa can plan what we will need."

"And where are you going?" asked Tonno, startled.

"To rest." Darrow rubbed his finger over the silvery scar that marked his eyebrow. "Forgive me," he said in a low voice. "I am — very tired."

The three who remained in the room stared for a moment as the door closed behind him; they all heard the slow, heavy tread of his feet as he walked up the stairs.

Tonno shook his head. "Seems we're going, whatever I say. Well, if you're paying, Princess, there's no need to hold back." He rubbed his hands together briskly. "We'll need a new sled, food, tents and groundsheets, sleeping-furs. Can you remember all this, Halasaa?"

"A hairdresser, my jewel-box, mirrors . . ." Keela ticked off the items on her fingers. "Dear me, darlings, don't look so horrified! Can't you tell when someone's making a *joke*? I fear this is going to be a *very* dull journey!"

The Frozen Forest

As soon as the gap in the Wall was wide enough, Mica flew through it and straight into Tonno's arms. "Calwyn were all set to leave tomorrow, hey, what'd you say then? This is Antaris, it ain't like I thought — I got so much to tell you! Did you find Samis? Is he dead, oh, say he's dead, go on!"

"How can I say anything while you're strangling the breath out of me?" growled Tonno, folding her in a bear hug.

Trout leapt forward to pump Halasaa's hand and ask a dozen eager questions about their journey and Gellan. The small group of priestesses who had sung the chantment of unmaking hung back, wrapped in winter cloaks. And Calwyn hung back too, looking for Darrow. When he stepped from behind the big sled, fair hair gleaming above his dark cloak, her heart rose into her throat.

"Calwyn," he said.

She nodded; she couldn't speak. Halasaa spoke into her mind. *My sister, is all well with you? Have your powers returned?*

She shook her head. Halasaa and Darrow exchanged a swift, unreadable glance, then Darrow stepped forward and wrapped his

115

arms around her. Calwyn pressed her cheek against the rough cloth of his cloak. Then, over his shoulder, she saw the fourth figure, standing apart from the others, wrapped in a fur-lined, cherry-colored cloak, a faint smile playing about her lips. Calwyn's mouth fell open.

Tonno was muttering to Trout and Mica. "— traveling with us. She says Samis has gone to Spareth, got some story — most irritating woman I ever met — not far behind him, we've seen his camping places. Darrow thought he might have stopped here —"

The former princess tripped daintily across the snow to kiss Calwyn on both cheeks, just as if they'd met at a grand ball at the Imperial Court. "Darling Calwyn, how delightful to see you again! Isn't Darrow a *wonderful* traveling companion? So amusing, so considerate! We sledged all the way from Gellan on the sea ice, then along the rivers, day after day, and he hasn't let me suffer a single moment's discomfort!" The princess slipped her arm possessively through Darrow's.

Calwyn stared from Keela to Darrow and back again. Darrow shook off Keela's hand. Without a word, he nodded tersely to the priestesses and stalked along the path to the Dwellings.

"Poor boy!" murmured Keela. "So brave! His illness is troubling him, of course, but he never lets us take proper care of him, and he *insisted* on singing all the way . . ." She shook her head and sighed, and set off after Darrow.

"Illness?" cried Calwyn. "What illness?"

"He caught the chanters' plague in Gellan." Tonno put his

strong arm around Calwyn's shoulders. "But Halasaa's helping him, he'll be right for a good while yet."

"Chanters' plague? The snow-sickness?" The chip of ice in Calwyn's heart spread its coldness through her body.

It is here too? Halasaa was grim.

"It began here. The sisters had an object called the Wheel. Tamen broke it, and it released dark magic. I have one part, but Samis stole the other. If we can mend it, we can undo the evil —" Calwyn spoke distractedly, her eyes fixed on Darrow's dark, slim back, and Keela's red cloak billowing as she ran up beside him. Keela's light, musical laugh drifted back to her.

Tonno whistled. "The Wheel, eh? Darrow'll want to hear this. And a missing piece, just like Keela said — So she's told the truth for once in her life, has she?"

"Darrow's wits has turned like a bucket of fish guts in the sun, to think of bringin' her along!" said Mica.

"I hoped we'd seen the last of her," said Calwyn.

Peace, my sister! It was Halasaa's turn to hug her. *There will be time to tell our stories. Come, help us bring the sled inside.*

On the way back to the Dwellings, Calwyn walked beside Mica, some distance behind the others. "Cal," said the younger girl, after a long silence. "I want to talk to you."

"What about?" Calwyn was barely listening as she craned to see what had become of Darrow and Keela.

"When you leave, Cal —" Mica drew a deep breath. "I ain't comin'."

"What?"

"I want to stay. I like it here. I been talkin' to Gilly, we reckon if we work together, we could melt the ice and keep the snow away. Then the grass might grow and the goats could feed and make more milk. Or we could even get some veggies started. Worth tryin', anyway."

Calwyn was so startled she hardly knew what to say. "But we need you, Mica! How will we keep the storms away, and . . . and clear the ice and play the Clarion?"

"You got Darrow to do that now. Reckon the sisters need me here more'n you will." Mica set her mouth in the stubborn line that Calwyn knew well.

"But Darrow's ill!" said Calwyn sharply.

"He's all right. Halasaa said so. He *looks* all right. He's walkin' quicker'n we are! Even if it is only to get away from Keela," she muttered.

"Mica! How can you be so selfish?"

"I'm tired out, Cal!" cried Mica. "I weren't born to the ice and snow, like you, I hate it, I hate it! And I ain't goin' off into the forests again, to live in a tent and be cold all day and night and never feel my toes, and be snufflin' all the time!"

Calwyn was white with rage. "Do you think any of us enjoy being cold and living on burrower meat and stale bread? Don't you realize how important it is that we find Samis and the other half of the Wheel? After all we've been through together —"

"After all we been through, I reckon it wouldn't kill you to give me a kind word now and then!" cried Mica. The two girls halted in the middle of the path, breathing hard.

"So that's what this is all about," said Calwyn quietly. "You think I haven't been *kind* to you."

"Well, you ain't."

"I'm sorry if I've hurt your feelings," said Calwyn stiffly.

Mica waved her hand dismissively. "My feelin's ain't hurt, it ain't that, I don't care what you say to me. But you ain't the same, Cal. I feel like I don't know you. You been like a sister to me. But now — well, I reckon you're the one what's selfish. I know you got good reason to be miserable and mean-mouthed. But that's all you ever are! It's like there ain't no one in the world 'cept you."

"Be angry with me, if you like," said Calwyn after a pause. "But what about the others? What about Tonno and Trout and Darrow? They need your chantments too. You'll be hurting them just to punish me."

"It ain't to punish you!" burst Mica. "There you go again! It ain't all about you! I told you already, I'm tired, I want a rest. Trout don't mind if I stay."

"You've spoken to Trout about this?" Calwyn was shaken; this felt like the greatest betrayal of all. The two girls stood in silence for a few moments longer, while their breath drifted across the path.

"You come back and fetch me when you're done with Samis," said Mica awkwardly. "I'll be waitin'."

"And what if we don't come back?" said Calwyn. She thrust her hands into her pockets and strode away, leaving the small, lonely figure of Mica behind.

It seemed to Calwyn that the time they'd spent in Antaris had vanished as swiftly as a dream, and she had woken again into a journey through the hushed, still forests that had never been interrupted. But she had said farewell to the sisters; she had exchanged a silent, awkward hug with Mica; and now they were headed southwest, following the course of the river downstream toward the great jagged mountain that Halasaa's people called the Peak of Saar, and then to the distant sea, where Spareth lay. Darrow and Tonno, the navigators of the party, stared at the quivering needle of Trout's which-way just as intently as they gazed up at the stars.

Darrow droned out a steady chantment of iron that sent the two sleds flying along the ice. The skaters were pulled along behind, careful not to let their lines tangle or catch their skates on ice flaws and debris that Mica would have blown out of their way.

For the first few days, the weather stayed clear. Snow-laden branches stretched overhead like the roof beams of a great hall, and the only noise was the hiss of their skates on ice. Icicles glittered like diamonds from every branch, and the heaped snowdrifts shone with stark blue light.

But then black storm clouds gathered, and they had another reason to miss Mica when the blizzards struck. They lost half a dozen days while the storms raged, squashed into the tents, huddled around the Clarion, sipping endless cups of steaming broth.

"You see?" said Keela. "If you'd let me bring some of those *unnecessary luxuries,* how much better off we'd be! We could have played fan-bones or eaten sugar-balls or strung beads." She sighed, then brightened. "But there's no reason why we couldn't have a poetry tournament! I'll begin . . ."

"Don't!" said Calwyn.

Darrow said wryly, "I thought we could not be more uncomfortable, but Keela seems determined to prove me wrong. Please, no poetry. Unless Tonno will take the first turn?"

"I'll tell you when I'm ready," growled Tonno, and that was the end of the tournament.

We must hope that Samis too has been trapped by the storms. Halasaa held out his hands to the Clarion's golden glow.

Trout shivered under his sleeping-fur. "We could have caught up with him, if Mica —" He saw Calwyn's expression and broke off. "Probably not."

"I'm surprised we're so close behind him," said Tonno. "Reckon he'd go quicker than this."

When Keela was out of the tent, Calwyn whispered, "Samis mustn't have known that the other half of the Wheel was in Antaris. He must be going to Spareth to search for it."

"So he can fix it?" hissed Trout. "Why would he want to do that?"

Darrow frowned. "Remember what Tamen said? The Wheel holds other dark chantments. Perhaps that's what Samis discovered in Gellan. It could be mended, then broken, mended, then broken again — and a different evil released each time."

"But Samis was in Spareth two years ago, and he had the half-Wheel," said Trout. "Why didn't he look for the missing bit then?"

Calwyn said, "But the winter, the snow-sickness, it all began slowly. Last winter was harsh, but not like this, and chanters didn't begin falling ill until after he left Antaris. Samis can't have worked out that the Wheel was to blame until he arrived back in Gellan."

It might have been Tragg who realized the truth, Halasaa pointed out. *From all accounts, he was a learned chanter.*

"Could Samis have gone to Gellan specially to talk to him?" wondered Trout.

"Squeezed out what he knew like juice from a mango fruit," grunted Tonno. "Then *phht!*"

Calwyn laid her hand on Darrow's arm. "If we can mend the Wheel, we will mend the world."

"I pray you're right." Darrow looked away and said under his breath, "Not everything that's been broken can be mended. Don't hope for too much, Calwyn."

He laid his hand over hers, but removed it almost at once as Keela pushed back inside the tent, shaking a crust of snow from her cloak and hood.

Calwyn tried to find a chance to talk with Darrow, but during the storm-bound days they all crowded into the larger tent and it was impossible to be private. He was resolutely cheerful, but Calwyn knew that his jokes and flippant remarks were a mask for his anger and his grief; his feelings were a shadow of her own.

Watching Calwyn as she brewed roseberry-leaf tea for Darrow and cleaned his boots, Trout was reminded of the small, loving attempts that Mica had made to comfort Calwyn. And he could see how, just like Mica, Calwyn tried not to be hurt by Darrow's silence.

At last the storms passed, but the sky remained heavy with brooding cloud, and for a day or two they were slowed by snow on the ice. But every day they saw signs of Samis's trail: a ring of blackened stones, a string of broken branches, and once the fresh remains of a trapped burrower, skinned and gutted.

That night, after Keela had retired into the girls' small tent, Calwyn took out the broken Wheel in its silken wrapping and turned it over in her hands. It was strange to think that this scratched chunk of dark stone could hold such deadly power and, at the same time, the hope of saving all Tremaris.

"Calwyn!"

Tonno was calling to her from near a gap in the trees. She carefully rewrapped the half-Wheel and thrust it deep inside her jacket before she clambered up to join him.

"Your eyes are sharp, lass. You see anything over there, in the next valley?"

Calwyn stared hard. After a moment she said, "A fire."

"*Him.* Who else could it be?"

"Do you think he can see us?"

Tonno shook his head. "I always make sure we're well hidden."

The two stood close while their breath rose white, gazing at the far-off flicker that could have been a distant star. They both knew that they would not tell Darrow; they didn't want to tempt him to try to reach Samis's fire that night. As the only chanter among them, he had to play the Clarion as well as drive the sleds onward, and he needed rest. But the fire was close enough for Calwyn and Tonno to want to keep the knowledge from Keela. Tonno turned away. "Time to sleep, lass. Skies are clear, we should have a long run tomorrow."

But Calwyn was slow to join Keela in their tent. She returned to the embers of the dying fire and stared up at the sky. Two moons bobbed low above the line of peaks to the west, and a spangle of stars was flung across the darkness of the east, like phosphorescence on a dark ocean.

Darrow had gone into the woods to empty the cooking pot. Calwyn saw him clearly in the moonlight as he returned, his head bowed; his footsteps were black indentations on the snow's blank silver. Softly she called to him, "Good night, Darrow."

He looked up, startled from his reverie. "Good night, dear love."

He had spoken from the heart. Even in the moonlight, Calwyn saw his face flush. She lowered her head, feeling an answering heat in her own cheeks. She heard the snow crunch beneath his boots as he strode to her, and then she was in his arms, and his lips were on hers. Calwyn's heart leapt into her throat. He murmured in her ear, an explanation or an apology, she couldn't make out the words.

"Calwyn!" Keela's imperious voice rapped out from the mouth of the small tent. "Hurry up, I want to seal the tent. It's freezing in here!"

Calwyn and Darrow sprang apart. "Go," whispered Darrow with a rueful smile. "We can talk another time."

It isn't the talking that I care about! lamented Calwyn to Halasaa in mind-speech, as she curled up crossly beside Keela. *I'm sure Keela interrupted us on purpose.*

Do not blame Keela. Since the day you met, you and Darrow have taken turns to push one another away, like children squabbling.

Calwyn smiled in the dark. *You're right.*

Halasaa's voice was sober. *There will be time to make up your quarrel with Mica. But do not wait too long to mend your friendship with Darrow, my sister.*

Calwyn did not answer.

The next day, as usual, they had to chivvy Keela out of the tent, and, as usual, she grumbled as she emerged into the cold, clutching her fur-lined cloak around her throat. "Why can't I sleep a little longer? It isn't even light yet! I don't want breakfast."

"You're lucky we woke you at all," growled Tonno. "If it was up to me, we'd let you sleep till we were well away."

"Now, darling, you know you'd never do that. You'd miss me *far* too much!" purred Keela.

Halasaa smiled to himself as he gazed at the line of the mountains and the curve of the river ahead.

"What is it?" asked Calwyn.

These forests are known to me. We are entering the lands of the Spiridrelleen.

"But Spiridrell is near the sea! We're a long way from where we first met you, Halasaa. These can't be the same forests, surely?"

These are the winter forests. He placed a picture in her mind: Tree People, huddled in caves for shelter, seeking food among the snowy trees. She remembered as he showed her that winter was especially difficult for his people, and she was ashamed that she had forgotten it until now. She touched her friend's arm. "Tonno and I saw a fire last night. Perhaps it belonged to some Spiridrelleen, not Samis after all."

Halasaa smiled a little sadly. *I think it must have been Samis, my sister. There are no Tree People here now.*

"I didn't know the Tree People came so close to Antaris, Halasaa. I could almost have seen you from my tower!"

I did not realize it either, Halasaa admitted. *But we have not come so far north for many years. Now we keep farther south, to make the journey shorter for the old ones and the children. There are fewer of us now than when I came here with my father. Every year, fewer. Every year, weaker.*

Calwyn was silent, wondering how the Tree People were faring in this hardest of winters. Halasaa had been treated harshly by his own people, but he was still one of them. As if he understood her without words, Halasaa smiled. *I will know if we come close to my people. I will tell you, Calwyn, when they are near.*

Thank you. But Calwyn turned away with a twinge of pain, knowing that a year ago she would have sensed the presence of the Tree People in the forests without Halasaa's help. He was the last of his people to have the gift of the Power of Becoming, and the discovery that Calwyn shared it had filled him with joy. Though the Power of Becoming was expressed in silent dances, not songs of chantment, Calwyn had lost that ability when she lost her other powers of magic, and she knew that Halasaa's sorrow for her, for what she had lost, had been compounded with the extra grief that he was alone once more.

As Tonno had predicted, the day was fine and the air crisp. By the time the sun had risen, they were out on the frozen river. Darrow's rhythmic growl of ironcraft droned beneath the hum of sled runners and the hiss of skates. The morning sun turned the snowdrifts on the bank to dazzling white, and Calwyn narrowed her eyes and blinked against the glare.

No one was prepared for the chantment that roared out of the forest and struck like a leaping roancat. The front sled, towing Darrow, Trout, and Keela, was wrenched violently sideways and slammed into the second.

The first sled tipped up, spilling its load of packs and bundles, while Darrow managed to fling himself clear. But Trout and Keela collided with the toppled sled and sent it crashing down so hard that it cracked the ice. Calwyn's breath exploded from her lungs as she was flung into the capsized sled. A jagged chasm split the ice apart; black water yawned beneath.

Tonno yelled, "It's Samis! Look out!"

Just in time, Darrow's strong hand seized Calwyn's and yanked her clear. The unmistakable throat-song of ironcraft was droning, not from Darrow, but from on the bank; Calwyn glimpsed a dark figure among the trees.

But the chantment was drowned out by the creaks and groans of the ice and Keela's shrieks of panic. She was a child of the deserts, and the water terrified her. The next instant, the ice gave way, and the first sled plunged into the black water. Trout's fingers scraped across the ice as he was dragged in after it, his skates tangled in the tow rope. Tonno lunged for him.

"No!" cried Calwyn and threw herself at Tonno's legs, for if he added his weight to the weakened ice, they would all go under. She called silently to Halasaa, who lay sprawled and winded beside the second sled. *The pole!*

Darrow was singing. Gradually, the nose of the submerged sled lifted from the river, but Trout still floundered in the freezing water. As Calwyn helped Halasaa to free the long, sturdy pole they kept strapped to the sled for just this purpose, she scanned the bank for Samis, but the shadowy figure had vanished.

Flat on their stomachs to spread their weight, Calwyn and Halasaa thrust the pole across the ice to Trout.

Reach out, my brother! called Halasaa. Blindly, his lenses lost, Trout clutched at the pole with numbed hands, and Calwyn and Halasaa hauled him from the water. Little by little, Darrow eased the dripping sled onto thicker ice until it was safe. Tonno gripped his knife between his teeth and crawled to the sled so he could cut through the rope that tangled Trout. Only then did he shout, "Where's Keela?"

But Keela had gone.

Clutching Trout, sodden and shivering, Calwyn fought for breath as she stared up and down the bank. *There!*

Halasaa nodded; he too had caught the scarlet flash of Keela's cloak between the black brushstrokes of the tree trunks. *She has gone with him.*

"Let her go!" barked Tonno. "Good riddance to her!"

"Which way?" demanded Darrow.

"I didn't see!"

It is too late. Only Halasaa was calm. *They are gone.*

"Too late? Aye, it's too late! We should have wrung her pretty neck when we had the chance!"

"Peace, Tonno, peace! We must get everyone dry and warm." Calwyn glanced around wildly. "The Clarion! Trout, where's the Clarion?"

Trout patted his clothes helplessly, squinting all around.

"I — I don't know."

"Did that rogue take it, as well as half-drowning us all?" roared Tonno.

Trout's shoulders slumped. "I must have dropped it into the river."

Calwyn's hand flew to her own jacket. The dense nugget of the Wheel was still tucked safely into her pocket; the silken wrapping was not even damp.

"If the Clarion's at the bottom of the river, I'll find it," said Darrow grimly. "Even if I have to pick out every last stone on the riverbed."

"You can't do that!" cried Calwyn.

Darrow glared at her. "I haven't lost my chantment yet."

"I wasn't —" Calwyn stopped herself. "I mean, we haven't time to wait. Tonno and Trout are wet through."

"You're not exactly dry yourself." Darrow frowned at her. "And what's *this*?" He snatched up her hand.

Blood was dripping bright red on the snow; she had sliced her hand open on one of the sled runners. She hadn't even been aware of the pain, but now the sight of the blood pouring out made her feel sick.

"Must've been waiting for us, the dog," muttered Tonno darkly.

"We saw his fire last night." Weakly Calwyn let herself lean back against Darrow, but he seized her shoulders angrily.

"You knew he was so close and didn't tell me? Didn't you *think*? How could we have caught up to him, unless he had waited for us? You know he does nothing, nothing, without a plan!" With a rough shake, Darrow pushed Calwyn away from him.

Halasaa was there; he caught Calwyn's hurt hand between his, and she felt the warmth of his touch as he began the dance of healing, his fingers tapping and kneading her flesh. *This will stop the bleeding. I will complete the healing later. Can you wait, my sister?*

Calwyn nodded. Her hand was stiff and swollen, and the red weal across the palm throbbed, but the cut was closed. The real pain had come from Darrow's fury.

Halasaa laid his warm hands on her shoulders. *There is shelter nearby. Come.* Swiftly, he extracted sleeping-furs from the dry sled and wrapped up Trout, then beckoned him to climb aboard. *The rest of us will pull; it will warm us. This way.* Already he had picked up a rope and begun to pull the laden sled up onto the riverbank. Tonno and Calwyn sprang to help him, and Calwyn winced as the rope bit into her injured hand.

Darrow called after them, "I'll stay and search for the Clarion."

We will leave a trail for you, my brother. We will not be far. Halasaa trudged down the thickly wooded slope. At times there was scarcely room for the sled to pass between the trees. Twigs snapped, and branches shook down snow on top of them.

"You all right, lad?" panted Tonno.

"Y-yes." Trout's teeth were chattering. "B-but I wish I'd asked D-Darrow to look for my l-lenses."

I will ask him, my brother.

Calwyn's hand throbbed painfully now, though she'd wrapped it in a fold of her cloak, and at every stumbling step her bones jarred, as though they had turned to brittle ice.

Halasaa led them down into a hollow, and there, hidden from

above, were the dark mouths of several caves. The nearest was partly
screened by a curtain of long-dead ivy; Halasaa held it aside as
proudly as if he'd led them to a palace. *Come. There is room inside for
us all.*

Calwyn ducked beneath the frozen lattice of ivy and gingerly
straightened up. But though the entrance was low, the roof rose
steeply inside and there was plenty of room to stand. The cave
reached so far back into the hillside that at first she couldn't see
the rear wall, but as her eyes adjusted to the shadows, she saw
sleeping ledges, lined with dried grasses, cut into the rock. There
were other, smaller shelves that held earthenware pots and plat-
ters, folded animal skins and woven cloths like those Halasaa had
once worn. There was a hearth-place, ringed with large stones,
close to the opening, and firewood was stacked neatly along one
side of the cave. Calwyn picked up something from the floor. It
was a bone brooch, carved with flowers.

Trout and Tonno stumbled in. Halasaa moved quickly around
the cave with his customary grace. *Help me to lay a fire, Calwyn. We
must have warmth.*

Awkwardly, Calwyn piled wood inside the blackened circle of
the hearth-ring. "But without the Clarion, how will we light it?"

Even in the dim light, she saw his teeth flash in a grin. *You think
the Tree People have lived so long without flint and tinder?* Without hesita-
tion, he crossed to one of the smaller shelves and found the fire
tools. He crouched beside the hearth, and soon a tiny flame licked
at the kindling.

Is this your place, Halasaa? Unconsciously she slipped into mind-speech.

Mine? No. I have come here with my father. But it is not mine, not as you and Mica speak of your cottage on Ravamey, or Tonno of his boat. The caves belong to all the Tree People.

Halasaa fetched wooden frames from another cave to hang their clothes, and more cloaks of stitched burrower hide. *These are old, worn cloaks, not very warm,* he explained. *But they will serve.* He sat down cross-legged beside Calwyn and took her hurt hand in his to finish the work of healing.

Tonno began to make soup from dried meat, beans, and the few withered vegetables that remained from their stores. Trout squatted near him, wrapped in burrower skins; occasionally he put his hand to the bridge of his nose, forgetting that his lenses were gone.

Drowsily, Calwyn leaned back and stared at the shadowy paintings on the cave walls. "Who are these people, Halasaa? I've never seen paintings like these before."

I do not know. They are just wall-pictures, like the carvings on the walls of the Palace of Cobwebs.

"I prefer these," said Calwyn. "They look alive."

In the wavering firelight, the figures seemed to stamp and whirl across the roof of the cave. Compared with the elaborate decorations of the Palace of Cobwebs, these paintings were simple, but the lean, energetic figures overflowed with life in a way that the stiff Merithuran friezes could not match. Halasaa's fingers pressed and brushed over the palm of Calwyn's hand with their own silent, insistent rhythm, until she almost felt that she could hear the beat of drums in time with the steady pulse of her own heart. The cave held her in a comforting embrace, as if Tremaris itself cradled her. The endless winter had prevented her from feeling the warm earth, from seeing green shoots push through the soil, hearing the whisper of growing things . . . As she sat there, Calwyn fell into a dreaming doze.

At last there came the thud of the other sled outside, and Darrow stooped to enter the warm cave. Every face turned hopefully toward him, but he shook his head. "The Clarion is gone."

Trout whispered, "I'm sorry."

"It wasn't your fault. He used chantment, there was nothing you could have done. We will survive without it." Darrow sought Calwyn's eyes. "I should not have spoken as I did," he said quietly. "Forgive me."

Wordlessly Calwyn nodded, and Darrow let out a long breath. Then he looked around at the cave, golden with firelight and fragrant with the smell of Tonno's hot, savory soup, and he smiled wearily. "No need for the Clarion here. Just like home."

Tonno glanced up. "You're in time for dinner. Bring those bowls, Calwyn lass, and we'll eat."

"Here, Trout," said Darrow, and handed him the battered lenses in their wire frame. Trout's face lit up. "They were a little scratched, but I've repaired them."

Tonno ladled out the soup, and they talked as they ate, pondering the loss of the Clarion and the disappearance of Keela.

Calwyn's thoughts had taken another track. Where was Darrow thinking of, when he spoke of *home*? Was it the Black Palace in Merithuros, where he had spent so much of his childhood, and where, now, he was lord? Surely it was not the island of Ravamey, where he had lived a bare half year, just one winter, with her and the others. Perhaps it was the cozy cabin of *Fledgewing*, where he had first known true friendship.

She felt Halasaa's questioning gaze on her. *I was wondering, where is home to Darrow?*

That is easily answered. Halasaa serenely spooned up his soup. *Wherever you are, Calwyn, that is his home.*

You think so? Calwyn glanced at Darrow, but his head was bent low over his bowl, and he did not look up.

The Time of One Egg

As soon as Keela entered Samis's camp she saw that it was much more luxurious than that of the other travelers. His arched tent was made from panels of doubled canvas, his sleeping-furs were thick and soft, and he carried fire in a brass pot. Keela lifted a corner of the tarpaulin and peered at the pile of large, strangely shaped silver containers hidden beneath it.

A low, powerful voice sounded behind her. "Touch nothing."

Keela jumped and let the tarpaulin fall. "Darling, you *never* let me play with your toys! I'm not a *child* anymore, you know. And I've been *so* good. Haven't I? Don't you think I deserve a little treat?" She twirled a tendril of golden hair around her finger and gazed at him. Her eyes sparkled blue and her cheeks were flushed. "Let me peek in your boxes, just one peek!"

Samis was unmoved. The flames from the campfire flickered over his face: the domed forehead with its thick, springing gray hair; the hooded eyes, intelligent and contemptuous; the beaked nose; the long, ruthless mouth. He wore an iron-gray cloak, the color of tarnished silver, that hid secret glimmers within its folds. "There is nothing in those boxes to interest you."

Keela tossed her head. "You *are* unfair! I've done *everything* you asked. I've brought you the wretched horn, the Clarion of the Lame or whatever they call it, I sent Darrow to the Lazar-House to get him out of your way, I've *lured* them into this *wretched* country, *and* I made sure they fetched that bore of a girl." Keela pouted, the delicious pout that her admirers in the Palace of Cobwebs had fought duels to receive. But her eyes were sharp. "I can't think why you're bothering with that plain, grumpy little thing. Singer of All Songs, indeed! I told you in Gellan, there's no more magic in her now than there is in me — and darling, you must admit, I'm so much prettier —"

Like a snake striking, Samis's hand shot out and jerked her head back. Keela cried out.

Samis's mouth curled. "You agreed, in Gellan, not to question me. Did you not? That plain, grumpy little priestess will be the Singer of All Songs." He tightened his grip. "Say it."

"She — will — be —" Keela choked out, "what you say —"

Samis released her. For a few moments there was no sound but Keela's stifled sobs and the crackling of the fire. Then Samis said in a bored voice, "You will have your reward, in time, just as I promised." He turned over the little Clarion; his fingertips caressed the swirling designs etched onto its golden surface.

Keela wiped her eyes. "I've been waiting so *long*."

"How you've suffered!" drawled Samis mockingly.

"Don't be angry with me, darling."

"I'm not angry, *darling.* Now listen. This is what you will do next."

After the soup, Calwyn slept. The next she knew, she was lying on her side, tucked under a sleeping-fur, and looking out through the mouth of the cave to a sky sprinkled with stars.

Someone touched her hand, and she sat up. Halasaa laid a finger to his lips and gestured around the cave with laughter in his eyes. The others were all asleep, worn out by the events of the day and lulled by the warmth and shelter of the cave. Tonno snored, his big boots poking from under a pile of skins. Trout was buried under sleeping-furs. Darrow slept sitting upright, as he often did, frowning with thoughts that never let him rest entirely. Calwyn felt a sudden impulse to reach out and smooth that frown away.

But Halasaa was beckoning. *Let us walk, you and I.*

Calwyn drew her cloak around her shoulders and followed his silhouette out of the cave. Their feet crunched in the snow, and their shadows stretched, stark and blue, in the light of the single rising moon. *The time of the Lonely Maiden.* Calwyn used mind-speech, not wanting to break the silence of this still night.

My people call it the time of One Egg, offered Halasaa. *There are no lonely maidens among the Tree People.*

But you were lonely among them, Halasaa. A lonely boy.

Yes. After my father died. He gestured ahead. *I will show you where we lived, my father and I, in the winters.*

The cave was smaller than the one they'd left, and some distance from the others. *Were you apart from your people even then?*

Yes. You know that most of the Tree People have come to mistrust those with the gift of Becoming, like my father and me. Halasaa shot her a sideways look. *Just as the Voiced Ones mistrust those with the gift of sung chantment.*

Calwyn sighed. *How sad that the two peoples of Tremaris should have that in common and nothing else.*

Halasaa put out his hand to help her climb the rocky path to the cave. *The peoples of Tremaris have much in common. Each of us is born. Each of us will die. In that likeness is all the bond we need.*

Calwyn laughed. *But we have that in common with — with goats, and fish, and with trees and grass!*

And so we do, replied Halasaa seriously.

Calwyn shook her head as they approached the cave mouth. *The peoples of Tremaris have stronger bonds with each other than we do with the other creatures of the world. Like the Power of Tongue.*

My people do not share that gift. We speak with our minds, not our tongues.

Halasaa, it's the same!

No. It is a different gift.

He was adamant. Calwyn smiled as she stepped into the cave that her friend and his father had shared in the winters of Halasaa's childhood. Moonlight streamed through the entrance, lighting the cave with silver. Halasaa found a flint and tinder and lit a tiny nut-oil lamp. He ran his hand along the walls. *In this alcove we kept our food. Here, my father slept. And here was my own bed.*

Touched, Calwyn laid her hand on the low, child-sized niche, still lined with dried grasses. *There are other sleeping-shelves here. Did you share this cave?*

With my mother and my twin sister.

"I never knew you had a twin sister!" Calwyn was so surprised she cried it aloud. "Or a mother!" She stopped. Of course, Halasaa must have had a mother. But he had never spoken of her.

As he so often did, Halasaa answered her question before she had a chance to ask it. *I do not remember them. I was only one year old when they died.*

One year old, repeated Calwyn. *I was one year old when my mother died.* There was a tingling in her hands that she hadn't felt since she'd lost her powers of chantment.

Halasaa groped on a deep shelf, hidden in the shadows. *We kept some things here, in memory of my mother. A hair-comb, a dish she made. Small things.* He drew out a bundle of cloth and spread it out on the floor of the cave.

Calwyn sank to her knees and fingered the pretty wooden dish and the delicately carved comb. Then she set them aside, and picked up a slender bone hairpin. Her face went pale; slowly, she reached back to her own hair, plucked out one of the pins, and held the two to the light. *Halasaa —*

What is it?

His face swam before her in the lamplight. Half laughing, half weeping, Calwyn lifted up the cloth that had wrapped the things. *These pins, and this — this is yellow linen. Where did this come from?*

It was my mother's, answered Halasaa. *I do not know how she came by it.*

Tears were spilling down Calwyn's face. *Halasaa, don't you recognize this? It's the tunic of a priestess of Antaris! Your mother came from Antaris!*

Like you? Halasaa's face was blank, and then suddenly it was transfigured with the light of understanding.

Your mother and sister did not die. Calwyn clasped his hands. *They returned to Antaris.* She turned their hands so that both their wrists faced upward. There were the ice-brands that marked her as a Daughter of Taris, the three moons, one in crescent, one half, and one full. The same marks were tattooed on Halasaa's wrist, almost hidden among the spiraling patterns that snaked up his arm and across his chest.

My father chose those signs for me. Halasaa's words were very quiet. *They are not known among the Tree People.*

"He chose them in memory of your mother," whispered Calwyn. "*Our* mother . . ."

My sister.

My brother.

Calwyn and Halasaa stared at each other as though for the first time.

Calwyn asked. *What was your father's name?*

Halwi. And your mother?

Calida.

The single moon traveled across the sky, their shadows crept across the wall of the cave, and still they sat, searching each other's eyes, as if the answer to every question could be found there. At last, without speaking, they stood, took each other's hands, and circled the cave in a silent, joyful dance.

"And you're absolutely sure?" asked Trout. He and Calwyn were sitting on skins by the fire.

Calwyn didn't mind repeating the story; she had already told it to Darrow and Tonno. "My mother, Calida, ran away from Antaris just after she'd been made a full priestess. Years later she came back with a baby."

"You."

"Yes. But she'd caught a winter fever on the journey, and she died that same night. She never said where she'd been or who my father was."

"And you think he was Halasaa's father?"

"The robes that Halwi kept, and the hairpins, were made in Antaris. They *must* have belonged to Calida. It's another reason why the Tree People shunned Halasaa, because his mother was a Voiced One. It shouldn't be a reason, but —" Calwyn's voice hardened. "My people are wary of me, too, because my father was an Outlander."

"But why did she leave? Why did she take you back?"

"Halasaa and I were about a year old. Calida and Halwi must have realized by then that I was born with Voice, but not Halasaa. We think perhaps I could always speak with my mind too, but I'd forgotten, until I knew Halasaa. Calida and Halwi must have wanted me to be raised with other chanters. I couldn't have learned all the songs among the Tree People." Calwyn smiled slightly. "Lia told me that Calida was gifted in many ways, but not in chantment. So she took me to Antaris. But the journey cost her her life."

"Wait till Mica finds out!" crowed Trout. "Calwyn, if your mother hadn't died, do you think she would have come back to the Wildlands?"

Calwyn dropped her eyes. "I don't know. It must have been a terrible decision to make. She had to abandon me or Halasaa and Halwi." *All so I could learn the chantments,* she thought wretchedly. *And now my gift is gone, and it was for nothing. If she and I had stayed in the Wildlands, then I would never have been parted from Halasaa, and our mother and father would still be alive, all of us together.*

The picture of what might have been was a dull ache in her heart. And yet she could not be sorry that she'd grown up in Antaris, with the rituals of the sisters and their reverence for chantment. If she hadn't lived there, she might never have met Darrow and her other friends, never experienced her journeys and adventures, never tasted all the different kinds of magic she'd learned.

With a shock, Calwyn realized that her memories of chantment were no longer purely painful. Gingerly, like someone exploring a sore tooth, she probed her feelings. There was still pain, but there was joy in her memories too, and thankfulness. Trout and Tonno, even Keela, would never know what she had known: the fierce strength of power flowing through her voice and her body; the pure delight, the sense of rightness when the magic caught, and she and the song were one, making up together the sum of the chantment, sung by the Great Power, by the Goddess.

We sing, but we are also sung. Marna's words returned to her, and for the first time, she began to grasp what they meant.

She poked at the fire. "Halasaa says Halwi always spoke of our mother and me with great love and sadness. But at last he must have known that she'd died, and he thought I'd died too. And then he lost his own joy in living. Once he'd taught Halasaa everything he knew about the Dances of Becoming, he died. Halasaa couldn't help him."

Calwyn fell silent, thinking of her father, who had died of grief, and of the mother she'd never known, who had made such a sacrifice for her sake.

"So you have Tree Person blood." Trout slid her a timid look. "You know — how you could do all those different kinds of magic — you think that's why?"

"It must be," said Calwyn simply. "We should have guessed before, when I could speak with Halasaa, and when I healed —" She stopped and looked away.

Hurriedly, Trout exclaimed, "As long as you and Halasaa don't turn out like Keela and Samis!"

Calwyn laughed shakily. "There's no chance of that!" She looked up as Darrow emerged from the shadows at the back of the cave into their patch of pale sunlight. "Did you go back to sleep?"

"Yes, I think yesterday's fishing tired me more than I knew." He spoke lightly, but a fist of fear clenched in Calwyn's stomach.

She said, "You must be careful, Darrow. Every time you sing a chantment, it takes some of your strength."

"But if I do not sing, we have no hope of keeping up with Samis," said Darrow sharply. "Please don't speak to me as though I were a child, Calwyn. I know the risks and I choose to take them."

Calwyn looked away, her eyes stinging.

Darrow reached out and clasped her hand. "I'm glad, very glad, that you and Halasaa have found each other. Don't let me spoil your happiness." He climbed stiffly to his feet and walked out of the cave, to where Halasaa and Tonno were repairing the broken sled.

Calwyn watched him go. She feared for Darrow, the man she loved, but also for them all. How could they hope to defeat Samis? Now he had the Clarion as well as half of the Wheel. Darrow tried to deny his illness, but he was so weary. She was useless, and Mica was far away. Last time they had confronted Samis with the strength of three able chanters and Halasaa, as well as Trout's ingenuity and Tonno's courage, and even that was not enough.

Halasaa! Calwyn called silently to her brother. *Darrow is feeling ill, but he won't admit it. Please, can you help him?*

Yes, my sister. Do not fear. He is tired, but he is not dying.

But even Halasaa's reassurance could not dissolve the dread in Calwyn's stomach.

* * *

That night Calwyn slept on the floor of the cave with her mother's carved hair-comb in her hand. Halasaa lay to one side of her, Darrow on the other. As Darrow turned in his sleep, his hand came to rest on Calwyn's arm and held onto it. His fingers were cool. Calwyn pulled a fold of the sleeping-fur over his hand, and she felt the comforting weight of it there, like an anchor connecting her to the earth as she slept.

At first, she thought she'd woken. She was still lying in the warm, safe darkness of the cave. She smelled wood smoke, the lingering traces of cooked meat, the scent of the dried grasses in the sleeping-alcoves. But three moons gleamed through the arched opening of the cave, not one. The interior was silver bright, and it was oddly empty, not crowded with packs and humped, sleeping bodies.

There was a low fire, no more than a handful of glowing embers. Two people sat close together, their backs to Calwyn. They were wrapped in gray-and-white burrower-skin cloaks, and their long dark hair was bound with vines. They were Tree People.

A young woman with dark, laughing eyes turned from the fire. "Go back to sleep, little one," she whispered.

The other person turned his head. He looked like Halasaa, with a high, thoughtful forehead and eyebrows as straight as Calwyn's own. He did not speak, but he shook his head in mock reproach, and his eyes smiled. Calwyn stared and stared. She wanted to leap up and embrace them, to feel their arms close around her, to be safe and warm between them, but she couldn't move. Then she knew that she was dreaming, and she began to cry.

"Hush, hush, my darling," whispered her mother. "Don't wake your brother."

A warm, breathing bundle was tucked in beside her: her twin, from whom she would soon be torn away. Calwyn sobbed as if her heart would crack in two.

Then a dark shape scooped her up and she was gathered into her father's strong arms, to be rocked and comforted. On the other side of the cave, her mother sang, an ancient, crooning song that Calwyn knew well. The darkness folded around her and she slept.

Calwyn woke before dawn, in the hush before sunrise. *Halasaa.* She knew that he was just waking too, ready to get up and build the fire.

Good morning, my sister.

Halasaa had often called her *sister,* but there was a special sweetness to it now.

Halasaa, I dreamed that our mother sang to us. Calwyn sat up on one elbow.

No one told me that my mother was a singer of songs. Halasaa's voice was sad. *My father did not share his memories of her. I have never seen her in my dreams.*

Calwyn put out her hand to keep her brother still. *Wait. I'll show you.*

And they lay side by side, while the others slept, and shared Calwyn's dream.

Without the Clarion to pass between them, fingers and toes were pinched with cold, and noses and ears were red. Darrow's chantment seemed less strong than before; now the skaters pulled the sleds, with Darrow's help, rather than being towed along.

"Sit on the sled, man, and rest while you sing," Tonno urged him. "We'll hardly feel your weight."

"I'm all right," said Darrow, tight-lipped.

"Go on! You can tend the fire-pot," said Tonno.

Before this, they had relied on a blast from the Clarion to send a blaze crackling up whenever they needed it. They had brought flint and tinder from the caves, and Trout had improvised a fire-pot from one of their lidded cooking pans. But it was not easy to keep the fire alight, and they wasted time fussing over the tiny nest of flames, feeding it with thawed moss and despairing when the fire went out.

Around midday Halasaa suddenly stopped. *Someone is coming.*

They halted, listening intently. A faint voice drifted through the trees, mumbling with a kind of hopeless exhaustion. "Oh, gods, help me. Is anyone there? Can anyone hear me?"

A pale, bedraggled figure emerged from the forest, hands outstretched, cherry-colored cloak drooping forlornly. The former princess of the Merithuran Empire was almost unrecognizable.

Tonno stepped forward. *"Keela?"*

The filthy, sodden figure launched itself at him with a sob, almost knocking him down. Tonno had never embraced a princess before, and he patted her back rather gingerly at first. But as her arms locked around him, he returned the hug with more vigor. "Oh, Tonno, Tonno!" she moaned. "I've never been so pleased to see *anyone!*"

"Nonsense," grunted Tonno, flattered in spite of himself. The whole group clustered around. "That wretch of a man tried to kill me!" Keela shivered as she clung to Tonno. "All the years I plotted and schemed to make him Emperor, the *disgusting* people I was sweet to, for his sake! How I crossed the sands of Hathara, swam that cursed lake, and sailed the four oceans in that stinking little ship, and lived in that poky hole in that *filthy* city. Do you know what he called me? He said I was a soft, sniveling *bore!*"

"Well, whatever else you might be, you're not boring," said Trout unexpectedly.

"Not soft either," said Tonno gruffly. "You had enough nerve to do all those things, and to come and find us in the forest on your own."

Keela gave him a wavering smile.

"How did you get away?" asked Calwyn sharply.

"He was asleep." Keela waved a vague hand. "And I brought *this* —" She drew something golden from under her jacket: the Clarion. "I can't use it, but I knew you would want it back." Her blue eyes brimmed with sudden tears.

"Tell us his plan." Darrow's voice was harsh; Calwyn could see that he too was still suspicious of Keela. "Now you have no reason to keep silent."

Keela looked pleadingly round at them. "He . . . he wouldn't tell me. All I know is that he's going to the Lost City. I swear, that is true!" Keela hid her face in Tonno's jacket.

Calwyn and Darrow exchanged a look, and Tonno glared at them. "What are you gawping at?" he barked. "Someone fetch the lass a cup of roseberry-leaf tea! Can't you see she's frozen through?"

"Thank you," whispered Keela, and Tonno's arms tightened around her.

By the Knot
of the Waters

The next day they came to the foot of the Peak of Saar. The Peak itself was a single jagged spire, shrouded in mist and surrounded by long stretches of barren rock. The winds raced across the rock, stirring the snow into restless flurries. Gnarled stone pillars rose alongside the river, like the remains of some vast ruined city, and the cold smell of stone filled the air.

Halasaa became more and more uneasy. *These are the Veiled Lands. Among the Tree People, only the Elders are permitted to enter here.*

The hairs stood up on the back of Calwyn's neck. Privately she asked her brother, *Should we go back?*

Halasaa looked troubled. *I ask myself the same question. But I do not know. Part of me is held back, but another part is called on.*

It was unlike Halasaa to feel uncertain, and his indecision made Calwyn nervous. She said aloud, "Perhaps we should go around the Veiled Lands on foot."

"It would be far slower than following the river." Darrow fumbled with his gloves and swore under his breath.

"You're getting clumsy, Darrow!" Keela laughed, but Calwyn's nervousness sharpened into fear. Darrow was beginning to lose the feeling in his hands.

"No. We must go on!" she cried, and she threw away her crust uneaten. But as they threaded between the uncanny, twisting columns of rock, Calwyn regretted her eagerness. The cold grip of fear tightened with every stroke of her skates.

At sunset they arrived in a sheltered gully at the very base of the mountain. By one bank was a small, flat area, heaped with snow, that they might use as a camping place. Laboriously they cleared the snow away.

"Mica could have done this in a flash." Tonno wiped his brow. "Aye, and given me cheek with the same breath. Come on, Trout, help me with the tents. No wood for a fire tonight. We need a blast on the Clarion. No, Darrow, don't you get up. Hey, Calwyn, where's that brother of yours?"

Despite her unease, Calwyn couldn't help smiling; the words *your brother* thrilled her. "Here he comes."

Halasaa had disappeared around a bend in the river; now he skated swiftly back. There was a strange light in his dark eyes as he glided up to the campsite. *It is as I thought. We have almost reached the caverns.*

"Like your other caves?" Trout looked up eagerly. "Can we camp there?"

Halasaa shook his head. *These caverns are a secret place of the*

Spiridrelleen. The river flows into them, deep into the belly of Tremaris. I have heard about them, but I was never permitted to come here.

"Caves?" Keela sidled closer to Tonno's side. "We don't have to crawl through any horrid caves, do we? Nasty, slimy, dirty places!"

Calwyn felt the needle of impatience that Keela always provoked in her. "There's no real danger, is there, Halasaa? If it's the quickest way — we can't waste time."

Keela widened her eyes. "Darling, *I'd* like to know what everyone else thinks, even if you don't care. We're not your slaves, are we? Trout? What do you say?"

Trout shifted from foot to foot. "If Halasaa says the caves are forbidden, there must be a good reason," he mumbled.

"I agree," said Tonno. His hand was on Keela's shoulder. "No point sailing into the rocks when there's a light to warn you off."

Calwyn's impatience curdled into rage; her fear was so strong that she struggled to speak calmly. "In Antaris, we have secret places too. Just because they're secret, it doesn't mean they're dangerous."

"Halasaa doesn't want to go on, that's obvious. I fear you're outnumbered, darling." Keela tossed her head. "You always place such store on your *votings.* Surely you won't argue now, just because the vote's gone against you?"

Calwyn was close to weeping with fury. Halasaa was torn and wavering. Darrow frowned as he rubbed his hands roughly together, as if to force some feeling back into them. Calwyn was sure that he wanted to go on, but he said nothing.

For the first time she had to face what she had tried to ignore for so long. In spite of Halasaa's help, in spite of his own denials, Darrow was seriously ill. If he was too exhausted even to argue, how could he lead them? His hands and feet were growing numb; before long he would lose the ability to sing chantment. Without his help to drive the sleds over the ice, they would founder. If they didn't reach Samis soon and mend the Wheel, Darrow would die.

Trembling, Calwyn took down Halasaa's pack from the second sled. As the others watched, dumbfounded, she returned to the lead sled and began to hurl baggage onto the ice.

"What are you doing?" cried Trout. "Careful! That pack's got all my tools in it!"

"We'll have to split up." Calwyn's face was set. "Darrow, Halasaa and I will go on through the caverns. If the rest of you are too scared to come with us, you'll have to make your own way around the Peak. We'll meet you in Spareth."

"Have you gone stark *mad*?" Trout's voice rose to a squeak of outrage. "Darrow, tell her! We can't split up, not in the middle of nowhere!"

Tonno grabbed Calwyn's arm. "Don't be daft, lass! Halasaa knows the way. And we need Darrow to push the sleds and play the Clarion, we can't go on without chantment."

"You must." Calwyn shook him off and threw Keela and Trout's packs up onto the second sled.

"We stay together!" Tonno swung Calwyn around by the shoulders. Calwyn tried to push him away, and they wrestled on the ice, feet sliding from under them, until they both tumbled over. The back of Calwyn's head banged violently on the ice.

Stop!

Halasaa stood, tall and commanding, his arms outspread. One by one they turned to look at him. *We must not quarrel, not here. The spirits of the Veiled Lands, the spirits who guard the caverns, feed on anger and fear.*

"Primitive nonsense!" said Keela, with a toss of her head.

Halasaa wheeled to face her. *You must be silent, you above all. You began this. If you will not be silent, I will bind your mouth with my own hands.*

It was so astonishing to hear serene Halasaa threatening violence that Calwyn began to laugh helplessly. Keela gaped, then turned away with a sniff and a flourish of her cloak. Shamefaced, Tonno helped Calwyn to her feet and brushed her down. "Sorry, lass," he mumbled. "Don't know what came over me."

And you, my sister — Halasaa's words sounded privately in Calwyn's mind. *The river flows as it should. Be at peace.*

Calwyn heard Marna's voice, too: *You must learn to listen. . . .*

There was no further debate. In near silence, almost in embarrassment, they made camp. As they pitched the tents, Darrow touched Calwyn's hand and smiled. Calwyn lowered her head, her eyes stinging with unshed tears.

Later, Halasaa stood behind Darrow, with his hands on the bowed, fair head. Darrow's stiff shoulders relaxed as the Power of Becoming flowed into him.

Halasaa, you must care for yourself too. Calwyn's words were for him alone. *Do not use all your strength.* The Dances of Becoming drew their power from the dancer; if Halasaa overexerted himself, he too might become ill and weak.

My homeland is helping me. The forests have given me strength.

Calwyn was only partly convinced. *There are no forests here, my brother.*

We are coming to a place with more power than forests. These caverns are called the Heart of Healing. Perhaps they will help Darrow.

"Stop talking to each other," said Darrow suddenly.

Startled, Calwyn stared at him. "How did you know?"

"The look on your faces. It's worse than whispering in a corner."

"I — I'm sorry."

Darrow smiled; the scar on his eyebrow gave his face the quizzical expression she had come to love. He admitted softly, "I wish I could speak to you secretly too."

Calwyn flushed. *But I can speak to you,* she reminded him silently.

For a few moments, Darrow sat very still, wearing the same absorbed expression as Halasaa as he listened.

Well done, my sister! Halasaa flashed her a secret grin. *You help him more than I ever could.*

Do I? Calwyn was startled. Perhaps she was not quite useless after all.

Calwyn had pictured the entrance to the caverns as a high, gaping black hole. But the frozen river dipped through a narrow crack in the rock, a mere sliver of dark, and vanished.

Darrow's chantment ceased abruptly, and the sleds slid to a stop.

"The sleds won't fit through there," said Trout flatly.

Halasaa looked at Darrow. *We will need the Clarion's light.*

Darrow drew out the little trumpet, a fistful of golden radiance, like all the weak winter sunlight compressed into one small, gleaming mass.

Keela shouted suddenly, "Catch me if you can!" and threw herself onto her stomach, sliding headfirst through the rift in the rock. Calwyn gasped as her skate blades flashed, a silver echo of the Clarion's golden light. Then she was gone.

"Keela!" shouted Tonno. "Come back!"

"I always *knew* she was crazy," said Trout with a certain satisfaction.

We must follow her. But Halasaa seemed frozen to the spot.

Calwyn hesitated. Then she too flung herself onto the slippery ice and launched herself straight for the crack in the rock. The opening was larger than it looked, and there would be plenty of room for the sleds to pass through. The river dipped sharply as it entered the gap; in summer, there would be rapids here. Holding her breath, Calwyn plunged headfirst down the icy slope into the pitch-black cave. She had never known such darkness, even on moonless nights; she couldn't tell if her eyes were closed or open.

Suddenly she was spinning out of control, sliding fast across a polished plain of ice. Desperately she flung out her limbs to slow herself. At last she slid to a halt, fighting for breath. She had no sense of the size of the cavern, no sense of direction.

"Hello!" she called aloud. Her voice was very small, and there was no echo.

She sat up, and groped with outstretched hands. Nothing. "Hello? Keela?" she called again, trying to keep the panic from her voice. She could make out a faint glimmer of light, high up and far off to the side, which must be the entrance. The faint light winked out, then reappeared, as someone else shot down into the cavern.

Then, to Calwyn's relief, a shaft of clear light blazed out from the Clarion, impossibly far away. The deep, rich hum of the Clarion's chantment grew steadily as Darrow played, and the light became brighter and brighter. Calwyn had to turn her eyes away, and she saw the cavern for the first time.

It was gigantic. The roof arched so high that all the Dwellings of Antaris could have fitted inside. The river widened into a pool that filled the enormous cavern from wall to wall, a floor of smooth black ice that reflected the distant walls and a roof dripping with huge icicles. As Darrow's breath and the light from the Clarion faltered, Calwyn realized that they weren't icicles but drips of honey-colored stone that glowed amber in the fading light. She heard Keela shout, half excited, half terrified, from somewhere on the other side of the cave.

Darrow's breath gave out, and the pitch-blackness engulfed them for a heartbeat, until another sweet note from the Clarion spread a pool of warm golden light. Calwyn struggled to her feet and struck out across the black ice. Out of the darkness Tonno appeared, drawn to the light like an insect to a flame. Then came Trout and Halasaa, glancing warily all around.

Keela glided toward them, smiling. "You see, Halasaa? It's not so bad, is it? Nothing to fear after all!"

Calwyn said, "You should have waited for us, instead of taking off like that."

"No harm done," said Tonno.

"*Yet.*" Trout gestured ahead. "The sleds are over there. They raced through so fast I thought they'd never stop!"

"Better keep the light going," growled Tonno. "We've no torches, and I don't want to be caught in the dark. That is, if Darrow . . ."

"I can manage, if the rest of you take the sleds." Darrow's voice was quiet but insistent.

Pulling the sleds, they followed Halasaa across the ice, past columns of amber-colored stone that soared overhead into the dark. At the far end of the cavern were the mouths of several dark tunnels; the black ribbon of the frozen river poured away into the lowest of them.

"Which way?" Tonno squinted over the direction-finder.

We follow the path of the water. Halasaa sounded calm now, as assured as if he'd traveled through these caves a dozen times. But Calwyn couldn't shake off the prickling at the back of her neck and the tips of her fingers.

Halasaa led them through the dazzling network of caves, each more splendid than the last: iridescent with blue and purple like a beetle's wing, glinting with deep green, or winking with the dark fire of opals. Without the guidance of the sun, it was hard to tell how time passed. The rumbling of Trout's stomach was their most reliable signal of midday, and then sunset, but deep belowground it was equally possible that only half a day had gone by or that they'd skated through the dark for a day and a night without rest.

They came to a cave carved from pure ruby. Blood-red gleams threw back the Clarion's light with answering flame, as if they moved through the heart of a fire. And yet it was so cold.

Calwyn fell back a little from the others. The stone reminded her of the ruby ring that Darrow had worn, the Ring of Lyonssar that belonged to the sorcerers of Merithuros. Suddenly she felt certain that the ring's gem had been cut from these very walls. This must be a place of power —

All at once she laughed aloud. Ever since they'd entered the Veiled Lands, a strange feeling had haunted her. Now she realized it wasn't fear: It was her sense of magic. It had returned to her here — not as strong as before, a mere glimmer of what it had been. But it was real and it was hers again. There was power all around them, deep in these caves, and she could feel it in the tingling of her hands and the hum behind her eyes. If not for the skates, she would have skipped for joy.

Keela, who was closest to her, turned around. "Please, do share the joke, darling!"

"It's nothing." Calwyn wasn't ready to share her discovery, not even with Halasaa, and especially not with Keela. But what if Halasaa were right, and these caves did hold the deepest secrets of healing? If Darrow could be made well here — if she could recover her powers? As she brushed the flickering wine-red walls with her fingertips, Calwyn almost dared to hope.

With no sunset to signal the end of the day, they pressed on for longer than usual. But when Keela flung down her towrope and declared that she wasn't going *one step* further, Calwyn was secretly relieved. Her body was heavy with fatigue, and the others, too, moved sluggishly as they prepared the camp.

They spread the tents on a wide, dry ledge beside the glassy band of the river and wrapped themselves in their cloaks and sleeping-furs. Darrow used the Clarion to melt and then boil a chunk of ice for roseberry-leaf tea.

"This is the best it's ever tasted!" exclaimed Trout.

"Mebbe it's because we're so tired," grunted Tonno. "But I will say, this tastes near as good as my own honey potion tonight."

This water is steeped in healing power. Halasaa's words were reverent. *It will restore us.*

Calwyn shot a look at Darrow. Was there more color in his face? He caught her look, and his gray-green eyes smiled. "We will all sleep well tonight."

Calwyn sipped at the fragrant tea; its nourishing warmth spread through her whole body. When she lay down close to Darrow's side, she might have been sinking into a feather bed, curled under a pile of duck-down quilts, rather than lying on layers of canvas on hard rock, in a cold, dark cave under the weight of a whole mountain, far from fresh air and sunlight.

And yet she was not afraid; no one was afraid. Calwyn felt the same sense of safety as in Halasaa's caves, as if Tremaris had curved sheltering arms around them, protecting them from danger. The last thing she knew was the steady sound of Darrow's breath beside her, the warmth of his body curved into hers, and the weight of his arm flung over her.

There was no sunrise to wake them, yet they all woke together, into the dark. Often on this journey Calwyn had longed for more sleep and tried to put off the moment when she would have to throw off the warm covers and plunge into the freezing air. But this morning she bounded up, bursting with energy, impatient to resume their journey. The little campsite buzzed with excited talk and laughter. The tents were rolled up and hurled onto the sleds, Tonno joked as he pounded out rounds of flat bread, and Keela was so charming that even Calwyn was bewitched by her. Darrow sharpened all the skate blades with an easy confidence that allayed any fears that his gift of chantment might be about to ebb away.

"Never thought it'd be so beautiful down here," confessed Tonno.

"I think I could stay forever," agreed Calwyn. "Even if I never saw the moons or sun again."

In the middle of that day, they entered the most remarkable cavern of all. Halasaa was in the lead, with Darrow and the Clarion just behind to light the way; the others were at their heels, still talking and joking, their spirits higher than ever. But the murmur of cheerful talk died away as, one by one, they skated into the cavern.

It was a high, vaulted chamber, almost as large as the amber cave. But as Darrow raised the Clarion high and swept the light to and fro, they saw that this cave was lined with sparkling white quartz, diamond bright as the snow that carpeted the ground far above. Calwyn shielded her eyes as the brilliant light of the Clarion dazzled back from the walls.

The black ice of their own river snaked forward and vanished, like a ribbon wound onto a spool, into three frozen whirlpools, cupped in white stone at the center of the chamber. The edges of the pools overlapped, and coils of ice surged and twisted like petrified rope flung into the air. Each pool was a different color. One was bright, deep turquoise; the second was the pale, fresh green of new leaves; and the third gleamed red-purple, as if it had been stained with mulberries.

Calwyn unfastened her skates. She knew instinctively that this was a place of such sacred power that to slide on the ice would defile it. On tiptoe, she crept to the very edge of the turquoise pool.

Behind her, Trout whispered, "When the waters aren't frozen, there must be a tremendous noise in here."

Calwyn hadn't thought of that. She imagined the deafening din as three whirlpools clashed together, noise reverberating around the chamber. But now it was eerily silent, save for their own breath and the muffled clink of skate blades.

"Halasaa, what is this place?" asked Darrow, and though his voice was hushed, his words seemed jarringly loud.

This is the heart of the Veiled Lands, the most sacred place of the Tree People.

Darrow nodded. "The most sacred place in all Tremaris."

More sacred than Spareth? asked Calwyn. *They say that Spareth is the breath behind every chantment.*

This place was here long before the songs of chantment came to Tremaris, replied Halasaa soberly.

Trout shivered. "I don't think we should stay here too long." It was unlike Trout to give in to what he called "superstition."

Darrow took his lips from the Clarion long enough to say, "There is a presence in this place. Some spirit, cold toward us."

"Ye-es. I feel it," said Calwyn. "But it doesn't seem unfriendly, to me."

Tonno grinned a little uneasily. "You're a Tree Person, ain't you? You and Halasaa, you're allowed to be here. But the rest of us, we don't belong."

"Tonno's right. We must go on." Darrow picked up a towrope to drag one of the sleds onto the rocky ledge that ran around the edge of the cavern, clear of the three knotted pools. "Where to now, Halasaa?"

Halasaa glanced around. Their own river flowed into the interconnected pools; other streams swirled into and out of them, leaving the cavern through half a dozen separate tunnels. For once, Halasaa looked nonplussed. *I do not know.*

Tonno and Trout bent over the which-way. "Blessed needle won't keep still!" growled Tonno. "Swinging around like a flag in a gale."

"Maybe we're too far underground." Trout frowned.

All this time Keela was silent. She had hung back, shifting from foot to foot. Suddenly she darted a look at Calwyn: Their eyes met.

A strange expression — cunning, frightened, triumphant — flitted over Keela's face. "Catch me, Calwyn!" she cried. She spun around on her skates, snatched the still-warm Clarion from Darrow's hand, and sped away, right across the ice to the center of the turquoise pool.

At once the glow of the Clarion began to fade. The dimming light wavered wildly as Keela swung the little horn back and forth, daring Calwyn to grab it back. Calwyn hesitated for a heartbeat, then sprinted after her. Keela twirled to face her, waving the Clarion like a challenge.

Darrow cried, "Give it back!" The yells and urgent footfalls of the others boomed around the cavern.

Calwyn leapt at Keela, and they crashed to the ice in a tangle of skates and cloaks. Calwyn felt Keela's small, strong hand pushing her away, and a sudden agonizing pain as Keela kicked her shins with sharp skate blades. Something smashed into Calwyn's knuckles: the Clarion. Keela's nails raked Calwyn's face, and she gasped, groping for the Clarion. Keela scrambled free and pushed herself backward; as she fled, she hurled the Clarion away as hard as she could, right into the middle of the interlocking pools, the ridged and knotted heart of the ice.

Like a burning coal on a slab of butter, the Clarion cut a neat hole in the thick crust of ice. A brief glow of gold lit up the ice of the three pools as the little horn sank, and Calwyn and Keela were suspended on a floating floor of gold. Then, in perfect silence, the ice dissolved, melting outward from the spot where the Clarion had disappeared. The ice beneath Calwyn gave way, then Keela screamed as she too tumbled into the water. At that moment, the light went out, and the whole cavern plunged into darkness.

This is how it feels to die, thought Calwyn. The water was so cold that her heart stopped beating. She was in a void of freezing blackness. It stopped her ears, blinded her eyes, filled her mouth. Everything was gone, snatched out of existence: the cavern, Keela, the ice, the Clarion. Her hands, her feet, churned the water, but there was nothing to grasp, nothing to save her.

There was time to feel regret, for Darrow, for Halasaa, for her quarrel with Mica. There was time to grieve for the very last breath that bubbled from her lungs. She was moving, carried sideways by the water. She felt her hair wrap across her face and the tug of the silver chain at her throat. The whirlpools were not frozen after all. Under the crust of ice that had seemed so thick, the waters surged and clashed as fiercely as ever.

Down in the depths, very far away, there was a faint greenish light, as dim as the stars when the moons were full, so dim it was hardly visible. Calwyn fixed her gaze on that faint starlight, and as she sank toward it, the light grew brighter. The Clarion was inside the light, a speck of gold, calling to her. Stars were falling around her like snow. And the blue-green light was singing, singing to her, and she had never wanted anything so much as to be wrapped in that radiant song.

Then Calwyn saw the limp body of Keela floating above her, lit from below by the blue-green light, hair swirling in the water. Keela was not falling into the light. Keela was drowning.

Anguish pierced Calwyn like an arrow. She would have to give up the light, give up the song, to help Keela.

Calwyn opened her mouth in a wordless cry of grief, and all her sorrow, all her loss, poured out of her, and the blue-green light poured in. It filled her, overflowed her, and she was breathing light as she breathed in water, and the force of it pushed her up and up. Suddenly her heart began to beat again. It was insistent as a drum, thudding so hard it seemed about to burst from her chest. Her heart dragged her upward, a cork rushing to the surface.

First Calwyn's hands, then her head, burst into the air, and she gasped, treading water in an ice-cold bowl of light. Keela floated beside her, facedown, circling in the current. Calwyn was dreaming, a dream where anything was possible. She had breathed the water in, but it had not killed her: Instead, it had filled her with a radiant, effortless strength. It was the easiest thing in the world to slip her arm under Keela as she drifted past and hold her face above the surging water. Keela seemed weightless. Calwyn could feel the fierce, slow tug of the water, but she kicked against it easily, gracefully.

The light from the bottom of the pools streamed upward, illuminating the whole cavern. A cluster of tiny, dark figures waved and gestured at the edge of the whirlpools. With one slow kick, then another, Calwyn swam to the rim, holding Keela afloat, and the shards of ice parted to let her through.

The others were there with eager hands to haul Keela's limp body from the water. Calwyn didn't need their help; she put her hands on the stone and raised herself effortlessly from the pool. She was made of starlight, and she laughed as she stood there, dripping wet, ecstatic. Blue-green light streamed from her fingertips, from her hair; she stood in a puddle of starlight. Then, like quicksilver, the puddle merged into the larger pool. And then the light went out, and the dark returned.

Only a dozen breaths had passed since the ice gave way.

In the pitch-blackness, everyone spoke at once.

"What *was* that, where did that light come from?"

"Is the lass all right?"

"Keela's not breathing — Halasaa, quick!"

"Calwyn?"

"Where's the Clarion? Darrow, play the Clarion!"

Calwyn stood oblivious. She was not cold; on the contrary, she was warm through and tingling all over. Every breath she took was charged with life, every sense was sharpened. She could feel the cold disc of the half-Wheel through her shirt. She could hear each individual breath of her companions, the tiny rustlings of cloth and fur; she could hear the knitting of the ice as the broken whirlpool began to refreeze. Just a moment longer and she would be able to see in the dark.

Halasaa's head swung round. *Look, there —*

A flaming torch appeared at one of the tunnel mouths, and the white quartz nearby burst into a million glittering fragments, gold and scarlet, yellow and orange, very different from the eerie blue-green glow that had shone from the pool. A hush fell over the travelers.

A band of half a dozen people stood in the pool of torchlight at the mouth of the tunnel. They were dressed in gray-and-white burrower pelts. Their long dark hair was bound or heaped onto wooden combs and, like Halasaa, tattoos covered their arms and chests and faces. Calwyn heard Darrow's sharp intake of breath. The last time they had encountered Halasaa's people — her own people! — they had been driven away and told, *Voiced Ones are not welcome here.*

Trout whispered, "We can see them, but they can't see us, not with the light in front of them."

"By the gods, where's that Clarion?" hissed Tonno.

But the Clarion of the Flame was gone, lost in the waters of the whirlpool.

Halasaa stepped forward. *Greetings, sisters and brothers.*

The torch swung to light them up where they stood clustered around Keela. An old woman stepped forward to answer Halasaa.

Greetings, brother. My name is Briaali. We have come to fetch you away from here.

Tonno said, "One of us — I think one of us has drowned."

The tiny woman bent her head gravely. *It is forbidden to enter the Waters. They quench life's flame.*

Calwyn used mind-speech without thinking. *Please — I was in the Waters too. And —* It was only as she formed the words that she knew they were true, and she felt a thrill of joy as she spoke. *Keela is alive too!* Calwyn's sense of Becoming had returned. Keela was weak and her pulse was feeble, but she had not been drowned.

"Thank the gods!" breathed Tonno.

The old woman stared searchingly at Calwyn. *To the one who gives life for the sake of another, the Knot of Waters gives a new life. You saved her?*

Yes.

Briaali gave a brusque nod. *You have been granted a rare gift, daughter.* With sudden impatience, she clapped her hands and beckoned. *You must come outside now.*

"Outside?" exclaimed Trout. "But we're so far underground!"

Briaali shook her head. *Not far. Your friend needs warmth and care.*

Tonno hoisted Keela into his arms, and in subdued silence the travelers edged their way around the cavern. The ice was hardening across the pools, but no one ventured onto it; those who had not already removed their skates did so now. Trout and Halasaa fetched the sleds, and Darrow sang a low chantment of iron to help move them to the tunnel where the Tree People were waiting.

Unnoticed by the others, Calwyn knelt by the rim of the

turquoise-colored pool. Her heart was beating hard, thudding against the broken Wheel inside her jacket. A thin crust of ice had re-formed on the surface of the pool. Calwyn broke it and scooped up some water. Swiftly, in a whisper, she sang the simple chantment that she'd learned as a little girl in Antaris.

As she sang, the little puddle hardened in her hand. Hardly daring to breathe, Calwyn took the clear disc of ice between her fingertips and held it up. The torchlight sent a scatter of tiny rainbows dancing through it. Calwyn laughed, a strange breathless laugh that was almost a sob of disbelief.

Darrow! Darrow! She ran across the cave toward him, flourishing the little disc. *I can sing — I can sing!*

She was about to throw her arms around him, but abruptly he flung out his gloved hand and thrust her away so hard that he almost knocked her down. "Calwyn, you fool! If you can sing again, you mustn't touch me!"

Calwyn stared at him, eyes wide. Then she covered her face with her hands. The disc of ice shattered into a thousand tiny shards on the white stone floor.

Come, all of you! Briaali's voice was stern. *It is forbidden to stay too long by the Waters.*

Calwyn stood still, her face hidden, as one by one the others trooped past her down the narrow tunnel. Halasaa was the last and, without speaking, he put his arm about her shoulders and led her from the cavern.

The Arrival of the Voiced Ones

In silence, they followed Briaali through the steep tunnel. The passage was so narrow and twisted that it blocked every particle of sunlight, but after a surprisingly short time they emerged into a cave that opened wide onto the snowy forest.

In the daylight, Calwyn saw that Darrow's face was gray and his hands shook. His eyes met hers.

"I tried to sing you out of the water," he said in a low voice. "I tried, but I —" His voice cracked, and Calwyn moved to him, but he held up his hand.

Tonno laid Keela down beside one of several crackling fires, sheltered behind a screen of branches. There were about forty Tree People in the camp; they stared at the strangers warily, but without hostility. All the travelers recognized on their faces the intent, preoccupied look that Calwyn and Halasaa wore when they spoke silently together.

Brother and sister knelt by Keela; she was breathing, but she was very cold. Halasaa turned her head and helped her to cough up the last of the water she'd swallowed. Together he and Calwyn restored the blood to her limbs and made sure she was wrapped up warmly. Halasaa's words were sober. *I do not know if she will survive.*

Calwyn smoothed the damp golden hair from Keela's brow. *She has come close to death. Perhaps too close to return.*

You saved her, my sister. Even though she tried to kill you.

Is that what she intended? Calwyn stared down at Keela's pale, beautiful face. *I don't know.*

Briaali watched closely as their hands moved over Keela. She was as old as Marna, perhaps even older. But where Marna had been soft and gentle, everything about Briaali was sharp-edged and glittering. Her small face was deeply lined, but her hair shone dark and glossy, barely shot through with silver, and her small black eyes were bright and shrewd. *You are healers?*

Halasaa stood, his body taut as he braced for rejection or abuse. *Yes.*

We are both healers. Calwyn stood too, shoulder to shoulder with her brother, ready to spring to his defense.

You are welcome here. Briaali wrinkled her eyes in an unexpected smile. *We have much to discuss.*

By the big fire, Tonno pulled Calwyn into a bear hug. "Is it true, lass, what Darrow says? You've got your chantment back?"

"Yes!" Calwyn laughed as she returned his hug. "There was a deep magic in that pool, deeper than I can understand."

When she heard Calwyn speak aloud, Briaali's eyes screwed up sharply. *You are a Voiced One, my sister? But the Voiced Ones do not have the gift of healing.*

We were born together. Halasaa answered for them both. *Our mother was a chanter of the Voiced Ones, our father a healer of the Spiridrelleen. Calwyn has inherited the gifts of both our parents.*

Briaali nodded slowly. *Then you are blessed indeed.*

"Yes," said Calwyn simply. In the past, it had seemed a fearful burden to be able to sing so many kinds of chantment. But now, glowing from her immersion in the Waters, she was sure that she could carry that burden with grace. The exuberant certainty that she could do *anything* was still with her. She felt as if she had come awake after a long sleep. The numbness that had wrapped around her like a cocoon of ice for the last half year was shattered utterly. She breathed the crisp, fresh air deep into her lungs, her heart skipping.

Your father was a healer? Briaali peered into Halasaa's face. *Was he Halwi, of the Blazetree People?*

For once in his life, Halasaa was startled. *You knew him?*

Briaali nodded. *We were friends. He shared the old knowledge with me, but I have no gift of Becoming and could not use what he taught.* She gestured around the cave to her companions. *My brothers and sisters here all wish the old wisdom had been preserved. We have suffered among our people, for believing so.* She laid one wrinkled hand on Halasaa's arm and one on Calwyn's. *I am glad Halwi fathered children, so that his gift was not lost.*

And now I must use that gift. Halasaa moved toward the fire. *Darrow has waited too long.*

Suddenly tears sprang into Calwyn's eyes. "The Clarion! The

Clarion is lost! I think I could have saved it — but I helped Keela instead."

"Mebbe we can fish it out of the pool," suggested Tonno, but the Tree People all drew back, frowning in disapproval.

"It's all right, Calwyn," said Trout. "Don't cry. It's worth losing the Clarion to have you back, singing."

"It's worth losing the Clarion to have you alive," murmured Darrow. "Chanter or not."

Again Calwyn had a wild urge to throw her arms around Darrow, to kiss his mouth and his hands. She didn't care if she caught the snow-sickness; she felt invulnerable. "The Waters have healed me — surely they will heal you too! Let's try!" She reached out to touch him, but Darrow pulled away.

Briaali's voice sounded sharply in their minds. *Do not look for such a gift to be given twice.* She turned to Darrow. *If you are ill, drinking from the Waters will strengthen you. But no more than that.*

"Change your clothes, Calwyn," said Darrow in a low voice. "Before you catch a fever."

While Calwyn hastily dragged on dry clothes, Halasaa laid his hands on Darrow's shoulders and poured healing power into his body. The others began the formalities of hospitality: making introductions and passing a cup of warm, sweet flower wine from hand to hand. One by one, the Tree People scattered about the cave, drew close and sat down. But as Calwyn rejoined the circle, she sensed that Briaali was impatient with the ritual. As if the

Elder had heard her thoughts, her glittering eyes fixed on Calwyn. *I am old, and soon my time will be over. I have no will to wait.* The light in her eyes went out. *The trouble that faces us is too urgent.*

"This endless winter —" Darrow raised his head.

"And the snow-sickness!" Calwyn interrupted.

Briaali leaned forward. *Snow-sickness?*

"An illness that attacks chanters," said Darrow. He looked away. "I am infected."

I am sorry, my friend.

The snow-sickness is beyond my healing, put in Halasaa. *I do not understand it.*

Briaali nodded. *Something is eating at the fabric of the world. This sickness may be a part of it —*

A faint memory chimed in Calwyn's mind, but she was so eager to interrupt Briaali that it vanished. "We know what caused the sickness and held back the coming of spring! An object called the Wheel holds dark magic, the chantments of the Tenth Power. The Wheel was broken two years ago, and those chantments were released —"

The Tenth Power? What magic is this? Briaali spoke over Calwyn.

"We don't know — not exactly. But the chantments must be very powerful, to alter the seasons and bring a plague on chanters all over Tremaris!" Calwyn's words spilled out faster and faster. "I have one half of the Wheel. A sorcerer, Samis, has the other. We're on our way to find him now. We must stop him before he releases more dark magic. If we can rejoin the Wheel, all the harm will be

undone. Spring will come. All the chanters will be cured!" Breathless, she smiled into Darrow's grave gray-green eyes, brimming
with confidence that their quest would succeed and Darrow
would be saved.

A powerful object indeed. Briaali held out her hand. *May I see it?*

Calwyn drew out the half-Wheel and passed it to Briaali. The
Elder examined it carefully, but after a moment she shook her
head. *There may be magic here. But what ails Tremaris did not come from your
Wheel. The troubles began long ago.*

Calwyn snatched back the half-Wheel and cradled it protec-
tively. "But — but Marna said — the Wheel and the Tenth Power
hold the answer!" she cried. "And so did Tamen — I know they
were right! When we mend the Wheel, we will mend the world. I
know it!"

Briaali gave her a cool, hard stare. *You are the child of two peoples, a
singer of songs and a dancer of healing. The Waters granted you a new life. Do
not waste it on broken rocks and idle prophecies.*

Calwyn folded her lips as stubbornly as Mica. Briaali was an
Elder and deserved respect, but she was wrong, wrong, wrong! It
was Briaali who wasted time sitting and talking, while Calwyn
burned to seize back the other half-Wheel, to make it whole. *That*
was the answer, no matter what Briaali thought!

And Samis knew that too.

The realization jolted through her. All through this journey,
they had spoken of the need to stop Samis doing more harm. But
why should he wish to damage the world he wanted to rule?

Wasn't it more likely that his quest was the same as their own, to repair the harm that Tamen had done? It was *power* that Samis craved, not destruction. Perhaps — perhaps they could work together? She was bursting to share this revelation with the others, but Briaali was still speaking.

I am old. You are all young. Too young to remember. The fruit hung heavy from the trees, and in spring the new leaves burst with life. But every year, the life in the forest weakens. The trees do not grow so high, the leaves turn yellow before their season. And now this terrible winter. But it is not the beginning of the trouble, and it is not the whole of the trouble. That began long ago.

Tonno broke in. "When my grandpa was young, the fish swam so thick in the oceans, he could bring up a day's catch in his two hands. Ain't like that now."

Darrow said, "The plants and the beasts have grown more feeble, and so has the power of chantment. Magic has faded all over Tremaris. I've seen it in my own lifetime. In Merithuros, there are fewer chanters than when I first went there, only twenty years ago."

Trout said, "Mica always says, when her grandma was a girl, every woman in the Isles could sing up a chantment of windwork. Well, *that's* not true anymore."

Halasaa looked at Briaali. *My sister and I are the last to know the dances of healing. Is that part of this nameless trouble too?*

Indeed. Briaali's face was grave. *These things are all connected. The pool of life and magic is not yet dry, but every year it becomes more shallow.*

"It's the work of the Tenth Power!" insisted Calwyn. "It must be!"

Briaali held up her hand. *These troubles are dreadful indeed, but there is another, more urgent danger that confronts us. We came here, as the Wise Ones did in the old days, to seek guidance. The Knot of the Waters holds the answer to every riddle and the completion of every dance.*

"There's another danger? What?" Tonno scowled and put his hand to the hilt of his knife.

Many young ones, young men, among my people believe that the seed of the troubles was sown when the invaders came.

"Invaders?" Trout was puzzled.

The Voiced Ones, rapped out Briaali. *Your people!*

"Oh," said Trout feebly. "Of course."

The young men call themselves warriors. They believe that the only way to restore the life to our world is to banish the Voiced Ones from Tremaris.

"War?" breathed Darrow. "They want war?"

"How can they hope to win a war against the Voiced Ones?" cried Trout. "There's no chance! Our weapons are superior — I should know, I used to build them! And there are all the trained armies — Merithuros, Rengan, Baltimar — they've been practicing fighting each other for years."

Tonno shook his head. "Your warriors must have lost their wits, old one. We'll wipe you out before the moons take half a turn."

Briaali's eyes flashed dangerously. *You speak of "you" and "we" as if you were warriors yourselves! I will not say that the warriors are right.* She drew her tiny body up as straight as a sapling. *But the Spiridrelleen have been driven from their lands, butchered and forced to live in hiding. Our forests have been slaughtered. The Tree People have much to win and little to lose by waging war on the Voiced Ones.*

"Then our quest is more urgent than ever," said Darrow in a low voice. "There is more at stake than we knew."

Yes. Unless we can stop them, the warriors will attack the lands behind the thicket of ice before next moondark.

Calwyn stared at Briaali in horror. "You mean Antaris, the Wall of Antaris?" A lump of dread sprang into her throat. She felt as if she were being torn into pieces. Of course the Tree People should not have to live in hiding, in suffering and sorrow. But fighting with the people of Antaris would not set that right. For all their faults, at least they lived in peace within their Wall. In an instant, all her exhilaration turned to despair. What was the good of regaining her chantment with so much misery everywhere?

Halasaa clasped her hand. *We will find a way to prevent this.* Her brother was reassuring as always, but Calwyn had to swallow hysterical sobs.

Prevent a war. Find Samis and mend the Wheel. And all before the next moondark! Oh, my brother, how can we do so much?

We must try, said Halasaa simply.

"I don't understand why the Spiri — Spirideen hate us," said Trout doggedly. "It wasn't *us* who killed the Tree People. That was all hundreds of years ago. It's not *our* fault."

"Let what's past, stay past," grunted Tonno.

Briaali fixed them with a shrewd look. *The tree bears the mark of drought long past; the forest changes its form with the pattern of flood and storm and fire. The shape of the present is created by the past. You do not know the story of your people, yet you would give lessons to mine, to the Spiridrelleen who fell at the hands of your ancestors? You must learn to listen, boy.*

Trout looked shamefaced. "Tell me the story of my people."

Briaali laid her hands on her knees and closed her eyes. Very gently, she swayed back and forth, and as she told her tale, she placed pictures into the minds of her listeners. *This tale was told to me by Halwi, of the Blazetree People, and it was told to him by his mother, Iaana. I tell it now to Halwi's son and to his daughter.*

Calwyn and Halasaa looked swiftly at each other.

Long ago, when the tallest trees were saplings, the Tree People lived in the endless forest. Hand to hand, the world's circle danced. The people danced with the trees, the trees danced with the land. The land danced with the sea, the sea with the moons, and the moons with the stars. So went the music and the dance, without beginning, without end.

Long ago, on a night of blood moon —

"Tree People call it blood moon too!" Trout whispered loudly.

"Shh!" Tonno frowned at him.

— on a night of blood moon, a silver boat sailed out of the dark between the stars. The Tree People gathered to wonder at the sight.

Then a door opened in the silver boat, and people came marching out: small, pale people, with hair of many colors. The people opened their mouths, and noise came out, like the noise of beasts, for these people were the Voiced Ones, and the Tree People were afraid.

The Tree People seated around the fire closed their eyes, as if they remembered the ancient scene. Calwyn could feel in her own body the shock and fright her ancestors must have experienced at that moment. And what of her Voiced ancestors? They must have been frightened too when they saw the silent strangers in the forest. But Briaali could not tell that part of the story.

The Tree People and the strangers found they could understand each other. Then was a time of peace. The Voiced Ones had singing magic. They commanded fire and ice, the stones of the land and the breath of the air. They made the beasts obey them, and they created images, not as we do with mind-pictures, but in the air —

"The Power of Seeming," breathed Darrow, so low that only Calwyn heard.

But the strangers could not help the plants of the forest to grow nor understand the speech of beasts. They could not heal a hurt to a living being: They knew nothing of the great river nor could they alter its flow. The singing magic of the Voiced Ones was an arrogant power. It bent the stuff of the world to the will of the singer. The Voiced Ones knew much of singing, but they did not know how to listen —

"That's not true!" Calwyn burst out, weeping with hurt and outrage, as if Briaali's story were an accusation directed at her alone. "If my father told you that, it must have been before he knew my mother, before he knew about true chantment! In Antaris, the priestesses teach us to be respectful of the power we summon. We're taught to listen for the voice of the Goddess before every chantment, and to do nothing lightly —" She stopped. For the first time, the lessons she had learned from the sisters struck her heart. At last she could see the wisdom in the discipline that she had always struggled against. She bowed her head, unable to go on.

Briaali watched her thoughtfully for a moment, then continued.

The Dances of Becoming do not benefit the dancer, nor do they alter for alteration's sake, but only heal what is damaged and nourish the whole. It was decided that the dances of healing should not be shared with the strangers.

But there was a girl of the Tree People who loved a man of the Voiced Ones, and she betrayed the secret. And when the Voiced Ones learned of the Tree People's magic, they feared that the Tree People would command the forest to destroy the Voiced Ones and their city.

At last the Voiced Ones burned the trees and left the land bare and barren, so the forest could never hurt them. The grief of the Tree People was heavy and some sought revenge.

Just as they do now. Briaali fell silent, and she placed no pictures into their minds. But everyone around the crackling fire was quiet.

The Tree People were many then, and the Voiced Ones were few. Terrible fighting broke out for many seasons, until the land was soaked with blood. The Voiced Ones used their singing magic to deceive and to destroy, and it was the Tree People who suffered more. When the last battle was over, the survivors of the Tree People fled, vowing to hide from the Voiced Ones forever.

But the Voiced Ones were also damaged by the warring. They quarreled among themselves. The ones who sang each kind of chantment clung together, and would not share their magic as they had done. One by one, the groups left the first city, to build their own dwelling-places elsewhere —

Calwyn leaned forward eagerly. "The ironcrafters went to Merithuros, and the windworkers to Doryus and the Isles. Those with the Power of Seeming went north, to build Gellan. . . ."

"And those with the Power of Beasts settled on the plains of Kalysons," said Darrow.

"The chanters of fire went to Mithates," said Trout. "That's right, isn't it?"

Briaali nodded. *Those who sang the songs of fire were the warriors of the Voiced Ones. They built the machines that slayed our people.*

"Soldiers and builders of war-machines," said Darrow. "With no war to fight, their powers were neglected, until they were forgotten altogether."

"All they left behind was the Clarion," said Calwyn. "And now even that is gone."

"Perhaps the war with the Tree People is the reason chantment fell from favor everywhere." Darrow stared into the fire. "Chantment was tainted by the way it had been used, to kill and destroy."

Calwyn looked up. "So, in the beginning, all the chantments were mingled together, overlapping and strengthening each other. But now they're separated, so each power has grown weaker, all the connections have been forgotten. We have to bring them together again!"

"Let us deal with one task at a time, Calwyn!" Darrow made as if to lay a restraining hand on her knee; at the last moment he remembered to snatch it back.

Halasaa turned to Briaali. *Wise one, how can it be that the Dances of*

Becoming have been lost? If a war was fought to preserve them, why were the Dancers shunned and forbidden to teach the dances of healing?

Briaali looked very sad, and she reached out to take Halasaa's hand between hers. *My son, it is a great sorrow of our people. Those who believed the Dances had brought death to our people forbade the teaching of the knowledge. But there were brave ones, like your father, who taught those who were willing to learn.*

Like you. Calwyn used mind-speech. *And you were brave too.*

Briaali smiled. *We who have studied the old wisdom hope that we may pass it on in our turn, though none of us has the power of healing. That power is a precious gift, my son. Guard it carefully.*

My sister and I will guard it together. Halasaa's face blazed suddenly, and Calwyn flushed with joy and pride.

Briaali looked at her. *It is said that the women who sang the magic of ice were so sickened by the bloodshed that they withdrew into the mountains. They built a peaceful place, a place of safety.*

"And they are the very ones the warriors are planning to attack!" cried Calwyn. Then she added sadly, "A peaceful place. But Antaris is isolated from the rest of Tremaris, just as the Tree People have been isolated, hidden away in the forests."

When the women of ice departed, the forest took back the city, and now it is no more.

Calwyn and the others exchanged glances. "That's not true," said Darrow. "We visited the city only two years ago. It is ruined and desolate, but it still stands."

Briaali wrinkled up her face. *I did not know that. Perhaps the Lost City is the seed of these troubles, spreading poison through the lands. Perhaps it should be destroyed before the sickness of Tremaris can be cured.*

"We're traveling to Spareth now," said Darrow. "And so is Samis —"

"Steady there!" interrupted Tonno. "We're not still going to Spareth, are we?"

Darrow frowned. "Why not?"

"Why not?" barked Tonno. "The Tree People are making war on Antaris! We have to stop them!"

"Mica's there," said Trout, in a small voice.

"Aye, she is, but it's not just that. We don't know what Samis is up to." Tonno glared around the circle, daring someone to argue with him. "But this fighting, that's a real danger. And there's something we can do. And I say we should. Nay, we must!"

"No, Tonno!" cried Calwyn. "We must go to Spareth! The Wheel —"

Darrow said wearily, "Whatever he is planning, Samis is a far greater danger to Tremaris than a group of Tree People armed with sharpened sticks."

Trout shook his head. "Tonno's right. We don't even know if fixing this Wheel of Calwyn's will help. But we could be back in Antaris in half a turn of the moons — less, with some luck from the weather. I know about weapons and defense. I could help."

Briaali gave him an approving look. *We came here to find answers. You were sent to us. You will help us prevent this war.*

Calwyn jumped up. "If I could, I would go back to Antaris —

I want to stop them fighting as much as you do! But everything depends on the Wheel, I *know* it! I'm going to Spareth, even if I go alone!"

You will not be alone, my sister. Halasaa spoke quietly. *I will go with you.*

"And so will I," said Darrow. "Though I suspect that from now on, my presence will be more a hindrance than a help to you."

Never, never! Calwyn spoke into his mind, and Darrow gave her his old lopsided smile.

Trout looked around the circle, slightly puzzled. "So, we are splitting up after all? What about Keela? And how will you manage without the Clarion?"

Do not be hasty. Briaali stood, a tiny figure, but regal in her long cloak of gray-and-white burrower fur. *Eat, talk together, sleep. Give me your decision in the morning.*

Calwyn did not want to talk anymore. Her mind was made up, and she was itching with restless energy. While the others argued around the fire, she walked through the blue-shadowed forest. It was a relief to find that she could put one foot steadily in front of another. The deadening numbness that had gripped her for so long was gone, but it had been replaced by a storm of emotions: soaring hope and bitter despair, fury and joy, had tossed her round and back until she was giddy. Her thoughts were so confused, and the singing lights of the Knot of the Waters seemed to pulse in her veins; she feared she would never sleep again.

As night fell and the moons rose, making the snow sparkle with silver, Calwyn returned to the cave. The Tree People had prepared a meal: vegetable cakes and a fragrant broth of dried herbs.

"Sit down, Calwyn, eat something." Darrow gazed at her with concern.

"No, no, I'm not hungry — I want to see how Keela is."

The woman who had once been the Third Princess of the Merithuran Empire was sleeping peacefully beneath burrower pelts, her cheeks pink and her golden hair curled round her throat.

Briaali's voice sounded in Calwyn's mind. *You and she will be bound together for all time. You were both reborn from the Knot of the Waters; you are sisters now.*

"She's not the sister I would have chosen," said Calwyn wryly, and she thought, with sudden violent longing — I would choose Mica! She would tell her that, as soon as she saw her again.

Calwyn sipped at the steaming broth, and the scent of the herbs sang in her nose and danced on her tongue. She wondered if this soup too had been made with the healing waters from the caverns. She leaned against the wall of the cave. There were tiny lively figures painted on these walls too, very faint and faded.

Briaali followed her gaze. *There were great dances held here in the old days. No longer.* The old woman laid her wrinkled hand briefly on Calwyn's head before she moved away. *Try to rest, child.*

Calwyn did not expect to sleep, but she wrapped a fur around her shoulders and tried to calm her racing mind with a round of the breathing exercises she had learned in Antaris.

"May I?" Darrow addressed her with the politeness of a stranger. He sat down, careful not to touch her even with the hem of his blanket. His face was pale, and he closed his eyes as he leaned against the wall.

Calwyn burst out, "Please, Darrow, let me try to heal you! I feel so strong now, I'm sure no harm can come to me! The snow-sickness doesn't hurt Halasaa, perhaps it won't hurt me either."

"But Halasaa is not a chanter," said Darrow patiently. "No, Calwyn. We cannot risk it." Lightly, with the tip of one finger, he touched the wooden hawk at her throat. "I say this not just for your sake, but for the sake of all Tremaris. You should have drowned today, but you did not. The Waters saved you. If you are to be the Singer of All Songs — and you may be, Calwyn, you must face that — then you are very precious to the fate of the world."

Half a year ago, Calwyn would have leapt to argue: *Of course* she wasn't the Singer of All Songs, she didn't want it. But now she said softly, "I can never be the Singer of All Songs. Without the Clarion, the chantments of fire are lost forever."

"Yes," said Darrow slowly. "There is that." He was silent for a moment. "In Merithuros, when you lost your chantment, you fought against the land, against the deep forces of magic. Was it different this time?"

Calwyn thought. "There was a light in the depths of the water, and I swam to it. And I breathed. I breathed in the water."

"The Waters embraced you, as you embraced the Waters."

Darrow closed his eyes again. "I am glad you have your powers back. I am not — as strong as I was. And without the Clarion, we . . ." His voice trailed away.

Calwyn swallowed. She whispered, "I wish —" But Darrow's head had tilted back; he'd fallen asleep between one word and the next. Carefully she folded the blanket over his legs, and with a heavy heart, she moved away until she was an arm's length from his side.

The Boat in the Clouds

Trout woke with a start. It felt like Mica was breathing cold air onto his face again . . . but of course Mica was far away in Antaris. Trout's sleeping-fur had come untucked, and the icy night air was nipping at his nose. He sat up sleepily. As he rearranged the fur, he glimpsed a shadowy figure prowling back and forth near one of the fires, bending over each sleeping body.

Trout called out sharply, "Who's that?"

The stocky, powerful figure straightened and gestured toward Trout, fingers outstretched. Trout jumped up. "Don't sing your songs of seeming at me, Samis, I can't hear them!" he yelled. "Darrow! Wake up! Calwyn, Tonno! He's here!"

Samis stooped and plucked back a sleeping-fur to peer at the nearest body. The sleepers stirred, rolling over and blinking in bewilderment.

Calwyn sat up groggily, her head thick with the artificial sleep the sorcerer had cast over them all. Keela was kicking and struggling back from Samis, screaming, "No! No! I won't go with you!"

But now Samis had seen Calwyn. In three strides he was beside her, growling out a chantment of iron. Calwyn tried to move away, but her limbs were heavy, and the sleeping-fur was tangled around her legs. Samis's strong, long-fingered hands flicked her effortlessly to her feet, as if they were dancing together. His hand clamped across her mouth. Beside her, Darrow made a strangled sound, and Samis swung Calwyn so she could see the silver rope twisted round Darrow's throat.

Calwyn sank her teeth into Samis's hand and nearly choked as blood flooded into her mouth. Samis didn't let go. He shook her hard, as if to say *Don't be a fool!*, and jerked her back across the stone floor of the cave. He was still growling out his chantment; Calwyn knew that with the alteration of one note, Darrow's windpipe would be crushed. Tree People came running from all directions. Keela still shrieked, "No, no!"

Don't fight him! cried Calwyn in mind-speech. *I'm all right, I'll be all right!*

Samis dragged Calwyn across the snow into the forest, under the trees. She couldn't breathe; Samis's hand was a band of iron across her mouth and nose. As they reached the edge of the grove, she collapsed, gasping for air.

An extraordinary craft waited in the clearing: a kind of boat, anchored by fine, strong, silver cables to a large, almost transparent bubble that floated high above the trees. This was what had been packed away in the mysterious containers Keela had seen in Samis's camp. Calwyn recognized the soft, gleaming metal from which the Ancient Ones had built Spareth. Samis swung her into his arms and dropped her over the side.

With swift, rough movements, Samis tied a silk scarf around Calwyn's mouth. He droned a chantment of iron, and more silver cables slithered from the floor of the craft to twine around her wrists and ankles. She was helpless, propped against the side of the boat, but able to peer over the edge. *Halasaa!* she called. *I'm not hurt. He is taking me away. Is Darrow — is everyone all right?*

Yes, my sister. Halasaa's words were jerky, confused. He sent her a mind-picture: The rope was still wound around Darrow's throat. *We will follow you — speak —*

Samis threw back his large head and let out a commanding growl of ironcraft. Silver cables snapped back into the boat, which rocked and swayed alarmingly. Slowly the bubble rose into the air, lifting the narrow boat higher and higher, level with the treetops. *We're flying!* cried Calwyn.

Halasaa and Tonno and the Tree People were just in time to see the bottom of the silver craft disappear above the trees. As the flying boat broke through the roof of the forest, Calwyn could make out a carpet of snowcapped trees below, and a ceiling of cloud above. The white sea of the forest lapped about the Peak of Saar, its shadowy spire bare and jagged, piercing the clouds. The bubble climbed steadily, and suddenly the boat was enveloped in a damp, muffling white fog. Then, just as abruptly, the boat broke through the layer of cloud.

The moons and stars gleamed in the clear dark sky, and above the boat the silver bubble gleamed too, carried silently by the wind like some huge dandelion seed. The air was icy cold. Calwyn couldn't hear any chantment from Samis. He manipulated some levers beside him, controlling the bubble, but not by magic. The only noise was the whistle of the cables that suspended the gently swaying boat from the bubble. *The wind is carrying us away,* she told Halasaa.

Yes, we saw you — heading south, to the sea.

To Spareth. Calwyn sensed that the connection with Halasaa was already beginning to weaken. *Take care, my brother, take care of Darrow! Don't worry about me, I'm strong now.* As the wind bore them swiftly away, she tried to think of useful things to say. *Help the Tree People! Darrow, I love you!*

But there was no reply, and Calwyn never knew if her last words had reached Darrow.

Now they were above the clouds, moonlight flooded the craft, and for the first time Calwyn saw Samis clearly. "So," he murmured, and Calwyn shrank inwardly as his cool, elegant hand caressed her cheek. "It is a pleasure to see you again."

Calwyn glared at him with all the contempt she could muster. Any noble ideas of working with this man had vanished.

"Come, little priestess. Sulking does not become you."

Calwyn wished she could spit in his face. Samis tapped her cheek lightly. "My dear, you must do me the courtesy of gratifying my curiosity. Did my scheme restore your powers?"

Calwyn's eyes widened in shock, and that gave him the answer he sought. The sorcerer chuckled in satisfaction, and Calwyn cursed herself for giving away her secret so readily. The boat swayed as he returned to his seat, while Calwyn lay still, her thoughts spinning.

Samis had planned it all! It was Keela who had led them into the caverns, Keela who lured Calwyn onto the ice. Samis had tricked her into the healing waters. Did he know, or care, that Keela had fallen in too and almost lost her life? He must have been waiting in the forest until they emerged.

The knowledge that she owed the return of her powers to Samis was dumbfounding. Why had he done it? He must want to use her gifts for some dark purpose of his own. But even so, she owed him a debt of gratitude. Thanks to him, she was a chanter again —

She was a chanter again. And more powerful than the last time she and Samis had met. Since then, she had learned songs of iron and dances of healing. And she was strong. Her immersion in the Waters had done more than restore her gift of magic: It had made her invincible —

For an instant, the giddy lights of the Waters pulsed and sang through her veins once more. But then she remembered something that chilled her. She had learned one more thing since she'd last seen Samis. She had learned the dark chantments.

No. She couldn't, she could never sing those terrible songs. But already, against her will, some of the simpler chantments were unspooling in her mind. A chantment to paralyze, a chantment to freeze his blood. There were a dozen ways to strike him dead.

Do not make the same mistake I made. Wouldn't Marna have wanted her to use the dark chantments against Samis? Calwyn's heart pounded. Samis could not keep her gagged forever. She would have to eat and drink; if he wanted her to sing for him, he would have to trust her. They were too far away for him to hurt Darrow or anyone else with chantment. She couldn't find any reason why she should hold back.

But then, with a flood of emotion that she was reluctant to admit was relief, she realized that she couldn't kill Samis. She didn't know where he kept his half of the Wheel. Perhaps he carried it with him, but more likely he'd hidden it somewhere in the vast, ruined city of Spareth, where it would take a lifetime to find. She would have to wait.

Samis said, "No doubt you are wondering where we are going and why I have brought you here." Calwyn stared at him over the top of her gag. The cables snapped and whirred against the side of the boat. "I wanted a chance to speak to you. It is a pity I have to go to such lengths to prevent your tiresome friends from interfering."

It took all of Calwyn's self-control not to scream at him in mind-speech. But some instinct told her to be silent.

Samis stared down at the moonlit clouds as though he were talking to himself. "You and I have much in common. We both possess unique gifts. You are a powerful chanter, my dear, but you are young. You need the wisdom of an experienced teacher to guide you." He smiled. "Darrow is a pleasant companion, but he is young too and not fitted for that task. Especially now that he's ill . . . He is ill, isn't he? Keela said so." He looked at Calwyn inquiringly, and she felt herself flushing with rage. Of course Darrow was ill; Samis had made sure of it. Samis and Keela together had arranged for Darrow to be arrested in Gellan and taken to the Lazar-House.

"Such a pity." Samis pulled down the corners of his long mouth. "I will miss my Heron — though I suppose you consider him your Heron now."

Calwyn had to look away; she couldn't trust herself.

"Of course, he doesn't have to die," said Samis. "That is, if you will help me."

Here was her own idea, mirrored back to her. But what had seemed logical and filled with hope in the caves of the Knot of the Waters was repugnant to her now. *Help you! Why should I help you? You tie me up like a dog, you've tried to kill Darrow twice over, you nearly destroyed Antaris. So much evil has been done to Tremaris, it's all your fault! And you want to make it worse!*

Samis stared at her. "So — you can speak with your mind! Why, this is wonderful. Your gifts are even more extensive than I knew. But you misjudge me, my dear. Why would I wish more harm to Tremaris?"

The snow-sickness — with no chanters to fight you, you could do whatever you please!

Samis snorted. "Why would I kill the chanters I need to serve me? I know you think ill of me, but credit me with some intelligence. I have no wish to be Emperor of a dead world, stripped of life and magic. That is why I'm taking you to Spareth, to help me find the answer to this riddle. If you and I together cannot solve it, then Tremaris is doomed indeed."

Calwyn's mind whirled. Was it possible that he was speaking the truth?

"Think about what I have said," said Samis softly. "Sleep."

An insect whine of chantment sounded in her ear as Samis began a high, almost inaudible song of seeming. Calwyn screwed her eyes shut. She would not give in! She must stay awake, she needed to think. But it was no use. She was drawn into the artificial sleep he had used to stupefy them all at the camp. Calwyn's head drooped and her body went limp. Samis watched her with narrowed eyes, swaying as the cloud-boat swayed, high above the trees. Then, casually, he drew a corner of a blanket over her sleeping body.

Keela sat very straight; her hair was twisted into a long rope down her back, and her face was pale but determined. The anger and bewilderment of the others beat around her like waves washing against a rock. In a low, steady voice, she said, "He told me that if Calwyn swam in the Knot of the Waters, she might recover her gift of chantment. And it was true."

"And what if she'd drowned? What if you'd drowned?" roared Tonno. "Did he care about that?"

Keela dropped her eyes. "He said that without her power of magic, she was as good as dead to him anyway."

"He has lost himself the Clarion, with his tricks," said Darrow quietly. He dabbed at his neck with a bloodied cloth.

"He said he didn't need the Clarion anymore." Keela twisted her hands in her lap. "I suppose he meant, if he had Calwyn, he didn't need anything else."

Halasaa touched Darrow's shoulder. *You know that Calwyn will not help him. She will fight so long as there is breath in her body.*

Darrow's face hardened into a stony mask. "That's what I'm afraid of."

Look at me, child. Obediently, Keela met Briaali's uncompromising, black diamond stare. *The Knot of the Waters is a secret place, a sacred place. How did your friend know of it?*

Keela shrugged. "He knows many things that no one else knows. What he doesn't know, he guesses." She gave a small smile. "And guesses right, most of the time."

"We must go after them," said Darrow. "They will travel faster than we ever could, but at least we know where they're going."

"He is returning to Spareth." Keela sought Darrow's gaze. "I swear to you, that was always true. Not everything was a lie." Her eyes were on Tonno as she whispered, "Forgive me."

Tonno scowled. "Why didn't you go with him last night?"

"I always planned to go with him when he came for Calwyn. But when I woke, I didn't *want* to go . . ." Keela's soft voice faltered.

The Waters have changed you. Briaali put her wrinkled hand on Keela's knee.

Leaning on Halasaa's arm, Darrow pulled himself to his feet. "We must leave as soon as it's light."

"Nothing else for it." Tonno clambered up too.

Briaali held up a hand. *Wait. The war of the Spiridrelleen is not set aside because your friend is gone.* The Tree People gathered behind her, silent and impassive.

"We cannot leave Calwyn alone with Samis." Darrow's gray-green eyes flashed with their old steely glint.

My son, I would not have you abandon one you love. But every one of the warriors of the Spiridrelleen, every one who dwells behind the thicket of ice, is beloved by someone. Must they be sacrificed to your love?

"Calwyn is the woman I love," said Darrow thickly. "But she is much more than that. She may be the savior of Tremaris."

Then she is a match for any chanter. Briaali challenged them, each in turn, with her flashing black eyes. *I appeal to you, Voiced Ones. We need you. Your people have brought untold harm to this world. Will you not help us now?*

There was a moment's silence.

"Calwyn *is* a powerful chanter," muttered Trout uncomfortably. "And she's still got that Wheel. If she can get hold of Samis's half, she can fix it by herself."

Tonno scratched his head. "I hate to think of Mica, stuck in Antaris, not knowing what's coming."

I do not ask that you abandon the girl or your quest. Only that you help us first.

"Very well," said Darrow. His voice was flat and weary. "Tonno, Trout, if you wish to go with the Tree People to Antaris, I will not prevent you. But Halasaa and I will go on to Spareth."

"May I come with you?" asked Keela in a small voice.

"If you wish," said Darrow brusquely. But Halasaa looked at her kindly, and in return, he received the first sincere smile of Keela's life.

Calwyn woke with the glare of morning sun in her eyes. A dark shape blotted out the sun's dazzle as Samis stood above her. Instinctively, Calwyn shrank back, but the sorcerer was holding out a hot, savory-smelling pastry.

Calwyn thought she must be dreaming. The silver boat still swayed beneath the floating bubble, under the pale blue dome of the sky. Below, a blanket of cloud hid the forest. Even the Peak of Saar had vanished. It was bitterly cold. How could Samis have produced a steaming hot pastry from nowhere?

I need water.

With one hand, he untied the silken scarf around her mouth and loosened the binding at her wrists, then handed her a tin cup of ice-cold water to gulp. "Eat!" he ordered. "Be quick, little priestess, if you want to enjoy your breakfast."

Calwyn was faint from hunger; how long had it been since she'd eaten? She reached out for the pastry. It was delicious. The buttery crust melted in her mouth, and the filling was hot and spicy. "How —?"

Samis's eyebrow lifted. "You surprise me, my dear. In your long journey, have you never improved the taste of dry bread?"

Of course. A spell of seeming. Already the spicy flavor of the meat was fading, and Calwyn found herself holding a stale crust. She said, "I don't know any chantments of seeming."

"Indeed?" Samis seemed surprised. "You've not troubled to learn them? Or was it too difficult for you?"

"I've never tried," said Calwyn, nettled despite herself.

"Perhaps you can't change your voice — like this?" He sang a shrill, falsetto note. "They say women find it almost impossible to keep these notes true."

Indignantly, Calwyn opened her mouth to show him that she could sing any note he sang. Then she saw the lazy smile spread across Samis's face. She would not be goaded or tricked into gaining another power of chantment. She would choose it of her own will.

"Sing it slowly," she said. "So I can copy you."

Samis raised an eyebrow and sang a dozen whining notes, pausing after each to be sure Calwyn had heard it clearly. Before the last note was complete, Calwyn was stringing the song together. The chantment tingled on her lips, and a tiny, jewel-bright butterfly fluttered from her hand. It gleamed briefly in the sun's light, then vanished like a burst bubble.

Samis gazed at her under hooded eyelids. "So. You can sing the Power of Seeming."

Calwyn was elated, but she would not let him see it. "One simple illusion doesn't make me a master of seeming."

"The Singer of All Songs need not know every chantment that's ever been sung! If that were so, there would never be a Singer." Samis stretched out his legs comfortably. "What of the other powers of chantment? You have the Power of Tongue, obviously. The Power of Beasts, yes, I have heard you use that, and the Power of Winds. I know that you have visited Merithuros. Did you learn the Power of Iron there?"

Calwyn shook her head. "Only men can sing the chantments of iron," she said. Then, without warning, she sang a swift throat-song of ironcraft. The tin cup shot up from the floor of the balloon-boat toward Samis's head.

But he was too quick. He lunged at Calwyn. The cup sailed harmlessly over the edge of the boat and was swallowed by the clouds below. A growl of ironcraft twisted the silver chain at Calwyn's throat, choking her until stars burst before her eyes.

Deftly, brutally, Samis jerked the gag into her mouth and yanked it tight. He held her close, almost embracing her. His muscular arm was around her shoulders, and she could smell his body. The edge of his cloak was cool where it brushed her cheek. He tightened the silver cable that knotted her wrists together, though this time he left it just loose enough for comfort.

Samis sat back, stretching out his legs once more, as though nothing had happened. "The Power of Iron, yes. And what of the Power of Becoming?"

Calwyn turned her head away to hide her tears of rage and humiliation. She cursed herself for trying such a stupid trick. She hardly knew whether she had intended to harm him or to show off what she could do.

"I don't want to hurt you, little priestess." He leaned forward and touched her cheek with his fingertip, turning her to face him. "But there must be no more foolishness. Do you want Darrow to live or die? We must work together. Believe me, there is no other way. Do you understand?"

Calwyn swallowed. Samis had said nothing about the Wheel; he was looking for solutions elsewhere, in Spareth. In an instant, she made up her mind.

I will help you.

Samis's thick eyebrows drew together. "You surprise me — I thought you would show more resistance. I confess I am disappointed."

There is one condition.

The sorcerer relaxed and laughed. "That's better. Name your price, my dear."

Calwyn hesitated. She must be very careful now. Whatever happened, he must not find out that she carried the other piece of the Wheel. *You stole something from Antaris, a sacred relic of the Goddess. If you give it to me, I will help you.*

"Ah!" Samis drawled. "Your yellow ladies were so generous — there were so many gifts. A sacred relic, you say? A statue, a jewel?"

A — a broken Wheel. Calwyn met his gaze unflinchingly.

"There may be something of that sort," said Samis at last.

"Among my possessions in Spareth. I will have to search for it."
He smiled.

Calwyn stared at him. It seemed too simple. She suspected
that, somehow, Samis was tricking her, instead of the other way
round.

"Now tell me," said the sorcerer. "Do you have the Power of
Becoming?"

Yes, said Calwyn, after a moment.

"The Power of Ice, you have, of course." He bared his teeth in
a smile. "All we need is the Power of Fire, and we will have our
Singer of All Songs."

Calwyn felt a surge of savage pleasure. *Thanks to your scheming, the
Clarion of the Flame is gone. Sunk to the bottom of the Knot of the Waters. There
can never be a Singer of All Songs now. The secrets of the Power of Fire are lost
forever.*

"Are they?" Samis gave her a strange smile. "Are they indeed?"
He glanced at the sun and held out a wetted finger to test the
wind. "Too much to the west," he murmured. "I've treated you to
breakfast. Would you care to return the favor?"

What do you want? Though Calwyn had already guessed.

"Sing a wind, my dear, to carry us south."

Aren't you controlling the bubble with chantment?

"Don't pretend ignorance, little priestess. You and I must be
honest with each other. Ironcraft would never work at such a distance from the ground, as you know perfectly well. Not everything

the Ancient Ones built was powered by chantment, though a spellwind would certainly be useful now."

Calwyn nodded. Samis gave a growl of ironcraft, and the cables that bound Calwyn's wrists and ankles slid to the floor, and the silken gag fell away. She swallowed painfully, but her heady confidence had returned. Everything would be all right. Samis would give her the stolen half-Wheel. She would deal with him somehow, then she would join the two pieces with chantment, and the world would be healed. She would go back to the others, spring would come, and Darrow would be well. Her voice was strong and glad as she sang a lilting chantment of the winds that streamed away until it was lost in the clouds. She thought of Mica, who had taught her the songs of the winds, and prayed she would be safe in Antaris.

All that day, Calwyn's spellwind carried them south. The clouds below were so thick that the boat seemed to float above another snow-covered landscape, with its own towering peaks and deep crevasses, shifting and dissolving with the movement of the air.

At evening, Samis used a chantment of seeming to transform their plain cups of cold water into spiced wine.

Calwyn held up her hand. "I don't drink wine."

"Never fear, my dear, this won't go to your head."

Calwyn pulled a face as she sipped. "It would taste better warm. If only we had the Clarion."

She was startled by the furious scowl on Samis's face. "You and your friends were not worthy to keep the Clarion. Keela told me how you used it — as a bed-warmer, as a frying pan! Where is your respect for the objects of power? Better that it lie in the Knot of the Waters than be profaned."

Calwyn's eyes stung; but why should she care what Samis thought? "Without fire, we would have died," she mumbled.

Samis snorted, but he let the subject go. "What would you like to eat? Name it, and you shall have your desire."

Calwyn hesitated. "Grilled trout," she said at last. She had a happy, well-guarded memory of eating trout by a stream with Darrow, long ago.

"No pigeons stuffed with myrtle berries? No oysters in seasoned butter? No mango fruit?"

"Whatever I ask for will have the same nourishment as dry bread," said Calwyn. "So it makes no difference, does it?"

"Your common sense is admirable. If grilled trout is your wish, then grilled trout it shall be."

This time Calwyn found it more difficult to give in to the illusion, and her fish was rather tougher than it should have been.

"Now for mine," said Samis when she was finished. "Tonight, I think, I would like a slow-cooked Hiberan pie."

"I've never eaten Hiberan pie. I don't know what it tastes like, I don't know what to sing."

Samis waved his hand. "I'll teach you. Never mind the look of the thing, for now. Let us begin with the smell." He sang a precise, high-pitched chantment, and a strong, gamy scent rose in the air. "Try that."

Calwyn breathed in and copied the shrill, keening chantment.

"Higher!" barked Samis. "Breathe from the bottom of your lungs! By the gods, girl, has no one ever taught you how to use your breath?"

Calwyn sang again and again, copying Samis's chantment to conjure the smell of the pie, then its taste, and finally the appearance of the tender strips of wader-bird meat in peppered gravy, cradled in a bed of steamed lily leaves.

Seeming was the most subtle power Calwyn had ever sung; the most delicate variations in note, inflection, pitch, and force of breath altered the illusion dramatically. If the Power of Winds was like pouring out a jug of paint and splashing it around, the Power of Seeming was like painting a tiny image with a single hair.

"Not bad, little priestess," said Samis at last. "The cooks of Hibera could not have served up better."

The sky was dark, and Calwyn realized she was exhausted. "I don't know how there can be so many Gellanese who practice the chantments of seeming. It's so difficult. They must all be very gifted."

Samis creased his nose in contempt. "Most of them learn — or buy — only one trick and content themselves with that. They learn a single spell to brighten shoddy cloth or spice up tasteless soup or make dull stones sparkle. Then they guard that one trick like a precious jewel. It cost more to buy the chantment of false sleep than I would have spent in Merithuros in a year. The so-called chanters of Gellan are nothing but peddlers, not worthy of their craft."

"I don't like the Power of Seeming," said Calwyn. "It's not honest."

She expected Samis to laugh at her, but he did not. "Like everything else in the world, it may be used for good or evil." He held up his finger to the wind. "We won't need a spellwind tonight. The breeze has shifted. If it holds, we will reach Spareth by morning."

"So soon?" exclaimed Calwyn.

Samis stretched out his legs in the cramped boat, forcing her to draw aside. "Are you looking forward to seeing the Desolate City again? Ah, they were great days, the days of our hunting, were they not?"

"You killed my friend Xanni, you almost killed all of us!"

Samis shrugged. "You are not a hunter. I'll wager Darrow sees it differently." He crossed his legs, and his cloak fell back, revealing leather boots that reached to his knees. "When you left me for dead in Spareth, I remained there a long time. I made many discoveries. There is one in particular that I look forward to sharing with you."

"Some new way of killing, I suppose."

Samis laughed. "Teasing me, little priestess? Excellent! We are becoming friends."

"As good friends as you and Darrow once were?"

She spoke sarcastically, but when Samis answered, his voice was sad. He said, "I will never have another friend like Darrow."

Again, Calwyn was acutely aware of his smell, like the spices of Merithuros, and the powerful, healthy body shifting beneath the folds of his cloak. "Sleep, my dear," he said softly. "Tomorrow will be a momentous day."

The Silver Ship

Calwyn woke from a natural sleep, not one imposed on her by a chantment of seeming. She sat up, stiff with cold, and drew the striped Gellanese blanket round her shoulders. The moons had sunk into the west, and a faint light in the east announced the coming of dawn.

Samis loomed above her, a black silhouette. He pointed down. The mass of cloud below had dissolved, and Calwyn could see the bumpy surface of the snow-covered forest. Then her heart skipped a beat as she glimpsed a sheet of smooth, glittering ice at the horizon: the sea.

Samis crouched beside her. "Spareth."

The boat swayed as they leaned over the side. The rising sun slanted through a tangle of silver spires and domes, tinting them in shades of rose and amethyst and gold. It was Spareth, the abandoned city, thrusting up through the forest.

Samis manipulated some levers, and the silver bubble drifted down toward the ruins. The towers and roofs loomed larger and larger, the city spreading itself around them, as Samis steered the craft down into an empty plaza with a spire in each corner. He sang a chantment of iron to hold the cloud-boat to the ground while Calwyn climbed out. She was tired and sore, and glad to feel the solid gray stone under her feet.

Samis stepped out of the boat and changed his growl of chantment. The silver bubble floated up and away into the pale sky, a dazzling globe lit by the morning sun.

"What are you doing?" cried Calwyn.

"We won't need it again." Samis smiled. "And to leave it here would be too great a temptation for you, my dear." His cloak billowed behind him as he turned and walked away.

Calwyn hurried after him along the empty streets. The crumbling walls and bare trees glittered with frost. Even the gentle curves of the silver domes and the tall, slender towers looked as if they had been carved from ice.

Samis strode past the site of their last encounter a year and a half earlier. The long splinters of the tower that had burst apart when Samis's magic failed lay where they had fallen, like segments of a discarded seedpod. Samis walked on without a backward glance, but Calwyn couldn't help staring at the place where they had left Samis's body, apparently lifeless, shrouded in his gray cloak.

"You dwell too much on the past," said Samis crisply, as if he had read her thoughts. "You must learn to look forward, as I do."

They climbed a hill and entered a small square bathed in morning sunlight, with a view of the city's shimmering spires and domes. The shallow fountain in the square's center was a sheet of ice, with dead leaves frozen into it.

Samis swept his cloak around him and sat down on the fountain's edge. "This place will do. Time for our lessons to begin."

"More chantments of ironcraft and seeming?" Calwyn remained standing. "What about your promise? You said you would give me the — the relic of the Goddess."

"Yes, yes. All in good time, my dear." His hooded eyes gleamed at her. "But first, little priestess, I will teach you something that the rest of the world has forgotten. I will teach you the Tenth Power."

"The Tenth Power!" Calwyn stared at him. "The power in —" She just managed to stop herself in time. Did Samis truly not understand the magic of the Wheel? Could he really mean to teach her these darkest, most powerful chantments?

"Sit down." Samis drew a slim silver tablet from his pocket and showed it to her. It was the size of his hand, and covered in tiny etched marks that shone like flecks of gold in the sunlight. He said softly, "The Tenth Power is the Power of Signs."

Calwyn blinked in confusion. This was not what she had expected.

"Signs?"

"Each of these symbols represents a sound," Samis explained, pointing to the tiny marks. "This one shaped like an egg is *aah*. This forked sign is *ee*. And this humped symbol stands for the sound *lll*. Do you understand?"

"I — I think so." Drawn in despite herself, Calwyn moved closer to peer at the silver tablet.

"The combination of signs spells out a chantment." Samis's arm was pressed against Calwyn's.

"So here, the humped sign and the egg together, is *laa*?"

"Bravo, little priestess! There are only three dozen or so signs. Once you have learned them, you can read the marks of every chantment."

As she frowned down at the rows of signs, Calwyn was pierced by the sudden sharp memory of Marna's pale face on a bed of straw. She whispered, "Marna knew about this. She tried to tell me. But I wouldn't listen. I was too busy asking my own questions."

Samis shook his head dismissively. "I doubt that this knowledge survived in Antaris. I found only one man in the whole of Gellan, where chantment is stronger than anywhere else in Tremaris, who knew of the existence of the Tenth Power. I saw nothing in my time with your yellow ladies to suggest that they had preserved this power."

Calwyn did not reply. All her certainties were tumbling around her. The Tenth Power was not the dark force she had thought it was. But even if the Tenth Power was not to blame for the troubles, the Wheel might have held some other kind of dark magic. Marna had said that the Wheel held the answer: Calwyn clung to that memory. Mending the Wheel would still mend the world, she was sure of it.

As Calwyn's thoughts whirled, her eyes flickered busily over the signs. "These marks give only the sounds of the words. How do you know the way to sing them? High or low, the length of the note?"

"See how the signs ride above or below this line? That gives the pitch. So far above for the high notes, so far below for the lower ones. The gaps between the signs show how long the note is held. It takes some practice to read the signs correctly. But I will teach you."

"This is — astonishing!" The Tenth Power was not a destructive power, but a way of preserving chantments. For a heady moment, she dared to restore her dream of setting up a chanters' college on Ravamey; she pictured rooms lined with these silver tablets, containing a record of every chantment, collected from all over the world. Nothing could be forgotten, no chantment would ever be lost again. She had no need to feign amazement. "How did you discover the Power of Signs?"

"There was some talk of a lost power among the scholars of Merithuros, though none of the sorcerers knew what it might be. Then, during my time in Spareth, I found many of these tablets, covered in signs. I have you to thank, indirectly, for that discovery." He looked at her sideways. "I took some of the tablets to Gellan, where I found Tragg, the man I told you about. He and I puzzled out the code together. It was mostly my work." He added with a smile, "You think I am arrogant? Perhaps I am. With the knowledge of these signs, I have discovered all the secrets that the Ancient Ones left behind."

"Darrow told me about your friend in Gellan. He said you killed him."

Samis gave Calwyn a dark, penetrating stare. "He was claimed by the chanters' plague. A terrible loss."

"You promised to tell me the truth."

"Ah, little priestess." Samis shook his head. "There are some questions better left unasked." He tapped his finger on the tablet. "Now, look at this. I copied these signs from the Clarion of the Flame, which Keela borrowed for me. The chantments of fire are not lost while the signs remain."

She stared down at the silver tablet. "They're here, all here? Are you sure? Have you sung them?"

"I have tried. But the gift of firecraft has been denied to me." Samis's hooded eyes narrowed, and he looked away for an instant across the cold, empty city. Calwyn felt a quick, unexpected beat of sympathy. Samis turned back to her. "Denied to me. But not, I suspect, to you." He pushed the silver tablet toward her.

Calwyn shrank back. "But — the Power of Fire can only be sung by men."

"Oh, and who spread that tale? Men, of course, just as they try to pretend that women cannot sing the chantments of iron. These fire-songs are pitched deep, but not too deep for you. Come now, try it. Haven't you discovered that with each power you acquire, the next becomes easier to master?"

It was true: Each new type of chantment had come more readily than the last. But Calwyn hesitated, clinging to the cold stone edge of the fountain. If she could sing the chantments of fire, she would be the Singer of All Songs.

Samis said, "You are afraid."

"The prophecy said that the Singer would be as powerful as a god," whispered Calwyn.

"Don't concern yourself with that, my dear," said Samis dryly. "If I believed that there was any chance of you becoming a god, I would not put this power in your hands. Here, take it!"

Reluctantly, Calwyn took the silver tablet and ran her finger along one row of the tiny symbols. Under her breath, she whispered the signs she had learned, guessing at the pitch of the chantment. "What's this? And this one?"

Samis told her. Calwyn found it easy to remember which symbol was which. It was as though her memory, as well as all her senses, had been sharpened at the same time as her gift of chantment had been restored and strengthened. She repeated the scrap of chantment, melding the sounds into a low-pitched, tentative song. Then she sang it again, the deep notes flowing with more confidence, and she felt the tingle in her flesh that signaled the rise of magic. A sudden burst of blue-and-orange fire flared against the pale winter sky.

Calwyn gasped, and Samis gripped her arm.

"Well done, Calwyn!" he cried, and his voice rang with delight and exultation. It was the first time he had called her by her name.

"The Power of Fire!" He wrapped his arms around her. "The Power of Fire, sung by human voice, for the first time since the death of the sorcerers of Mithates!"

Exhilarated, Calwyn returned his embrace, enveloped in the spicy smell of his iron-gray cloak. His hands were firm on the small of her back. They were larger than Darrow's hands. Awkwardly she pulled away, avoiding Samis's gaze.

Am I the Singer of All Songs now? she wondered. She didn't feel any different. She said aloud, "How will this help us end the winter and cure the snow-sickness?"

"Every chantment ever sung is recorded and kept somewhere in the storerooms of Spareth," said Samis expansively. "I have found many already, but with two of us to search we will soon discover the spell to reverse the damage done. But you must practice hard, little priestess, to be sure you are capable of singing the chantments when we find them. Now, let us hear more songs of fire!"

One by one, Calwyn sang the chantments that had been inscribed on the Clarion of the Flame: songs to create pools of light, songs to make soft warmth and intense heat, songs to make blazing columns of flame and fiery starbursts. If only she and her friends had understood the symbols before, she realized, their struggles to use the Clarion would have been far easier. There were patterns to the chantments, elegant affinities that she had never noticed.

"Enough," said Samis. "Time to work on the Power of Seeming. You hold your jaw too tightly, my dear; stretch your mouth, like this."

The two chanters created illusions for the rest of that day. Huge trees sprang up, flowered with flames; cascades of molten diamonds foamed through the little square. Samis showed Calwyn how to make time seem to slow down, so that the journey of an ant across her hand lasted for a day. Then he made the sun race across the sky and back in the space of a breath. As he sang, they sat on a raft in a blank green ocean, then swam with the fishes in the emerald depths.

At last Samis stood. The declining sun lit him in orange and gold, and opal glimmers sparked from his dark cloak. Calwyn realized that the whole day had passed. Guiltily, she thought of Darrow. But Briaali had said the healing Waters would hold off his illness; he was safe for now.

Samis said, "That will do for today. Tomorrow we will practice the Power of Iron."

Calwyn bit back a yawn. She didn't dare ask after the Wheel again; she didn't want to seem too eager, in case he guessed how important it was. If he didn't give it to her tonight, she would hunt for it herself tomorrow. "It's almost night. Where will we shelter?"

Samis smiled broadly. "I have a story that will surprise you. Come, I'll tell it as we walk."

He held out his large hand to her and, dazed with fatigue, Calwyn took it. As he led her through the chilly, darkening streets, he said, "No doubt you believe that our people have lived on Tremaris as long as time itself."

Yes, my people, the Tree People, have lived here forever! she wanted to reply.

Samis glanced up at the sky. "Our ancestors came to this world in a silver ship." There was a strange yearning in his voice. "They sailed across the stars as if the sky were a great ocean. That ship is still here, Calwyn."

"The ship is here? You've found it? It's in Spareth?"

Samis threw back his shaggy head and gave a rich, deep laugh. "Spareth *is* the ship!" He swept his arm across the silvery towers and domes. "The ship is all around us and beneath us. What you see is only a fraction of what lies below. The Ancient Ones built their first city on the foundation of the vessel that brought them to this world. You will see! You think that Spareth is an empty place, but there are storehouses of supplies, tools, clothing, medicines, devices like the cloud-boat, everything we will ever need."

As she stumbled by Samis's side, Calwyn stared with new eyes at the vast, mysterious structures that surrounded them. Were those silver towers the ship's masts? Were the domes its sails, its watchtowers, the captain's bridge?

She shivered. "Imagine if the ship could sail again!"

Samis glanced down at her. "But it could, dear heart. The Singer of All Songs could make it fly like a great silver bird. When this ship sails again, we will conquer Tremaris as easily as plucking an apple from the tree."

Calwyn pulled her hand from Samis's grasp and halted in the middle of the empty street. "You told me you wanted to save Tremaris! But you don't care about that at all! You lied to me."

Samis halted too. A breath of breeze caught his cloak and it billowed around him like a thundercloud. "No, Calwyn. I told you the truth. With your help, I will stop the chanters' plague and return spring to Tremaris. But after that —" His teeth gleamed as he bared them in a wolfish smile. "I have grand plans for us, dear heart."

"I've heard enough of your plans," said Calwyn, but her words were hollow; she was too tired to summon up proper outrage. And after all, what Samis wanted was a peaceful, prosperous Tremaris. That was not such a terrible plan. "And don't call me *dear heart*," she added.

Samis stalked off, and after a moment, Calwyn followed. He used a chantment of iron to open a doorway in a low, featureless dome, and led her up and up, along countless empty corridors, all lit with the soft glow she remembered from her previous visit.

She followed him into a round, airy room with curved windows that overlooked the whole city. A band of sky circled the room, scattered with stars, and the three moons were all visible, small and sharp and white as pearls.

The room was furnished with divans and long tables, littered with silver tablets. A spiraling ramp in the center led to another room above. Samis threw open paneled doors to show Calwyn shelves stacked with canisters and boxes.

"Food. Enough to feed us for centuries." He laid out a curious feast for them: slabs of crumbling cake made from spiced beans; broken biscuits tasting of salted meat; unfamiliar dried pink fruits.

Samis mixed a powder into a flask of water and asked Calwyn

to heat it with one of her newly learned chantments to make a hot, foaming drink that tasted of cinnamon and chocolate. He raised his cup.

"To the Singer of All Songs," he drawled.

Calwyn clasped her cup with both hands until she felt it burning her. The Singer of All Songs. She had traveled so far since that spring day when she and Marna walked beneath the apple blossom in the orchard of Antaris, and Marna had told her of the prophecy. Marna had not believed that anyone could master all the different chantments of the Nine Powers. What would she have said if she'd seen Calwyn today, summoning fire and spinning dreams from the sky? *Of course, I am not the Singer yet,* Calwyn told herself. *I need more practice, much more practice.* She smiled privately, then looked up at Samis. "How did you know the Knot of the Waters would restore me?"

Samis waved his hand at the piles of silver tablets. "Stories, legends. I took a risk, my dear. But aren't you glad I did?"

"The risk was all mine —" Calwyn began indignantly, then stopped. "Mine and Keela's."

There was silence in the room; Samis sipped at his drink, watching her over the rim of his cup.

Calwyn picked up a silver tablet and read at random: *dressed in animal skins and woven vines . . .* "So, it's not only chantments that are recorded here?"

"Our ancestors made observations of their new home. They

wrote down information about the primitives, their beliefs, their customs."

"The primitives? You mean the Tree People?" Calwyn's face had gone white, and her voice rose. "The Spiridrelleen are a wise and ancient people. They lived here long before the Voiced Ones came with their weapons and their — their powdered drinks!"

Samis laughed. "You are sentimental, like all the yellow ladies of Antaris." His voice hardened. "The Tree People are doomed."

"You're wrong." Calwyn's hands shook. She wrapped her cloak around her shoulders and lay down on one of the divans with her back to Samis.

"Good night, little priestess." A low throat-song of chantment filled the room, and the lights dimmed. There was a sighing sound as the doors sealed, and the soft tread of Samis's feet on the spiral ramp. Calwyn knew she was alone. She could search for the Wheel or read more from the silver tablets scattered on the table. But she was so worn out that she fell instantly asleep.

Tonno, Trout, and Briaali's party pressed northward. The Tree People had their own paths through the forest, and they made rapid progress toward Antaris.

"We've been marching two days," muttered Trout. "How long before next moondark?"

Tonno said grimly, "Time enough to warn the sisters and help them defend themselves."

No. We must persuade our brothers to abandon their attack. Briaali's words were steely. *There must be no fighting.*

"But you've already tried to argue with them," said Trout. "Without weapons —"

At that instant, a spear whistled past his nose and thudded into the trunk of an ember tree. With a muffled yelp, Trout threw himself onto the snow. The Tree People whirled around, and Tonno snatched the knife from his belt, shouting, "Who's there? Show yourselves!"

It is the warriors! cried Briaali. *Peace, brothers! We will not harm you!*

But another voice screamed into every mind: *Death to the Voiced Ones!*

The warriors rushed from the cover of the trees, brandishing spears, their faces streaked with red and white war paint.

Trout grabbed a fallen branch, shouting, "Keep back!" and Tonno yelled, "Hold your peace! Hold your peace!" as he swung his knife. At the sound of their voices, their attackers fell back, teeth bared in silent snarls of fear. But they did not fall back for long.

There were more than a hundred warriors; they had the advantage of numbers and weaponry. Before long, it was clear that the warriors would win. The struggle that followed was curiously silent. Trout was slashed across the shoulder by a stone knife and quickly disarmed. Briaali's wrist was sprained, and most of her followers suffered hurts of one kind or another, surrendering before they could be badly injured. Tonno fought on alone, but a group of the warriors surrounded him, and he was felled at last by a blow to the head that knocked him unconscious.

The leader of the warriors was a young man called Sibril, no older than Trout. He picked up Tonno's knife and thrust it through his own woven belt. He watched with satisfaction as the voiced travelers were gagged and bound, and roped together with the other captives. *We have won our first battle!* he exalted. *Let us go on to the lands behind the thicket of ice!*

Trout struggled as the ropes were twisted round his wrists, though he was glad to see that Tonno was conscious and sitting up groggily. As the warriors forced a gag between his lips, the burly fisherman gave a bearlike roar. Two or three of the Tree People took a hasty step back.

Call themselves warriors! thought Trout scornfully. But then the prisoners were all hauled to their feet, the wound in his shoulder began to throb, and he had other things to think about.

The days that followed passed like a strange dream for Calwyn. If she hadn't been comforted by the knowledge that Darrow had gained strength at the Knot of the Waters and had Halasaa to help him, she couldn't have delayed so long. She and Samis practiced chantments together, and she learned to adjust her voice with ease from ice to fire to ironcraft, from windcraft to seeming, and back again. Samis was a stern teacher, but Calwyn learned more in this short time than ever before. Samis helped her to see connections between the different forms of chantment that she had never understood, the overlap between powers that Marna had spoken of but never explained.

Every day, Calwyn asked about the Wheel, and every day Samis made some excuse: He had searched, but not found it; he was sure it was in this cellar or that storeroom. Tomorrow — she would have her precious relic tomorrow.

And every night, Calwyn vowed that soon, soon, she would use the dark chantments to force Samis to tell her where his half of the Wheel was hidden. She could hear Marna's words in her mind. *I lacked the courage to act. Do not make the same mistake.*

Then she would hear Mica's blunt voice. *So you're goin' to torture him?* Calwyn knew that was exactly what she must do, and day after day she hesitated. Tamen, or Samis himself, would have called that weakness. But if that was weakness, did Calwyn want to be strong?

One day she said to Samis, "You wanted to be the Singer of All Songs. Why are you happy to teach me instead?"

"Do you think I'm happy?" said Samis.

"No," said Calwyn, after a pause. "Do you expect me to serve you?"

"You have a timid spirit."

His words echoed her own thoughts so closely that she started. Samis smiled. "I will guide you. Or —" He fixed his dark, hooded gaze on her. "I could repeat the proposal I made to you once before. You might be my queen. My empress."

Calwyn's mouth was dry, and she struggled to keep her voice light. "Keela would have been your empress willingly."

"Poor Keela! How jealous she would be if she could hear us now!" Samis's smile faded and a brooding look came over his face. "These last years, since Darrow abandoned me, I have had no friend, no companion, no one to share my thoughts and plans. Keela thought she could be my partner. But she cares only for jewels and servants and compliments — that is all power means to her, flattery and fine clothes."

Calwyn said, "But she isn't stupid."

"No," agreed Samis. "But she has no interest in knowledge or the wise use of that knowledge — " He stopped suddenly, as if he'd said more than he intended. Beneath his breath, he murmured, "It is not easy to be alone."

"I know," Calwyn whispered. "I was lonely too, growing up in Antaris."

"I do not expect your answer now," said Samis. "Think on it, Calwyn. Think on it."

For a time they were both silent, and then they went back to their work.

In the evenings, Calwyn and Samis returned to the round tower. They would prepare a meal from the strange foods in the stores, and then they would talk. Samis told her stories of his peculiar childhood in the Imperial Court of the Merithuran Empire, and one night Calwyn told him about her friends' adventures in Merithuros the year before.

Samis had heard a version of events from Keela, but he listened with deep interest to Calwyn's story. When she came to the part where Darrow was proclaimed Lord of the Black Palace and became, in effect, the ruler of Merithuros, Samis roared with laughter. But his laugh was warm, not mocking. "To think of my Heron, who always shied from power, ruling the Empire!"

"It's a Republic now." Calwyn looked down. Where was Darrow? How much had the healing waters helped him? Was he weaker than before? Suddenly she was seized with a sick panic. How many days had slipped away while she sang? How could she have wasted so much time?

Samis had said something. He was watching Calwyn across the table, waiting for her reply.

"I'm sorry. I — I didn't hear you."

He whispered, "Sing for me, Calwyn."

Calwyn walked to the curving window. The empty streets and plazas of the moonlit city spread below, an island of silver hemmed on all sides by the white sea of the frozen forest: cold, silent, beautiful.

Calwyn closed her eyes and breathed in. The first tremble of power ran through her, from the soles of her feet to the top of her head. For an instant she paused, feeling the magic suspended within her, like oil stirred into water. And then she sang.

As her song of seeming unfurled, the streets of the empty city were transformed, clothed in brightness, bustling with people as they would have been in the time of the Ancient Ones. Painted walls, green gardens, and singing fountains flowered into being under her chantment; music and laughter drifted up to the round tower. Far below, Mica looked up and waved; Marna strolled arm in arm with Lia. Heben of Merithuros was deep in conversation with merry-faced Xanni, who had died long ago, and the children from the island of Ravamey shouted as they chased one another across the square. And Darrow and Halasaa smiled up at her as they threaded their way through the crowd.

Calwyn's body thrummed with effortless power as magic trembled from her lips. A mixture of feelings whirled inside her: mingled joy and sorrow, for the ghosts of the people she had known and the phantoms of the friends she might never see again; for the Ancient Ones, so hopeful in their new world, so blind to the harm they were about to do; and for herself, her own intertwined hope and fear.

The chantment died away, and the bustling, noisy, colorful square blurred before her eyes. The babble of talk and music faded. And then the image was gone. The square was empty once more. Snowflakes whirled softly through the streets. Calwyn shivered, though it was warm inside the tower, and drew her cloak around her shoulders.

Samis was beside her. Calwyn held out her hand, and he grasped it. She was surprised by the coolness of his fingers. He raised her hand to his lips. "Are you ready, little priestess? Are you ready to call yourself the Singer of All Songs?"

Calwyn opened her mouth to speak, but no sound emerged. The Singer of All Songs. She had spent the past two years running from this moment. But if it was truly her destiny, it would be cowardice to turn her face away. What if the salvation of Tremaris did lie in her hands, in her voice, and from false modesty, from the shying of her timid heart, she allowed the world to wither and die? What was more dangerous: too much pride, or not enough? Perhaps she had learned more from Samis than she'd realized. Was the Singer of All Songs the person she had become, or was it the person she had always been? It didn't matter: The answer was the same.

Her heart pounded. Samis was watching her carefully, as if she were a wild, dangerous animal that he held at the end of a slender string. "My queen," he said softly. She had expected him to smile in triumph, but his dark eyes were shadowed with sorrow. "There is one more lesson for you to learn."

"No," murmured Calwyn. "No . . ."

"You must." His hand tightened around her fingers. "Did you think there would be a flash of light? Did you think your Goddess would stoop to kiss you? No, little priestess. Becoming the Singer of All Songs is not accomplished in one leap. It is one step, then another, some steps in the light, and some in the darkness. The Singer's powers are not only of the light, Calwyn. It is time to walk in the dark." His eyes searched hers. "You want your Wheel; you must have it. But I will not give it to you. You must take it. Take what belongs to you, Calwyn. Take it!"

Calwyn made a small sound, a moan of protest, quickly stifled. Then she turned to face him and reached up to kiss his mouth.

She had never kissed anyone else but Darrow. Samis's lips were dry and cool; his back stiffened briefly as their mouths met, but then he seemed to relax. Calwyn's heart thudded in her chest as she wound her arms around his neck. Her lips brushed his ear.

And, in a whisper, she sang.

The Secret of the Wheel

Samis cried out and staggered back in pain, clutching at his eyes.

Calwyn faltered, but she forced herself to keep singing. The dark chantment hissed and spat; her lips were numb, as though venom dripped from them. Samis sank to his knees, driving his fists into his eyes. His mouth was stretched wide with pain.

In mind-speech, without pausing in her song, Calwyn formed the words, *Where is the Wheel?*

Samis moaned and shook his head.

Where is it? Calwyn demanded. *Where is the broken Wheel you stole from Antaris?*

Tears streamed down her face; it took all her self-control to keep her breathing even. Her heart was jumping in her chest.

Samis fumbled, one-handed, with the many tiny hooks that fastened his jerkin; the fingers of his other hand were jammed into his eye sockets as Calwyn's chantment forced needle-sharp splinters of ice beneath his eyelids. The dark song writhed around them both.

Calwyn felt the power of the shadow chantment build within her. Samis pulled the chunk of dark stone from inside his jerkin and flung it at her feet. As he hunched into a tight knot, Calwyn could just hear him moan, "Please — please —"

But Calwyn kept on singing.

This was the man who had made Darrow sick, who had killed her dear friend Xanni and crippled Lia. He had brought so much suffering to those she loved; it was only right that he should feel some of that pain. The chantment burned through her, feeding on her anger. She was no *little priestess* now! The thrill of her own wild, dark power surged through her, growing as her grim joy in her vengeance grew —

Calwyn realized she was *enjoying* it. Appalled, she stopped her song mid-note.

The only sound in the round tower was Samis's jagged breathing. His hands were pressed to his eyes; blood seeped between his fingers. Calwyn looked down at him. A few moments more, she knew, and she might have killed him with her chantment: not to regain the Wheel, but simply because, in that instant, she had wanted to.

Marna's words echoed in her mind: *a time for song, and a time for silence.* As she stood there, Calwyn began to understand that the true power of the dark chantments lay in the choice to leave them silent and unsung.

Slowly Calwyn stooped and picked up the precious half-Wheel. She did not not know how much time passed as she stood there, staring at the broken disc of black stone. She was aware that Samis had rolled over and was watching her through swollen eyes, rimmed with a dark crust of blood. When he blinked, he closed his eyelids slowly, wincing, and his breath still came in ragged gasps of pain.

Calwyn's hands shook as she drew her own half of the Wheel from the inside pocket where she'd kept it ever since leaving Antaris. Then she fitted the two halves together.

Darrow, my brother? Are you awake?

"Let him sleep," begged Keela in a low voice. "He needs to rest."

He needs to hear this also, my sister. Darrow, my brother, wake!

Darrow was breathing deeply, buried in sleeping-furs. He had fallen asleep over his meager dinner as the snowstorm rose outside the tent, and Keela and Halasaa had bundled the furs around him where he sat. But now he snapped cleanly out of sleep, his eyes alert as ever. He croaked, "What is it?"

I heard her.

"Calwyn?" Keela looked from one to the other. "Calwyn spoke to you?"

Halasaa shook his head. *She did not intend to cry out to us.*

"Is she in pain?" said Darrow sharply. "Where is she, what's happening? Can you still hear her?"

"Is she with Samis?" asked Keela.

I cannot tell. I have called to her, but she cannot hear me, the distance is too great. Halasaa hesitated. *There was pain in her cry. But it was pain of the heart, not of the body.*

Darrow passed a hand over his eyes. "How far did we come today? How close are we to Spareth?"

There is still far to go. But this is the river that leads to the ruined city.

"Here, drink." Keela pushed a cup of broth into his mittened hands. "Halasaa kept it warm by the fire-pot."

We will go far tomorrow, when this storm is past. Halasaa put his hand on Darrow's shoulder. *The wind will drive the snow from the ice.*

"No need for Mica's chantments after all." Darrow's hands trembled as he sipped at the broth.

"We should go back to sleep," said Keela. "But we need more fuel for the fire-pot. Is it your turn or mine, Halasaa?"

"Don't go out." Darrow put down his cup. "I'll sing some more wood into the tent." He had done this before, slipping firewood through the tent flaps to spare them a trip out into the snow.

As usual, Darrow parted his lips to growl out a chantment of ironcraft. But though he sounded the words and the notes, the chantment would not catch. In that instant Darrow knew that the last trace of his powers had slipped away. He did not speak, but something changed in his face. In a heartbeat he looked ten years older than before.

Keela swallowed. "I'll go," she whispered. "I need some fresh air."

* * *

Calwyn held the Wheel together, one half in each hand, and sang a chantment of ironcraft to join the two pieces together. Gradually the crack down the middle of the little disc sealed and vanished. When the Wheel was whole, Calwyn stroked her fingers over the stone as she sent the healing magic of the Power of Becoming into the disc. Then she rested the Wheel on her knees and lifted her hands away.

She stared down at the object of such power, the dread secret that the High Priestesses of Antaris had guarded for generations, the stone that had stopped spring from coming and released the snow-sickness across Tremaris.

The Wheel lay lifeless and inert in her lap. It was a dead thing. The Clarion had pulsed with life and power, even when it was not being played; it was always charged with magic. But the Wheel was not like that. There was no power in it. Mending it had achieved nothing. There was no magic here.

Clutching the Wheel tightly, Calwyn ran to the window and pressed her forehead against the cold glass. Snow was falling, thicker than before, hiding the silver towers and domes. Heavy clouds blotted out the sky. Even as she watched, frost crackled across the window. The world was deep in winter; the chanters were still sick. Darrow was dying. In her blind arrogance, she had fixed all her hopes on a worthless chip of granite. She was the Singer of All Songs, and there was nothing, nothing she could do.

A sound behind her made her turn. Samis had sat up; he took

his hands from his face, and Calwyn saw that he was not weeping, but chuckling softly.

"Well done, little priestess!" His deep voice hummed with pride. "I thought you would be afraid. But the Singer of All Songs must embrace the dark as well as the light. Do not be afraid of the dark, Calwyn. There is power in darkness."

"But there is no power in the Wheel!" cried Calwyn. "Nothing's changed. Nothing!" She turned back to the glass. Shadowy snowflakes danced before her eyes, and her head felt dull and heavy. She pushed the useless Wheel deep into her pocket.

Samis's voice echoed behind her. "So. The stone is worthless." He came up and kissed her lightly on the forehead. "But you have proven yourself tonight, my queen, my empress! Power flows through you. Day after day I watched it growing stronger, but now — you are alive with it." He lowered his voice. "I can hardly look at you. You are the Singer of All Songs at last." He seized her hands and spun her around and around. "This is the dawn of a new day for Tremaris! The old gods are dead. We are the new gods!"

Round and round the tower they whirled, until Calwyn was dizzy, and the stars and moons blurred together. *He is mad,* she thought, but the knowledge did not frighten her. Her long plait came unbound, and her hair tumbled around her shoulders. When Samis halted, she collided with him, breathless, and he threw his arms around her and held her tightly. Her face was turned up to his, and his heart pounded madly beneath her hands. The whites of his eyes were yellow, with tiny spots of red where the splinters of ice had pierced. He brushed back the hair from her face with blood-blotched hands, and murmured, "With the secrets of the Tenth Power, and our mighty ship, nothing can be denied to us. Forget Tremaris! We can leave this frozen, wasted, sickly world to rot. Together, my Calwyn, you and I —" He whispered, "We will rule the worlds beyond the stars."

Calwyn stared up at him, unable to tear her eyes from his. His madness seemed to call up a madness within herself. In a sudden frenzy, she pulled his face toward her and kissed his burning, bloodied eyes over and over, his forehead, his lips. She tasted salt: Samis's blood, Samis's tears. One of his hands was in her hair, while the other slid down her body. Calwyn pressed herself against him.

"My queen," he murmured. "My empress." All at once he sprang up, grasping her hand, and tugged her up the spiral ramp and into the smaller room above, which she had never seen. "Come, let me show you, the greatest secret of all —"

The small room at the very top of the tower was also circled by a seamless window, with a low shelf running below. A group of high-backed chairs clustered in a ring, facing out to the curved window.

Samis spread his arms wide as if to embrace the chamber and all it held; his dark cloak swirled behind him. "This is where the Ancient Ones sailed their ship! Sail it for me, Calwyn, my queen. Let us make Spareth sail!"

He whirled her into one of the high-backed chairs. Calwyn clutched at the arms of the seat. Her hands sank deep into the soft, shining metal and were held there. It was a strange but not unpleasant sensation, like resting in cool jelly. She sensed the first faint twinges of chantment coursing from her fingertips, down into the cool receptive material of the seat. Intuitively she understood that this cluster of chairs acted as a magnifier, weaving together and intensifying the power of the chanters who sat there.

Samis lowered himself into the seat beside her, and the yielding material encased his hands up to the elbow. He gave Calwyn a long look from his weeping, blood-crusted eyes.

"Let me go," he murmured. "Let me go."

Calwyn stared at him, the taste of his blood sharp on her tongue. The fog of madness, misery, and grief that had clouded her mind dissolved, as though a cold breeze had blown through her.

"Samis?" she whispered, but he had leaned back in his chair, a trancelike look masking his face. He began to sing a steady drone of chantment, and with a strange, fateful sense of calm, Calwyn added her voice to his.

A jolt of immense power ran through the base of the seats and into the floor of the chamber, shuddering down into the base of the tower. The two chanters were singing a chantment to prise loose something held fast, and Calwyn felt the magic build and build below her, as if she perched on the rim of the fire-mountain of Doryus as it was about to erupt. She tried to grip the arms of the chair, but her fingers just sank deeper into the fleshy metal.

The tower shook violently, and there was a vast, thunderous rumbling all around them, as the foundation of the city strained to free itself. Like a tree being pulled up by the roots, the city, the silver ship, lurched. Through the window, Calwyn glimpsed toppling trees and clods of frozen earth flying through the air as the ship tore itself from the ground where it had been buried for so long.

Samis's head was thrown back; his closed eyes were two rusted slits. Calwyn sat bolt upright on the edge of her seat, every nerve tingling. The rumble became a roar that drowned out the sounds of their chantment. Calwyn's teeth rattled; her hair fell into her eyes. Still she and Samis ground out their song, and still the power built. Once before, Calwyn had summoned up a chantment that was beyond her control, and it had nearly destroyed her. This magic was almost as great as the strength of that chantment, and she prayed to the Goddess to protect her.

Just as the vibrations reached such a pitch that it seemed Spareth would shake itself to pieces, the ship broke free. Calwyn was slammed back into her seat, but almost at once she felt an exhilarating sense of lightness as the immense silver ship soared into the air. Miraculously, everything fell quiet. There was no roaring or rumbling now, only their jerky, breathless throat-song of iron. Calwyn leaned forward. The vast silver ship was clear of the ground, suspended over the forest. Below them was the enormous crater of raw, churned earth where the city had been, and the white sea of

the frozen forest that lapped around it. Flurries of snow were set-
tling in the crater as the snowstorm died.

Samis's eyes were squeezed shut, his face gray, showing none of
Calwyn's exhilaration. Calwyn realized that his voice had failed;
she was singing alone. The vast swooping ship was under her
control.

Swiftly, subtly, she changed her song, and the ship angled
to the ground and swung so low that it barely skimmed the treetops. The flat, silver-lit, winding river was just below. In one
smooth movement, Calwyn wrenched herself from her chair and
dived onto the long, low shelf that ran beneath the curving window. As she sang, she clung to a section of the silver shelf. She
altered the chantment again, and the shelf tore free and was
hurled at the window. Calwyn ducked her head and braced for the
shattering of glass, but the window parted and resealed as she
hurtled through it, like the membrane of a soap bubble.

The icy air outside made her gasp. The long silver shelf
plunged with Calwyn clinging to it, her hair streaming behind her.
She sang out and the shelf swooped clear of the ship, down
toward the treetops. Just as her feet brushed the snowy twigs, the
shelf leveled and paused. Calwyn hung in midair for a heartbeat,
then crashed down, knocking the snow from the intermeshed
branches as she fell.

The deep snow broke her fall. She tumbled against a tree trunk,
scratched and bruised, but not badly hurt. Instantly she scrambled

up. Only the space of a breath had passed since she'd torn herself from the high-backed chair. The ship was still afloat, directly above Calwyn's head, a huge, round silver platter. It was as if one of the moons leaned across the gulfs of sky to aim a drunken kiss at the face of Tremaris. The ship's pocked and pitted underside was so low it blotted out the sky; and it was slowly falling closer. Calwyn threw back her head and sang with all her power.

The strength of the chantment surged up through her body as if the whole sphere of Tremaris pushed behind her. Her voice was stronger and more confident than it had ever been, the double notes of ironcraft buzzing from her lips. Magic poured forth to repel the silver shape that had been Spareth, the vessel that had carried the Voiced Ones across the stars.

The silver platter hovered and steadied. And then, slowly, it began to retreat. A dark fringe of night sky appeared around its edge, a margin that grew steadily bigger as the silver disc moved higher and higher. When it was the size of her hand, Calwyn felt her first twinge of doubt. Ironcraft worked by pushing from the ground. As the ship moved farther away, would the chantment buckle and let the ship crash down? Would a chantment of the winds be safer?

But the magic coursing through her was still strong, and she sang on, thrusting the ship higher. Now it was the size of the largest moon at harvest time; now it was as small as her thumbnail. Suddenly Calwyn felt the connection snap. The power of ironcraft had stretched as far as it could. Calwyn held her breath as she gazed up through the lacework of twigs overhead.

But the ship did not fall. The tiny silver ball gathered a cloak of blue fire around itself. Was Samis performing some chantment? Had he helped her to thrust the ship away? There were secrets of Spareth that Calwyn did not know, devices and machines Samis had never shown her.

The small, bright sphere did not grow any larger. The ring of blue fire that licked around it flared briefly. And then it streaked away across the night, trailing a spectacular tail of blue-and-green flame. In a moment it was gone, swallowed up into the darkness between the stars, the same darkness it had come from so long ago.

Calwyn stood staring up at the sky. She thought of Samis, alone in that huge vessel, hurtling past the moons and out into the vast ocean of stars. He would be peering from the window in the round tower through his swollen eyes, watching the green-blue marble of Tremaris shrink smaller and smaller, knowing that he could never return. He would sail that empty ocean forever, a lonely man wandering the rooms and storehouses of his deserted ship. Had she understood him, was that truly what he had asked of her? If he were not already mad, such a life would surely make him so.

Calwyn shivered. *It is not easy to be alone . . . my queen, my empress . . .* She covered her face with her hands.

Then she swept the tears from her face. Her arm ached; she had bruised it when she fell. She laid her other hand on the hurt place. Though she barely made the effort to summon the Power of Becoming, the tips of her fingers tingled with sudden magic, and the flesh of her arm grew warm. Instantly the soreness was gone. The scratches were not worth healing, but she soothed a swelling on her ankle and sealed up a deeper cut on her shin.

Her eye was caught by a dark shape against the snow: The Wheel had fallen from her pocket, and she bent to retrieve it. Marna had valued it: For that reason alone, she should treat it with respect. Gently she brushed the snow from its surface, and as if in response to her touch, a carved pattern flowered about the rim of the disc. She had never noticed any carving before — then she remembered the faint pits and scratches that had always marked the Wheel's surface. Until now, they had been meaningless. It was too dark to see clearly; the pattern was very faint, only just perceptible beneath her fingertips.

Calwyn sang one of the deep, resonant chantments of fire that she had practiced with Samis, and a small yellow-white globe of light blossomed at her shoulder. She tilted the Wheel carefully to make out the carvings, and as the light struck the rim of the disc, she saw that the marks were indeed signs of the Tenth Power.

Calwyn traced the symbols with her finger, sounding each sign as she'd learned. It was not a chantment, only a string of words.

When the Singer of All Songs shall dance, and the dancers shall sing, then will be the coming of the Goddess, and the healing of the world. For this world breathes chantment as we breathe the air, and drinks in the dance like water, and the song and the dance are one music.

Calwyn lowered the Wheel. This was the secret! This was the message locked in the signs of the Tenth Power, the answer that Marna had known was there. But what did it mean? *The dancers shall sing . . .* The only dancers Calwyn knew were the healers of the Tree People. And they had no voices, they could not sing. It made no sense.

"Taris, help me!" Calwyn whispered. But the Goddess did not answer.

Calwyn's hands were numb with cold; she sang a chantment that shook the ball of light and warmth into a gossamer cloak that she could wrap around herself. *The Singer shall dance, and the dancers shall sing.* Whoever had made the Wheel knew the worship of the Goddess and the Tree People's Power of Becoming. Was the message simply a plea for harmony between the two peoples of Tremaris? But Calwyn felt certain that the words held a more particular meaning.

She smiled faintly as she remembered how Briaali had warned her against wasting time on "idle prophecies" . . . Briaali — An echo of memory chimed in Calwyn's mind. Briaali had said something else that night. Calwyn had not paid much attention at the time, and now she struggled to remember the wise woman's words.

In the wake of the storm, the night was clear and cold, and Calwyn gazed up through the trees at a slice of dark sky and a sprinkling of stars. She recognized the constellation of the Bell that gleamed in springtime skies. Though it was still deep winter below, the stars wheeled in their proper patterns above, following their stately dance.

There were great dances here, in the old days. The lively figures painted on the walls of the cave by the Knot of the Waters.

Dancers twirling and stamping their feet, lit by the flickering of the scattered fires. The murmur of music, the beat of drums, the call of flutes. And the distant sound of voices, all the sisters of Antaris singing together.

It was all one, *one music*, the singing and the dance, the magic weaving ice and fire, wind and iron, the spark of life and the cold breath of stone.

The three whirlpools, the three twining waters, surging together to form one knotted, living whole.

The light of the stars, the light in the depths of the Knot of the Waters, the living light bursting inside Calwyn's heart.

Briaali's voice echoed: *Hand to hand, the world's circle danced, the people, the trees, the land, the sea, the moons, the stars . . . without beginning, without end . . .*

This world breathes chantment, and drinks in the dance.

And Mica's song, an old song of the Isles where she was born. *From the river, the sea; from the sea, the rains; from the rains, the river . . .*

Her mother, her father, their love merging as the whirlpools merged, to create new life, Calwyn's life, child of two strands of magic.

A clear note suddenly rang across the heavens, like a chime struck with a small silver hammer. Calwyn was lying on her back in the snow, but she didn't feel the cold as she stared up with wide eyes. The brightest star at the top of the Bell, the star called Lenari, flared blue-white, then faded gold as the sweet note faded. One by one, the stars rang out, each one glowing brightly as it sang. Calwyn lay breathless beneath the song of the stars, watching as the pattern of their song was picked out across the dark of the sky, each note a sign etched in silver, marked with gold.

Calwyn opened her arms, and the music of the stars and the forest wrapped around her and carried her into the light.

When she woke, her head was spinning. She stood and brushed the snow from her clothes. She was barely cold; she could only have been dreaming for a moment. She threw back her head and shouted for joy, there in the middle of the forest. "Darrow! Halasaa! My dear ones, I know what we must do!" She knew they were too far away to hear, even with mind-speech, but the words sang themselves through her whole body.

She knew how to preserve Tremaris and its chanters. She knew it as surely as she knew the chantments of ice-call, knew it deep in her bones, etched in her soul with signs of golden fire. Whether the Goddess had spoken to her, or the spirits of the Knot of the Waters, or some ancient chantment of the Wheel, she did not know, and it did not matter.

Calwyn tucked the Wheel reverently inside her jacket, then twisted her hair into a long rope and wound it around her head. Her mother's carved comb was still safe in her pocket, and she pushed it into place. She held her head high: She was no longer a little girl.

It was time to go. She had no cloak, no provisions, no skate blades, nothing. She had no cloud-boat, no sled —

She spun around. The long section of silver shelving had landed some distance away. And she was not far from the river.

With a chantment on her lips, the Singer of All Songs began her journey.

The Flight of the Goddess

The captives marched through the wilderness, roped in a long line behind the victorious warriors. Trout and Tonno were tightly gagged at first and treated warily. On the second day, Briaali demanded that Sibril remove their gags. *How can they eat and drink with their mouths stopped?*

Sibril was unmoved. *I cannot risk it.*

Young fool! Not all Voiced Ones make magic with their mouths. These are not chanters, but ordinary men.

You are the fool if you believe their lies, old mother. The chanters must die.

Briaali lost her temper. *If these two were chanters, they would have used magic to fight you when they had the chance. You would not allow a beast of the forest to starve thus.*

Be silent, old one! You have no authority here. I am the leader!

Briaali held up her hands and said nothing more, but the next morning one of the warriors removed the gags. Tonno and Trout were allowed to eat and drink their fill, but as soon as Tonno began to speak, the alarmed warrior jabbed him in the ribs with a spear tip and roughly pulled the gags back on.

Trout reflected miserably that all the other hardships — the forced march through the forest, the inadequate food and warmth, the chafing of the ropes — did not make him feel as helpless as being unable to speak. If only he could have one brief conversation with Tonno, he thought as he stumbled through the snow, the rest would be bearable.

Seven days after their capture, much sooner than Trout and Tonno had expected, they came to the Wall of Ice. When the great rampart of ice reared out of the forest before them, every one of the Spiridrelleen, warriors and Briaali's followers alike, reeled back in dread and wonder. Trout shivered, and Tonno felt a prickle of hope. Surely it would be impossible for the Tree People, armed only with spears and without the power of chantment, to pierce this immense barrier.

A few warriors approached the Wall and stared up at it speculatively. Trout and Tonno exchanged a horrified glance and began to jerk the rope and stamp their feet, trying to catch Sibril's attention. *The Voiced Ones wish to speak!* cried Briaali with mind-speech, but the warriors ignored her too.

Tonno and Trout could only watch helplessly as one of the warriors picked up a stick and poked it at the Wall. Instantly, his whole body stiffened and jerked as the current of protective magic rushed through him. He fell to the ground, rigid and lifeless, his blood frozen in his veins. The other warriors leapt back. Some turned to stare accusingly at Briaali and her friends.

They tried to give you warning! Oh, my brothers, do you not see the madness of this attack? Briaali berated them, and she kept up a stream of remonstrance all through the afternoon as the warriors cut down trees around the clearing. The forest rang with the thud of stone axes and the crash of timber.

What are you doing, my brothers? Briaali lamented. *What is the purpose of this slaughter? How can you condemn the Voiced Ones for mistreating the forests when you yourselves kill the trees without reason?*

We have our reasons, old mother, replied Sibril grimly.

The felled trees were piled high near the Wall, though not touching it. It was soon clear that the warriors intended to make a huge bonfire to melt the ice. The wood was too green and damp to burn readily, and when the Tree People first ignited a stick from their fire-pot and poked it deep into the pile of fuel, there was no result but a cloud of smoke. But the warriors did not give up. They fed the first tiny flames with kindling and coaxed the fire to grow, twig by twig, branch by branch.

Trout shook his head unhappily, and Briaali's words echoed his thoughts. *If they are patient they will melt this ice, and we cannot stop them.*

Tonno widened his eyes at Briaali and jerked his head toward the Wall.

Briaali understood him. *Yes. I have spoken a warning to your friend within, and the other chanters inside the thicket. I cannot tell if they have under-stood, and it will not prevent the fighting. But it is all that we can do.*

All that day and into the night, the warriors felled trees to feed the bonfire, until the flames blazed up in a roaring, crackling inferno.

The captives were forced back into the forest to shield themselves from the heat. Tramping feet and dragged logs had churned the clearing into mud, and the Wall glistened as the flames shot high into the clear sky.

Briaali had given her warning to Mica and the Daughters of Taris, but there was no sign they had heard her. As night wore on, the captives huddled together in despair while the warriors dragged log after log into the blaze. Briaali stared ahead, her wrinkled face set like carved stone in the glow of the fire. *Foolish children! What can you hope for? When the soil is muddied with your own blood and the blood of the Voiced Ones, will you be content?* But her words were more sorrowful than angry now, and her followers beat their breasts with their bound fists in a slow, dull rhythm of grief.

Sibril flung out his hand, and his triumphant words rang through all their minds. *See, my warriors! The thicket is melting!*

The surface of the Wall was dripping now; steam wreathed through the clearing, and puddles spread from the foot of the Wall, mingling with melted snow to further muddy the ground. Slowly, the Wall behind the bonfire was shrinking.

Prepare, warriors of the Spiridrelleen! cried Sibril. *Prepare to take back our homeland from the Voiced invaders! Prepare for battle!*

The warriors left the fire to care for itself while they daubed their faces with white-and-red war paint and sharpened their spearheads and stone knives for the fight.

Trout nudged Tonno in the ribs. A faint noise could be heard above the roar of the fire: the sound of voices. Sibril heard it too; his head swiveled round, and the rest of the warriors froze, listening intently.

Briaali's words sounded in the minds of the captives and the approaching chanters. *Be warned! The warriors of the Tree People await you! Take care, take care!* And she showed them a mind-picture of the fire and the preparations in the clearing. *This battle must be stopped!*

The sound of singing faltered, then rose again, stronger than before. A gust of wind swept around the clearing; the bonfire guttered wildly so that the warriors had to dodge the flames. Tonno gave Trout the thumbs-up at this sign of Mica's presence, and Trout nodded, grimacing through his gag.

The warriors hefted their spears to their shoulders, preparing to rush through the Wall when the gap appeared. But the chantment of the priestesses was mending the breach, building and firming the ice that had dissolved. For a time the two groups struggled in a tense balance, invisible to one another, the warriors frantically feeding the fire to melt the Wall down, and the sisters singing to rebuild it. Trout fidgeted with the rope that bound his wrists. Why didn't the priestesses simply put out the flames instead of fussing with the Wall? Tonno was pacing, two steps one way and two steps back, as far as the rope would take him.

Then, suddenly, a compelling cry sounded in the mind of every person there. It was Briaali, her words vibrating with emotion, a command that was impossible to ignore.

Look up! It is the sign, the Star of the New Days!

One by one, the warriors halted and stared upward, open-mouthed. The captives shuffled out from under the trees, faces turned to the sky.

An enormous, white-hot star was racing across the sky, with a long tail of green-and-blue fire. It burned a trail across the vision of those who watched, until they were unable to distinguish the true star from the ghostly image it left behind.

Tree People, both warriors and captives, priestesses of Antaris, windworker, fisherman, and scruffy youth, all stood as if they'd been turned to stone, faces lifted to the sky. The priestesses' song of strengthening died away. For a few moments, except for the roar of the fire and the hiss of steam, there was silence in the clearing. Then a murmur rose from the chanters beyond the Wall. "A portent, the Star of the Goddess — the coming of Taris — the Goddess flies down from the skies —"

For shame, to shed blood in this place and under this sign! Briaali's words were a heart-torn whisper. *Whatever happens under the light of this star will spread across the whole of Tremaris. . . .*

The warriors hesitated, looking about for Sibril, confused and uncertain. Tonno clenched his fists with a savage hope. Perhaps Briaali could convince them to abandon this senseless attack after all. . . .

But then Sibril's words shrieked inside his mind. *Attack, my brothers!* The warrior leader leapt onto a tree stump, brandishing

Tonno's knife, his face fiercely striped with white and red. *Kill the chanters!*

Even before the words were out, a volley of spears and arrows was whistling over the Wall into the midst of the priestesses gathered on the other side. The women cried out in pain and fear. Some sang chantments in retaliation, and a hail of huge ice-stones rained down on the attackers, knocking some of them to the ground. But the strong cohesion of the priestesses' chantment was dissolving into chaos.

At long last someone did what Trout had been waiting for all night, and sang a chantment to douse the bonfire. With a deafening hiss and cloud of steam, the flames went out.

But as soon as the fire was out, Trout realized why no one had done it before: Now there was nothing to prevent the warriors from pouring through the gap in the Wall, and the sisters could not mend the breach fast enough to keep them back. As the tall, silent warriors of the Spiridrelleen leapt across the remains of the fire and inside the Wall, the sisters screamed, some in fury and some in terror. The war of the Tree People had begun.

"Halasaa!"

It was Keela's voice, low and urgent. Halasaa struggled to wake from a deep sleep as Keela shook his shoulder. "Halasaa, I saw something while I was fetching the wood. It was a shooting star, but — oh, *huge*, and so bright! I've never seen a star like it!"

Halasaa knew the legend of the Star of the New Days, the omen that foretold sweeping change for the whole world. But somehow he was sure that Samis, or Calwyn, or both, were responsible for what Keela had seen. Her eyes were enormous as she stared at him in the dim light from the open fire-pot. She whispered, "I think we should wake Darrow."

Halasaa hesitated. *No. Let him sleep.*

Keela bit her lip. "All right. But, Halasaa — it was a wondrous thing. It must mean something. I wish you'd seen it." She replaced the lid on the pot and extinguished the faint glow. In the darkness she settled herself under a pile of furs, and soon her breathing slowed and deepened.

But Halasaa lay staring into the dark, waiting. Time passed; perhaps he drowsed. And then a whisper at the back of his mind made him jerk upright. *My sister? Is that you?*

Halasaa, my brother! Calwyn's words were faint, but unmistakable.

My sister, are you hurt? What has happened?

I'm as well as can be! Her words fizzed with a wild, irrepressible happiness. *Where are you?*

Darrow and Keela and I have traveled downstream, on the river that flows through Spareth.

Yes — yes. I'm following that same river upstream. I will reach you soon. Already Calwyn's voice was stronger, as if she was moving toward them very swiftly indeed.

What of Samis? Is he with you?

No. Some powerful emotion stirred beneath Calwyn's words, an emotion that Halasaa found difficult to read. *Samis is gone. How is Darrow?*

Halasaa wanted to spare her pain, but he had to be truthful. *He is weaker, my sister. He can no longer sing any chantment.* Halasaa hesitated. *Come quickly.*

There was silence, and at first he thought that the connection between them had been broken. But then he heard Calwyn's voice again, less elated than before, and unsteady. *Speak to me, Halasaa. It will help me to find you.*

Yes, if you will speak to me. Tell me what has happened.

As Calwyn sped through the freezing night on her silver sled, singing a throat-song of chantment that trailed behind her in a white mist, she told Halasaa in mind-speech everything that had happened in Spareth. She told him of becoming the Singer of All Songs. She told him about mending the Wheel, and of her vision for the healing of Tremaris. But she did not tell him she and Samis had kissed, nor of the strange bond that formed between them. If Halasaa sensed gaps in her story, he did not question her. And while Darrow and Keela slept, he told her how Trout, Tonno, Briaali, and the others had set off for Antaris, and of the change in character that had overcome Keela.

Calwyn's words became stronger and clearer until Halasaa sensed the flame of her presence flickering through the forest. She was moving so swiftly that he thought he must be mistaken. When

Darrow had sped the sledges with ironcraft they had never traveled so fast. He crawled from the tent and gazed down the river. There she was, a slim, dark figure in the moonlight, a blur of shadow skimming along the ice. She raised her hand in greeting, and now he heard the hum of chantment that drove her on.

In a moment she had leapt off the flat silver sled and come running to embrace him. Keela poked her tousled head out of the tent. "Darrow's awake," she whispered.

"Good," said Calwyn briskly. Her eyes were very bright. "We must leave for Antaris at once."

Halasaa shook his head. *My sister, we have been traveling down this river for ten days. Even if you speed our sled with chantment, we can't hope to reach Antaris more quickly than that.*

Calwyn laughed aloud. "We'll reach Antaris by morning, my brother!"

"Calwyn?" Darrow stood behind her, a sleeping-fur clutched about his shoulders. As she turned, he flung up his hands instinctively to ward her away. Her eyes locked with his. Deliberately, she raised her arms to embrace him through the sleeping-fur. *My love,* she said in mind-speech. *Be brave, be strong. I know what we must do to make you well.*

"My heart —" Darrow lifted a hand to touch her hair, her new queenly hair, then dropped it to his side. He gave her his old lopsided smile. "Too late, I think."

"No," said Calwyn. "It is not too late. I wouldn't say so unless it was true."

Keela arched an eyebrow. "Antaris by morning? Is that true too?"

"Climb onto the sled, and hold on tight." Calwyn threw back her head, and her eyes blazed. "Leave the tent, leave it all! We are going to fly."

Tonno could not block out the clamor of the fighting, much as he wanted to: shrieks and sobs; the sickening, meaty thud of spearheads into flesh; high, panicked singing; the gurgle of blood in the throats of the dying. But then, through it all, he heard Mica's voice, howling in pain and rage. Without thinking, Tonno ran, forgetting that he dragged all the other prisoners in a stumbling line behind him. He didn't know what he intended to do, or how he could possibly help Mica, tied and gagged as he was; he only knew that he had to find her.

Wait! called Briaali. *The fire — we can free ourselves!*

Trout had heard Mica's voice too, and he understood Briaali at once. He flung himself down by the remains of the bonfire, where some coals still glowed, and held his bound wrists as close to the embers as he could bear. With a swift flare of flame, the vines shriveled black and fell away, and Trout tore his gag free. "Mica!" he shouted. "We're coming!"

Tonno threw himself on his knees and copied Trout, then he was up and staggering through the gap in the Wall and into the thick of the battle.

The struggle was fierce and bloody. The priestesses were fighting with chantment. Blinding snow flurries swirled everywhere, blown by Mica's songs of windwork, while a hail of sharp ice fragments rained from the sky. Even through the driving snow, the warriors hurled their stones and spears with deadly accuracy. Injured women lay moaning on the ground, tangled in their dark cloaks; bleeding warriors writhed in the mud, gashed with razor-edged shards of ice. The warriors were gaining ground as they forced the sisters back into the woods, farther and farther from the Wall.

"Mica! Mica, where are you?" shouted Trout, snatching up a dropped spear shaft. A dark shape blundered into him out of the whirling snow, and he felt a searing pain in his shoulder as his earlier wound was torn open. Trout struck out blindly; his opponent wrenched the spear from him, and suddenly they were grappling hand to hand, stumbling over the uneven ground.

Tonno's hand had flown instinctively to the empty knife-sheath at his belt. He growled in frustration and grabbed a fallen branch, whirling it furiously around his head. "Sing ice under their feet!" he bellowed. "Freeze their hands!"

A handful of sisters sang as he suggested, and for a few moments the warriors' advance was checked. Then came the sound of yells from the woods behind them: Tonno whirled around to see the villagers of Antaris, hoes and pitchforks in their hands, pouring over the slope to help the priestesses, screaming in rage against the invaders. Tonno held out his tree-branch to bar their way. "Wait! Wait!"

One of the villagers bared his teeth, lowered his pitchfork, and ran straight at Tonno. Roaring, Tonno parried the thrust, but the force of the movement sent him careering into one of the sisters. She spun around, wild-eyed with panic, her fingers spread and shaking as she sang out a chantment to imprison Tonno's hands in a lump of ice.

"Not me, you fool!" Tonno yelled, but it was too late. His hands were frozen, encased in ice, and someone else was rushing at him. Tonno kicked and rolled over, and brought down the lump of ice on someone's skull. He no longer knew who he was fighting against; it didn't matter anymore. Now he was fighting for his own survival.

Trout had lost his assailant; somehow they'd blundered apart in the snow and failed to find each other again. His injured shoulder burned with pain, his jacket was soaked with fresh blood and his left arm dangled uselessly as he stumbled and dodged between the fighters.

"Mica! Mica!"

If he kept heading into the wind, he thought doggedly, he should find her. . . .

Something squelched and crunched beneath his boot. He lifted his foot and saw the hacked-off stump of a hand, a bloody pulp trodden into the mud.

Stomach heaving, he reeled on. A clump of blanch-trees loomed out of the blizzard and he half-fell into their shelter.

Sobbing and breathless, he slumped against a slim tree trunk. Strong fingers clamped around his ankle, and he yelped in fear.

"It's me, you goose!" cried Mica, her breath hot in his ear, and there she was beside him, one eye swollen shut and her thick, honey-colored hair matted with blood.

"What happened?" groaned Trout, touching her head. But Mica just shrugged. She sang and the blast of wind that her chantment summoned bent the tree trunks nearly double. She leaned into Trout, and a spear thwacked into the spindly blanch-tree near their heads.

"It ain't safe here!" cried Mica, scrambling farther back under the trees. "Where's Tonno?"

"I don't —" Trout began. There was a sudden whistling sound, and a handful of arrows trembled in the ground beside them. Dazed and disbelieving, Trout stared at his side; an arrow was sticking out of his ribs. "Oh," he said weakly. "Oh dear."

Mica's face went white. "Don't — don't move," she stammered. "We'll get it out of you." She looked around wildly, but there was no one to help. There was total confusion in the muddy area between the Wall and the woods. People staggered back and forth, or collapsed to the ground, whimpering for help. A villager in a green jerkin sprinted by, knife in hand, his mouth stretched in a grimace of mad rage. A woman stumbled across the battlefield, her bloodied hands clutched over her mouth. A Tree Person with a painted face sprawled close to Trout and Mica, staring sightlessly at the sky. Nearby, hidden in the trees, someone was screaming, one shrill note, on and on. And still the random hail of spears and arrows and ice-stones whistled through the air in all directions, deadly, unpredictable.

Then Briaali's voice sounded inside their heads. This time she spoke in a faint, despairing whisper: a plea, not a command. *Stop . . . stop. Look up, brothers and sisters, look up.*

Trout and Mica clutched each other tightly. To their left, someone cried with a disbelieving sob, "It's true, it's true! Taris is come!"

Outlined against the moons, poised high on the back of a dark eagle, the Goddess rode across the sky. She was tall and slender, lit with silver; her hair was black as a moondark night, and her eyes shone like stars. The comet had come, and now the Goddess flew, wrathful, beautiful. She wheeled above the scorched land and the wreckage of battle, above the smoke and the snow.

Mica pinched Trout's arm. "That ain't no old goddess! Look, Trout! That's Cal, our own Cal up there!"

Calwyn wheeled the sled above the ragged gap in the Wall, the blackened scar where the huge fire had been, and the battle in the clearing. Here and there a frightened face turned upward, but most people still staggered about or raised their arms to strike or hurl a spear or lay motionless on the mud-churned ground.

Calwyn's companions clung to the sled behind her, peering down. Halasaa's voice sounded in her mind. *They have not stopped fighting.*

Keela said softly, "I thought — when they saw you —"

The few who had seen the vision in the sky were struck dumb with awe and terror. But most of them had not looked up.

Darrow whispered, "Do what you must, Calwyn. Put an end to this."

She nodded. *Hold on.*

Subtly Calwyn changed her chantment of the winds, and the sled swooped low over the Wall, onto the broad canopy of a spander tree. Even with her new powers, she could not sing two songs at once. But the moment the sled landed on the stiff branches, and she knew that the spander tree would hold their weight, she began to sing a different chantment.

She sang one of the high-pitched, bitter songs that she had learned at Marna's deathbed, the chantment to paralyze. The dark chantment numbed her lips and tongue as it unfurled across the battlefield, rippling out from the tree like a black mist of poison gas. One by one the fighters were struck by the dark magic; one by one they froze in mid-action and toppled into the mud, stiff as ninepins. Calwyn struggled against a rising nausea as she sang, and she wrapped the ropes tightly around her wrists to hold herself upright.

Dawn was breaking. A watery light and a dreadful silence spread across the valley. Smoke and steam billowed from the remains of the fire. The last snowflakes of the priestesses' chantments settled into the mud, and the last ice-stones dropped from the sky, until the only sound was the uncoiling of the high, discordant chantment. Calwyn let her poisoned song fade, then she spoke into every mind, with a quiet, terrible authority. *Hear me. It is finished.*

No one could raise their head to stare, no one could quake or tremble, but she knew that her voice held them in thrall, and she felt the thrill of that power. Briefly, she thought of Samis. From her viewpoint high at the top of the tree, she scanned the sea of bodies until she found the one figure she sought. *Briaali. Rise up.* Using the skills she had learned from Samis, she sang a directed chantment of undoing that freed the old woman. *Find your people. You will gather the weapons and throw them on the fire.*

Briaali moved among the fallen, touching a shoulder here and there, and Calwyn freed those she touched. Without moving her eyes from the scene below, she sang to release her three companions from their frozen positions behind her. The sled rocked as Keela and Halasaa sat up. The Tree People moved back and forth, prising stone knives and spears and hoes from paralyzed hands and piling the weapons on the smoldering embers of the bonfire. Calwyn sang out a deep, ringing chantment, and at once the fire leapt into blazing life, belching black smoke as the weapons were consumed.

I release you all. There will be no more fighting.

Calwyn sang and all over the battlefield, slowly, stiffly, people sat up.

Now Calwyn spoke aloud; her voice carried effortlessly. "Where is the High Priestess?"

"I am here," came a low, clear voice. Lia stepped forward; her hair was disheveled, her pale oval face smudged with dirt and blood. Her chin thrust upward, and she clasped her hands tightly before her. If she was destined to meet the Goddess face-to-face to answer for her actions, she must do her best to meet her fate bravely.

The Goddess, more clearly visible now in the strengthening sunlight, turned to face her. "Lia, Lady Mother."

Lia's mouth opened, but no sound came out. This was not the Goddess, but somehow, it was not Calwyn either. The girl shone, as if she had bathed in starlight.

Calwyn spoke. "People of Antaris, People of the Trees, be at peace. The wounded among you must be tended. The High Priestess welcomes you all within the Dwellings."

"But — so many men . . ." murmured Lia.

"The High Priestess welcomes you *all*," said Calwyn.

Lia croaked, "The Wall — the Wall must be mended."

Calwyn gave her a stern look. "Leave it! The harm has already been done. I have more important work for you."

Lia swallowed, abashed. Then she cried, "Sisters, did you hear her words? Help the hurt ones back to the Dwellings. Fetch goat-carts from Areth for those who cannot walk. Gilly, run ahead. Warn Ursca that we're coming."

Limping, bleeding, holding onto one another, people began to move. Calwyn looked over her shoulder. "Are you all right?"

Keela nodded. Halasaa was supporting Darrow, who slumped against his shoulder, his breathing shallow. *He needs warmth, my sister.*

"I'll take us to the Dwellings," said Calwyn. But as she gathered breath to resume her chantment, she heard a faint voice calling from below.

Trout? Calwyn glanced swiftly at Halasaa, then she sang. The sled leapt from the treetop and swooped to the ground. Calwyn and Halasaa jumped from the sled and ran to the little group who had been hidden from view under the trees: Trout, gulping for breath, with pale tear-tracks on his dirty face, and Tonno, kneeling with his back to them.

"Trout, you're hurt! Keep still, Halasaa and I can take the arrow out —"

But Trout pushed her furiously away. "Not me, not me! Mica!"

Mica was cradled in Tonno's lap. Halasaa and Calwyn flung themselves down by her side.

Trout's words jerked out, faster and faster. "She couldn't — the spell came and she fell and the spear was coming, we saw it coming, we saw it, but we couldn't move, she couldn't get out of the way —" Trout sobbed for breath. "But she'll be all right, won't she, won't she, Halasaa, she'll be all right, you'll heal her, won't you, it's a clean wound, you can heal that, can't you, Halasaa, can't you?" The last words were almost a scream.

The spear shaft stood upright in Mica's chest, like a sapling reaching for the sun. Her eyes were open, her lips parted in surprise. Halasaa pressed his hands flat down on either side of the wound, his palms sticky with her blood.

Calwyn sought his eyes.

Yes, I know. Halasaa looked at her steadily. *She has gone. But sometimes we dance for the sake of those who remain behind.*

They knelt under the trees, anchoring her beneath their hands, until Trout's frantic words dissolved into sobs and Tonno covered his face. Calwyn was numb, paralyzed as if her own chantment had engulfed her. She stared down, dry-eyed, at her own slender hands, white with cold, and at Halasaa's brown hands beside them, with the darker tattooed spirals that curled and uncurled across his skin. The numbness crept through her body; she was floating, far away, flying high above the forest, back and back, far away from here.

Someone touched her shoulder, and she returned to her body. It was Keela. "Go to the Dwellings. There are things you must do." She put her arm around Tonno, and he sagged against her, his face still hidden in his hands. Keela stared at Calwyn with fierce blue eyes. "I'll take care of them. Go."

Halasaa looked up. *Wait, my sister. I will take care of Trout's wound, and then I will come with you.*

The goat-carts had begun to clatter down the track from the nearby village of Areth. The sun had risen in the clear sky, flooding the woods with light and revealing the drab, dirty muddle of the battle site. Wisps of smoke and breath-fog mingled in the crisp air. The wounded staggered along the narrow path to the Dwellings, leaning against each other, makeshift bandages slipping from their limbs. But there were many who had not risen when Calwyn's chantment ceased. The ground was littered with bodies and pieces of bodies.

Calwyn stood. The snow where she had knelt was stained with blood. Her heart was a cold, hard stone in her breast, twin to the small, dense disc of the Wheel. Slowly Calwyn climbed back onto the sled. A few moments later, Halasaa joined her, holding Darrow. But Calwyn sat in silence, unable to think what she should do next.

Halasaa prompted her. *Sing, my sister. Sing.*

One Music

A fire glowed in the hearth of the High Priestess's room, and morning light spilled through the narrow windows, softening the gray stone with pale gold. There was little furniture, but the high-backed chairs and the table had been worn to a rich polish with beeswax and the loving touch of many hands. The rugs on the floor and the tapestry on the wall were threadbare with age, their colors faded to soft pinks and blues and greens. At the sight of the familiar room, where she had sat at Marna's feet and learned the long songs, Calwyn felt a tug of yearning. This, more than any other place in the Dwellings, had been home.

It was the day after the battle, and everyone came crowding in, finding places to sit or stand. Briaali and Darrow had the warmest seats beside the fire, but with so many bodies crammed inside, the little room was soon warm and stuffy. Tonno sat on the windowsill, Keela perched on a stool nearby, and Trout leaned against the wall, gnawing at his lip. Tree People of both factions sat cross-legged on the floor. The headwomen of the villages of Antaris crowded shyly together, wary of so many strangers. Lia and several of the most senior priestesses were near the front of the room, Ursca and Janyr among them. Halasaa and Sibril stood, tall and silent, by the door.

Sibril was leaning on a stick; he had been badly wounded in the battle. His knee was smashed, and his face was heavily bandaged. One of the villagers had wrested Tonno's sharp knife from him and used it to gash his face; half his ear had been sliced off, and his cheek slashed open to the corner of his mouth. Calwyn and Halasaa had not yet been able to heal everyone, and Sibril had refused their help while there were other warriors still injured. He meant it as a noble gesture, no doubt, but Calwyn saw beneath it a sulky boy's hostility. He was beaten, but he could not admit it.

As she glanced at Sibril's dark, sullen face, half hidden by bandages, it struck Calwyn that since she'd sung the shadow chantments, her awareness of others' anger and misery, their cruelty and grief, had sharpened in the same way as her sense of life and magic had sharpened after the Knot of the Waters. She could read Sibril's defiance, Lia's doubt, Briaali's fierce impatience, as plainly as she read the signs on the Wheel. When she looked at Darrow, she saw loving encouragement. But she shied from meeting Trout or Tonno's eyes; she was afraid of seeing blame in their faces, as well as searing grief.

Calwyn stood in the center of the room with the Wheel in her hand. "We are all grieving this day," she said. "There is not one of us in this room who has not lost someone dear. But I must ask you to set aside your anger and your blame, and listen to what I have to say.

If we do not act, and act swiftly, we will find ourselves mourning the death of Tremaris itself, and after that, there will be no one left to mourn for us."

Everyone in the room was still, and Calwyn knew that she had their attention. "This is no time for keeping secrets. For all our sakes, I am going to speak of matters that have been kept hidden, secrets of the Tree People and secrets of the Voiced Ones. If anyone here objects to that, now is the time to speak." She looked around the room and though she saw doubt on several faces, no one spoke. Calwyn took a deep breath. "Very well."

As briefly as she could, she told them about the Power of Signs, the Tenth Power. She read out the message of the Wheel for them all to hear and told them of the vision that had come to her in the forest.

She mouthed the words, and she knew as she spoke that she was persuading her listeners. But her argument seemed empty to her own ears; though she tried to speak with passion and conviction, she was no longer sure that she believed what she was saying. She could read the emotions of everyone in the room, but she could not read her own heart; it was a lump of ice, a frozen stone. She had not yet shed one tear for Mica.

"The Wheel says: *This world breathes chantment as we breathe the air, and drinks in the dance like water.*" Calwyn looked from one face to another. "I believe Tremaris needs our magic to live, to nourish itself. But for many generations now, chantment has been neglected and the dances forgotten. It is we who are killing our world through our own ignorance and folly."

They did not understand her. All around the room she saw blank faces. Calwyn sought Briaali's gaze. "Our magic is woven into this world, and this world is woven of our magic. It's like the forest. The trees draw up their food from the soil, and when they fall and decay, they enrich the soil in their turn. We, the peoples of Tremaris, are nourished by this world, but we have neglected to feed it in return."

Briaali's eyes were like chips of black diamond, and she pulled her cloak of burrower pelts close. Her words were thoughtful, as if she puzzled it out while she spoke. *The Tree People are born of Tremaris. Our magic, our dances of becoming, were born here. But the Voiced Ones came from the dark between the stars and brought their sung magic with them. How can your chantments feed our world?*

"Hear me, wise one. Hear me, all of you." Calwyn's words were emphatic. "The Wheel says the song and the dance are one music. One music, one magic. Marna once told me that all kinds of magic are like different faces of the same jewel." She held up her fingers to count them off. "The Power of Tongue, which allows us to speak and sing together. The Power of Beasts, which tames animals. The Power of Seeming, which creates illusions and hides reality. The Power of Winds, which governs winds and weather. The Power of Iron, which can move any object, except for fire, water, air, or living creatures. The Power of Becoming, the magic of life and change and healing. The Power of Fire, which makes heat and light. The Power of Ice, which is the magic of dark and cold. And the Great Power, the mystery that lies beyond us all, the mystery at the heart of every magic." She paused, to let her words sink in. "I have been blessed with the gift of Becoming, as well as the powers of chantment, and I can tell you, the same magic breathes in both. Chanters and dancers, it is the same. Tremaris is parched and dying. This world thirsts for the offering of our magic."

For a few moments, there was silence. Then Darrow said in a low voice, from far back in his chair, "What must we do, Calwyn?"

She took a deep breath. "Briaali, Halasaa, all of you who have been to the Knot of the Waters, will remember the figures painted on the wall of the cave. They are dancers. I believe that the Tree People gathered there — perhaps once a year, perhaps more often — to perform a great dance of healing, a Dance of Becoming." She looked around, impressing her words into their minds. "We must do the same. We must dance, singers and dancers together. The interweaving of our magic is the only thing that will save Tremaris."

A dance of healing? Halasaa's forehead creased, and he exchanged a glance with Darrow.

"You don't want to try that again, lass," muttered Tonno, and his voice cracked as he added under his breath, "Can't lose you too."

Calwyn said steadily, "Yes, I attempted a dance of healing before, in the desert, and it went wrong, but I know why. I shouldn't have tried to do it alone. This will be different. This time the dancers must work together, so the magic will not be too strong for them."

Lia said, "Here in Antaris, the priestesses sing together. Magic is stronger when many voices sing the same song."

"And strong magic does not harm those who sing with the protection of many voices," said Calwyn. "The same will be true of this great Dance of Becoming."

Halasaa turned to Briaali. *Wise one, you are learned in the old ways. Do you know of such dances of healing, with many dancers together?*

My learning is like a net, more holes than string. Briaali's words were wry. *But Halwi, your father, who knew more than I, never spoke of such a ritual. A dance of healing is performed by one alone, not by several together.*

"But the paintings in the cave show many dancers," insisted Calwyn.

My child, there are dances for birth and for death and for the celebration of pairing. At these times we dance together. It is those dances that are painted on the walls.

Calwyn opened her mouth and closed it. All at once she was sure Briaali was right. Her so-called vision had been a hollow dream, the message of the Wheel no more than a plea for peace. She looked down, feeling the weight of the Wheel in her hand, and said nothing.

But then Darrow whispered, "Sometimes the form of a ritual is preserved when its original purpose has been lost. The dances of celebration may be an echo of these great life-giving dances that Calwyn has described."

"She saw them in a dream," said Lia skeptically.

"She saw a vision of the truth." Darrow cleared his throat impatiently, and whispered, "Perhaps your Goddess spoke to her."

His voice was faint, but his gray-green eyes were as alive, as keen and bright as ever, and a respectful muttering ran around the room as he spoke. If she could, Calwyn would have seized his hands and kissed him. *Thank you,* she murmured to him in mind-speech. Aloud, she said, "Maybe it was the Goddess. Or maybe it was the caves, the Knot of the Waters, the forest that remembered, and spoke to me."

Briaali nodded slowly. *I have said it often, we must learn to listen. But what is the use of listening if no one heeds what is said?* Her sharp eyes twinkled. *Only you and your brother among us have the gift of the old magic. Who else will dance this Dance of Becoming?*

"The sisters have the gift of chantment, and Darrow . . ." His name slipped out before Calwyn could stop herself. When she saw how he flinched, she wished she could have bitten out her tongue. She hurried on, "Briaali, if you and your people will teach us the dances you have learned, and the High Priestess and the sisters join the Dance of Becoming, the magic will work. I know it." She looked at the village headwomen. "The villagers are welcome to join the ritual too. I know you have your own dances, your own music and festivals. Please, bring your dancers and your musicians to help us."

A mutter of dissent broke out among the priestesses.

Darrow said clearly, "This is work for everyone, not just

chanters! The villagers were fit to fight and die to protect Antaris. Are they not fit to make music, to save all Tremaris?"

The murmur of protest died away. Briaali inclined her head. *We will teach you. Let the Dance of Becoming be the rain that quenches the thirst of our world.*

Trout murmured, "From the rains, the river; from the river, the sea; from the sea, the rains . . ." His voice was thick with unshed tears. Tonno covered his eyes with his hand.

Calwyn said, "Yes. Chantment flows in a circle — a wheel." She pressed the Wheel between her hands, fully understanding the meaning of its shape for the first time.

Lia said in her dry, matter-of-fact way, "The wheel turns, as they say. I must confess, I find it hard to believe that any amount of dancing will help us. But I suppose it cannot hurt." She shot a look at the senior priestesses. "I must consult with my sisters. Do you propose to travel beyond the Wall, to this cave by the Waters, and hold the dancing there?"

Calwyn shook her head. "There's no need for that. The valley of the blazetree is a sacred place, as sacred as the Knot of the Waters. In six days, the three moons will be full. That gives us little time to prepare; I hope it will be long enough."

One of the priestesses cried out, "Lady Mother, the time of the full moons is reserved for Strengthening the Wall! And the valley is sacred to the Goddess. Bad enough to invite in the common folk of Antaris. But you cannot allow these men, these Outlander savages, to enter there!"

Before Lia could reply, Calwyn cut in sharply. "The Outlander savages, as you call them, lived in these lands long before the Daughters of Taris came. No doubt the valley of the waterfall was a sacred place to them before we ever set foot there. And what is the strengthening of the Wall compared with the strengthening of Tremaris?"

Lia said quietly, "If any priestess considers this ritual to be an affront to the Goddess, she need not join us. But I will dance."

"Sibril? What do you say?" Calwyn turned to the leader of the warriors.

I will not dance. He stared at the floor, and the words were dragged from him. He seemed very young, a sulky boy acting the part of a man. *My warriors will not dance.*

Do not be so sure! Briaali's black diamond eyes flashed at him, and she sent private words into Calwyn's mind. *Do not be angry with the boys. They are young and foolish, but they could see no other way.*

Suddenly one of Sibril's lieutenants stood up, straight as a spear, head high. *We have had our taste of war, Sibril. It was not as you promised, and we want no more. We have held a council. You are not our leader anymore.*

Sibril still looked at the ground, but he flinched as though he had been punched. The young lieutenant nodded toward Calwyn. *The men have agreed to follow this daughter of the Tree People.*

Calwyn tried to catch Sibril's eye, but he would not look at her. *I respect the ways of the Tree People. So do we all. We want to use the Tree People's magic to heal Tremaris. Surely you cannot object to that?*

Sibril made no reply.

Young man! rapped Briaali. *You have been treated with more honor than you deserve. In any other place, you would be imprisoned or worse for the trouble you have caused. Lift your head! Show the Singer that courtesy, at least.*

Sibril raised his head and darted a look at Calwyn. But then his eyes slid away again.

Calwyn turned to the young lieutenant, and said gravely, *I thank you and your men. I hope to be worthy of the trust you have shown me.*

The young man flushed, crimson through copper, and abruptly sat down.

Briaali stood. *We will all dance, Tree People and Voiced Ones together. The day you propose would be the longest of the year, if the seasons ran as they should. We will dance on that night beneath your sacred tree.*

The young lieutenant and his friends ducked out of Lia's rooms before the priestesses and villagers began to move. Sibril limped out painfully, his head hung low; the other warriors did not wait for him.

Darrow said quietly to Calwyn, "They will put all the blame on him, so they can cleanse themselves of shame and begin again. That will be harder for him to bear than all his injuries, he is so proud."

Calwyn stared after them. "They seem such awkward boys, for a war party."

They were not awkward during the fighting. Briaali was behind her. *It is you who have made them so.*

Why should I make them awkward?

Briaali gave her a shrewd look. *Child, you cannot see yourself. Magic flows so fierce in you that the ends of your hair, your shadow, the very prints of your feet are alive with it.*

Calwyn remembered Samis's words: *I can hardly look at you. . . .*

Briaali took Calwyn's hand and spoke to her alone. *In time, child, you will be stronger yet. The power of the woman is greater than the power of the maiden. Do you understand? The power of the mother is even greater, and the power of the Elder is the greatest of all.* She smiled. *When you are my age, you will be strong indeed.*

Calwyn looked across to where Darrow struggled to his feet, waving Halasaa away with a crooked smile. He could still smile. If Darrow could not be healed, she would remain a maiden forever. She could never love anyone else.

Unbidden, the memory of Samis flashed into her mind, the taste of him on her lips, his hands on her body. She closed her eyes. Briaali patted her hand. *Come, child. You and I and your brother must puzzle out the form of this great Dance together. We have much work to do.*

The sisters gathered in the great hall, murmuring with curiosity and nervous laughter. A handful of villagers had come up to the Dwellings too: fewer than Calwyn had hoped. Perhaps there would be more tomorrow. The Tree People settled themselves around the walls to watch; most of the young warriors were among them. Keela had offered to be one of the teachers. "I don't know anything about sorcery," she said. "But I do know how to dance."

The priestesses of Antaris were not used to dancing. The

villagers danced in their own festivals, after harvests and at the coming of spring. But the priestesses did not join these celebrations of the seasons. All the sisters' festivals were centered on the Goddess, and the turnings of the moons. *We have been divided from the breathing of the land,* thought Calwyn, with a sudden flash of insight. *That is how we lost our way.*

This great Dance of Becoming would bring together the rhythms of the moons with the turning of the seasons, the longest day, the shortest night. If the ritual worked, it would bring all the rhythms into harmony again.

Take off your shoes! ordered Briaali. *Grip the ground with your bare feet.* She threw off the gray-and-white burrower-skin cloak and stood before them bare legged and bare armed, a tiny, wiry figure with her feet planted on the floor. *I will show you a dance of the women, the dance for a child's birth. This will be the middle part of our great Dance.* She nodded to the two Tree People crouched in the corner; one held a pipe to his lips, the other had his hands poised over a drum. *Begin, my brothers.*

The Tree Women danced with their feet rooted to the ground. Their bodies rocked and undulated to the simple music, graceful and sensual. *Sway as the sea sways,* Briaali told the watching priestesses, her body rippling as easily as a candle flame. The sisters looked at one another in confusion; they had never seen the sea. Briaali shook her head. *Bend as the trees bend in the wind.*

None of the sisters had danced since they were little girls prancing by the fire. They knew how to use their voices, but not their bodies, except for work, and their movements were jerky and embarrassed.

"Briaali said, be like the trees, but she didn't mean you should be made of wood!" called Keela, and everyone laughed.

With that laughter, the stiff, awkward bodies began to relax. "That's better!" Keela seized the hands of two of the village girls, who moved with more grace than the sisters, and shook them vigorously. "Shake out your hands, shake your legs, make them loose, loose! Yes, laugh, laugh at each other, laugh at yourselves, *enjoy* it!"

The movement begins in your knees! called Briaali. *Let it flow up through your thighs, into your hips and belly.* The dancers jiggled helplessly, laughing as they tried to copy Briaali's smooth, curving movements. Keela swayed easily back and forth; but she could not remember to keep her feet still.

Then Halasaa showed them the dance that men performed when someone died: the wild, stamping dance of mourning, arms outspread like birds' wings, flying as the spirit flew. This would be the beginning of their Dance, grieving for the dead year.

Then Halasaa and Briaali danced as men and women danced together at marriage rituals, a complex weaving of the two forms, planted and whirling. This would be the climax of the great Dance, and soon the hall was filled with earnest, thumping dancers trying not to collide with one another.

After that, it was the turn of the Tree People to listen while Lia explained, as simply as she would explain it to the novices, how the breath of the Goddess breathed through the chanters as they sang Her songs. She told how the hand of the Goddess reached down from Her realm between the stars to touch the sacred valley and intensify the power of magic there. If Calwyn was right, this was the power they would summon with their dance, wreathing the movement, the music, and the magic of chantment together. Those who had been warriors listened passively. Briaali's followers listened and nodded, as if they were remembering something they had half-forgotten.

The villagers listened in wonder, and Calwyn realized with a jolt that the work of bringing chantment back to Tremaris had to begin here, in Antaris. She had always believed that here, at least, where chantment was revered and protected, there was no more work to be done. But outside the Dwellings, chantment was as mysterious and fearful as anywhere else in Tremaris. Calwyn went away from that first rehearsal with much to think about.

After the first day, Calwyn had missed some of the practice sessions. There were many wounded from the battle who still required healing, and Calwyn felt driven to use her gifts to help wherever she could, especially now Halasaa was needed to teach the dances.

But today Ursca had scolded her and shooed her away. "Most of them will recover just as well with good clean bandaging and herbal potions and rest. But you'll be no good to anyone if you're tired out! Be off with you, go and visit your sweetheart. Day after day he lies there, biting off my head when I poke it around the door, because I'm not you!"

So she had gone to see Darrow. But though he tried to be cheerful, he was weaker than before. Mica's death had been a terrible blow, and the snow-sickness was progressing rapidly. Calwyn was horrified to see that he could no longer hold a spoon or comb his own hair, and his voice was very faint.

"The preparations are going well? For the dance?" he whispered.

"Yes. Yes, very well," Calwyn replied mechanically.

"I must be there . . . I insist . . . even if Tonno has to carry me into the valley."

"We could push you there in Lia's chair, if you weren't so heavy!"

He smiled at her feeble joke, and she tried to smile too, but she felt as if the stone that was her heart was cracking in pieces as she sat there.

After a time, he whispered, "You must be careful, Calwyn, in the days to come. This new knowledge will bring great changes to Tremaris."

"I hope so," said Calwyn in puzzlement. Why else were they holding the Dance of Becoming, if not to bring change?

"I don't mean the Dance. I mean the Tenth Power. The Power of Signs will change our whole world, perhaps even more than the Dances of Becoming." Darrow broke off into a cough. He motioned to Calwyn to hold the cup of water to his lips, and went on in an urgent whisper. "Anyone can learn to master the Power of Signs, just as anyone can learn the Power of Tongue. But with this difference: When I speak to you, what I say flies into your memory or onto the wind. Once you have forgotten my words, they're gone forever."

"I've never forgotten your words," said Calwyn with a smile, but Darrow made an impatient gesture.

"This is important, Calwyn! Listen. If I write a message with the Power of Signs, the message remains for others to read after you. Do you understand? If everyone had known how to read the signs, the message of the Wheel would never have been lost."

"All Marna's knowledge — lost when she died — could have been saved," said Calwyn slowly. "The Power of Signs shouldn't be secret. Everyone should learn to read and write the Signs, so no more knowledge is lost. The chantments — we must write down the chantments —" A thought struck her. "Anyone who can read will be able to learn the chantments for themselves. They won't have to come to Ravamey to be taught! The chantments will spread all over Tremaris, just as we've always dreamed."

"Not only the chantments." Darrow coughed again and his voice was hoarse as he fought to speak. "Songs and stories, histories, messages, instructions . . . The recipe for Tonno's honey potion . . ."

"Tonno won't like that," said Calwyn wryly. She tried to imagine how the world might be different. "You could write a message to Heben and Fenn in Merithuros," she said. "You could send it with any trader, you wouldn't have to rely on Tonno or Trout or someone else you trusted to remember what you said."

"Yes," Darrow whispered. His eyes were almost closed. "Yes. I will do that. There are things I must tell them, before . . ."

You are not going to die! Calwyn said fiercely in mind-speech. *Do you hear me?*

But Darrow had drifted into sleep. Calwyn stayed by his bed, breathing with the rise and fall of his breath. From the window she could see the stone walls of the vegetable gardens. Gilly and Mica had worked tirelessly, Lia said, to keep them clear from snow, coaxing new growth from the frozen ground. Mica had never given up. "A little longer," Lia said. "And they might have succeeded." But now the snow had drifted back again, nipping the fragile shoots as soon as they uncurled from the soil.

Calwyn stood there, staring, then she wandered away, past the rooms where the others with snow-sickness lay, hardly aware of where her feet were taking her.

After a time, she found herself in the gallery of the great hall, watching the dancing practice below. The sisters rocked back and forth, eyes closed, their hands dangling forgotten by their sides or jerking awkwardly in the air. Someone twirled on the spot and almost knocked over her neighbor, and both of them collapsed in giggles.

Calwyn sank back in despair. It was hopeless. The chanters could not dance, the dancers could not sing. She herself was among the better dancers, but she knew that even she was clumsy compared with Briaali and the Tree People.

She caught sight of Gilly, spinning wildly below. Her round face was flushed, and her yellow tunic billowed round her knees. Calwyn had seen her, sobbing and sniffling for Mica, with her apron over her head. Calwyn felt a surge of sudden rage. What right did Gilly have to mourn for Mica? She'd only known her two turns of the moons. That should have been Mica down there, not clumsy Gilly: Mica could have done this! Calwyn remembered how she had pirouetted on the ice in her fur cap. Why couldn't it have been Gilly who stood in the way of that spear? Mica could sing and dance, she was beautiful and brave and loyal . . .

Calwyn covered her eyes with her hands, but even now she could not weep.

Down below, the dancing petered out. Briaali called for attention; everyone stood fidgeting while she demonstrated a rapid, shimmying movement of the legs. Calwyn watched dully as the sisters tried to copy her. No one, not even Keela, could do it properly. It was three days before the moons became full; she should have been excited, thrilling with hope. But instead she felt nothing but dreary despair.

On her way downstairs she ran into Trout. His eyes were red. "Why aren't you in there, dancing?" he asked.

"Why aren't you?" Calwyn felt a kind of envy for his tears.

Trout shrugged. "Oh, you know. I'd only make a fool of myself. I never was much of a dancer. If Mica were here —"

"If Mica were here, she'd want you to help." She spoke more

sharply than she'd intended; Trout winced as if she'd slapped him. Calwyn felt that everything she did was coming out wrong.

"All right, all right," mumbled Trout. "I'll go in." He turned away.

"Trout, wait. Please." Calwyn held out her hand and, after a moment, Trout grasped it, crushing her fingers.

"I'm sorry, Calwyn. I can't —"

"Don't. Don't speak. Words are no good."

Trout grimaced, trying not to weep, then abruptly he threw his arms around her in a fierce embrace. For a long time he clung to her, while Calwyn held him tight and pressed her face into his shoulder. But still she couldn't cry.

Calwyn's numb hopelessness persisted until the very evening of the great Dance. As Ursca had predicted, the long days among the wounded had left her very tired. "It's lucky that Halasaa healed your broken back when he first came here," she said to Lia. "We might not have had a chance to help you, this time."

"I could have waited," said Lia. "I was in no pain." She smiled and touched Calwyn's hand. "But I am glad indeed that I will be able to dance in the ritual that heals the world."

As Calwyn's doubts deepened, everyone else had become more confident. In the last day or two, the Dwellings had buzzed with excitement. Calwyn wished she could share Lia's certainty, but to her the Dance seemed nothing but folly. She had tried to sleep that afternoon, but without success, and her feet dragged as she walked the path to the sacred valley. If this didn't work, what would they do?

The sisters, the Tree People, and the villagers filed down into the valley, exchanging smiles and nods, touching one another on the shoulder. One of the novices earnestly twisted her hands in the air, showing a movement to a village woman. As was their custom when preparing for a ceremony, the priestesses did not speak; the only noise was the shuffle of feet and the crack of twigs underfoot. They carried no torches. All the moons were full, and the valley overflowed with light like a silver bowl. The frozen pool and the column of the waterfall were like black glass, and the blazetree, stripped of leaves, thrust its bare branches into the sky.

Tonno and one of the village lads had carried Darrow to the valley in Lia's wheeled chair, and Calwyn heard him whisper his thanks. His voice was fading, as Marna's had faded before the end; Calwyn bit her lip so hard that she tasted blood.

Calwyn and Lia stood beside Darrow beneath the blazetree, watching as the silent dancers came down into the valley: two dozen villagers, half a hundred priestesses, and twice as many Tree People. In the end, almost all the warriors had decided to join the dance. But not Sibril; he was up in the Dwellings, nursing his wounds alone.

Once everyone had crowded into the clearing between the frozen pool and the blazetree, Lia gave a signal. Without speaking, everyone stepped back to form a circle around the edge of the clearing, where half a dozen huge mounds of firewood had been laid at intervals. The ground within the circle was bare and frozen hard, trampled flat by generations of priestesses who had held their rituals there.

Calwyn moved into the center of the ring. In the night's first sound of chantment, she sang out a song of fire in her clear, strong voice. All the bonfires blazed up together, and the black ice of the pool reflected the dancing flames.

Musicians were spread through the crowd, Tree People, Daughters of Taris, and villagers mixed together, holding drums and pipes and chimes. Tonno stood ready with a flute to his lips. "I played a fair whistle when I was a boy," he'd told Calwyn. "Surprised you there, eh?" He chuckled. "Just because I'm no singer doesn't mean I can't make music."

Now that the moment was finally here, Calwyn felt small and scared and foolish. When she'd flown above the battlefield, she was strong and brave, conscious of her own power. That sense of effortless control had gone. Every face in the grove was turned to her. It was because of her that they were all here, waiting to begin a performance that might be nothing but a senseless charade. Calwyn held a drum in one hand, and suddenly she felt unsure what to do with it. But as she looked around the circle, she sensed no such uncertainty among the waiting dancers. They were all tense as harp strings, eager to be plucked.

The three moons sailed above the trees. Clouds scudded across the sky, and the silver light flickered as it mingled with the golden light of the fires. Calwyn breathed deep; the cold air burned her throat. Briaali looked at her impatiently. *Now, daughter!*

Calwyn raised her hand and brought it down on the drum, and a deep *boom* echoed out into the night. The noise startled her, and the palm of her hand stung. She brought her hand down on the drum again and again, until the beat rang out, strong and sure as her own heartbeat. The drummers of the Tree People struck up a softer, more complicated rhythm.

Halasaa stamped his foot, once, twice, in time with Calwyn's drum, and slowly began to circle the clearing, within the ring of watchers, his knees bent, his bright eyes shining. He danced the dance of mourning, the celebration of death which brought life, and the ground trembled beneath his stamping feet. Calwyn felt the tension in the waiting dancers wind even tighter, as if Halasaa wound them on a spindle as he turned.

The chimes and flutes wove a gentle thread of sound through the drumbeats, and now Briaali began to dance. Calwyn realized she was beating the drum slightly faster, and her heart was beating faster too. No one who saw Briaali would have thought she was an old woman; she moved with the lithe grace of a young girl. The sisters and the village women began to clap their hands and sprang into the circle. Suddenly the clearing was filled with joyful, swaying, graceful women, calling up the life in the soil through their feet, up through their own life-giving bodies, shimmering out from their fingertips as they danced.

At the edge of the circle, the village men and the men of the Spiridrelleen stamped out their own insistent rhythm with bare feet on the frozen ground. One by one, they whirled into the clearing with their arms outstretched, the men and the women dancing together.

Calwyn stood at the center of the circle with dancers spinning and swaying around her, the still point, the pivot of the dance. And now she began to sing. This was the day when the sisters sang to strengthen the Wall of Ice. But the chantment that rose to Calwyn's lips was the song of unmaking, the song that dissolved the ice. It was a song of opening, a chantment to melt down barriers and let in what had been shut out. The magic rose within her, warm and tingling as fire, and Calwyn felt the numbness in her heart thaw at last. The tears that had been frozen inside her spilled down her face, and she tasted them on her lips as she sang.

One by one, the sisters joined Calwyn's chantment, and the song and the music, the pipes and chimes and drums, all wove together into one seamless, intricate whole. Everyone was part of the dance now. Calwyn glimpsed Lia, singing strongly. Tonno's foot tapped time as he played a simple, swooping melody. Gilly clapped her hands, her cheeks pink with exertion. With their heads flung back, sweat pouring down their faces, the dancers twirled and looped, weaving a pattern as complicated as the music. The clearing was filled with flying figures, but unlike the days of practice in the great hall, no two ever collided, or even brushed each other's fingertips.

The bonfires crackled and leapt, and shadows flickered over the dancers, whose movements echoed the flames. There was the gleam of Keela's golden hair, the flash of her dainty feet, the sound of her laughter threading through the music. There was Darrow's face, pale in the shadows. He was leaning forward, his gray-green eyes fixed eagerly on the dancers, on Calwyn herself. Her palm struck the drum, but she no longer felt the sting on her hand. She was singing, her voice lost among many voices; she was dancing, her body moving unconsciously with the sway of the music; she wept, and she was laughing.

All around the clearing were watchers, who had fallen out of the dance to catch their breath. But they were clapping or playing drums or chimes. Their lips moved as they sang or shouted encouragement, they nodded and swayed to the lilt of chantment. Suddenly Calwyn understood that this watching and listening was just as important, was just as much a part of the dance, as the movement of the dancers and the singing of the chanters.

Beyond the circle of the fires, the moonlit trees whispered in the breeze, as if the woods joined the dance. With a rush of elation, Calwyn knew that the lifeblood of the land, frozen for so long, was stirring at last, called by the magic of the dance. From below the thick ice that imprisoned the waterfall, a deep, muffled murmur blended with the sound of chantment, as the living water wakened from its long sleep.

Someone plucked the drum from Calwyn's hands, and she was free to thread her way through the pattern of the dance. The smell of smoke and sweat filled her nostrils, and behind it the cold, fresh smell of the woods and the ice. Familiar faces dipped and blurred away: Trout, Gilly, Tonno, Ursca, Halasaa. Was that Mica whirling by, her head flung back, her golden eyes glowing? *Mica, I'm sorry!* cried Calwyn in mind-speech. Tears streamed down her face as the music spun faster and faster. Keela came up and grabbed both her hands, and they danced together. Keela pointed her toes and kicked high in the air, and Calwyn copied her, laughing through her chantment. Keela's face was alight with joy, her hair flying free in a golden cloud, and for an instant the two young women clasped each other close, thudding heart pressed to thudding heart, before Keela whirled away.

But now the music, as if at some silent command, began to slow; the wild rhythm calmed. Drums and chimes were abandoned as everyone surged into the middle of the clearing. The fires had died down, and the embers glowed deep red. The dancers circled slowly, hands linked; the priestesses still sang the chantment of unmaking, but there was no other music.

Calwyn returned to the center of the circle, slowly spinning with her arms outstretched. As she looked from face to face, she read every emotion from rapture to exhaustion to inexpressible grief. Tears gleamed in the eyes of many dancers. Feet dragged, hair hung limp, clothes were in disarray, and the circle revolved more and more slowly.

There was a moment at the end of every ritual when the chantment ceased. Calwyn found herself gathering the attention of the singers like threads in her hand. The end of the chantment was near; they would follow her lead. Calwyn brought them to the last phrase, the last note trembling in the air. And there was silence.

Into that waiting silence, like a wave building, the magic surged to its crest. Hand to hand, power flowed around the ring. It came from the ground beneath them, warmed by the tread of their feet, and from the ice-cold air they gasped into their lungs. Chanters and those without the gift of chantment, Tree People and Voiced Ones, all were links in a great chain of living magic that strengthened with every step. As the slow circle turned, the power heightened, spiraling in a great coil. This was the axis around which the whole of Tremaris pivoted, the solemn wheeling of the whole world.

Like warmth spreading from a white-hot fire, the healing magic spread across the valley. It passed effortlessly through the Wall of Ice and melted it away. It rippled across the forests and the mountains and down across the plains, wider and wider with every turn of that inner wheel of dancers. Calwyn, the Singer of All Songs, was the center of the wheel. And it was her hand that had set it turning.

Calwyn felt flooded with light, just as when she'd emerged from the Knot of the Waters. All her tiredness vanished. She didn't want to stop; she wanted to dance until morning. Then she saw the faint pale sky behind the trees. It *was* morning! And there was a sound she had not heard for a long time: the clamor of birdsong. They had danced all through the night.

With the coming of dawn, the force that had connected the

dancers diminished and released them. Only then, with a pang, Calwyn remembered Darrow. She craned to where he had sat, in the blazetree's shadow. There was Lia's chair, but it was empty. Darrow was gone.

"Calwyn!"

She whirled around. Darrow broke free from the circle of dancers and ran across the clearing toward her. His head was held high, his eyes sparkled. He had shouted, clear and glad, and he was running, running . . .

Calwyn cried out. With one leap she was in his arms, and he buried his face in the dark hollow between her throat and her black hair.

Once broken, the circle dissolved quickly. People flung themselves down by the remains of the fires. Others embraced and kissed and sobbed in each other's arms. Halasaa had slipped away between the trees. Someone fetched kettles from the Dwellings and began to brew roseberry-leaf tea over the coals. Keela sat beside Tonno with her head on his shoulder. Trout was almost asleep, propped against a tree trunk. And one by one, greeted with cries of joy, the priestesses who had been too ill with snow-sickness to leave their beds were stumbling, skipping down into the valley, cured as Darrow had been cured by the great healing magic.

Darrow released himself from Calwyn's arms and said quietly, "Is there a place where we could be alone?"

Calwyn hesitated. She could sense Briaali's impatient black eyes on her back. She took his hand. "Come with me."

She led him away from the clearing, around the rim of the black pool, and up the slope, between the bare trees. Her body thrummed with the awareness of magic; the whole world hummed with chantment. Below them in the little valley was a quiet buzz of conversation, the crackle of the fires, the whistle of a boiling kettle, the first trickle of falling water.

She led him to a secret place, a place she had discovered as a child. The branches of the bower-tree drooped down, and Calwyn and Darrow crawled through them into a dry, sheltered space. There was no frost beneath the tree, and the ground was carpeted with soft moss. The two sat close together under the arching roof of the bower-branches. Darrow began to say something, but Calwyn touched a finger to his lips, and he kissed it. Gently he turned up her palm and traced some signs on it with his fingertip. Laughter trembled on her lips, and then they were kissing hungrily, as if they had never kissed before.

Darrow reached up and tugged at the carved comb she wore. She shook her long hair free, and it shimmered like a dark opal, with the same lights they'd seen inside the sacred caverns. Darrow ran his fingers through the silken curtain as he drew her down beside him, and her hair fell around them like a waterfall.

The Singer of All Songs

The soft spring breeze was scented with starflowers and sunsweet. Calwyn breathed in deeply as she followed the path that led to the village of Anary. The pale sky soared above the new green of the valley, and the normally sleepy river was so swollen by the thaws that it thundered like a cataract. Trout had warned of floods downstream; by the time they arrived in Kalysons, he'd predicted gloomily, the canals would be overflowing, and they'd find the streets waist-deep in water.

It was on a day much like this one, in the first part of spring, that Calwyn had found Darrow lying injured, just inside the Wall. She remembered the awkward, rebellious girl she had been then, unsure of herself, filled with vague longings and fears. More than two years had passed since that day; she had changed. The world had changed.

Today was to be her last day in Antaris, and Calwyn did not know how long it would be before she returned. She was on her way to bid farewell to Mica and to Marna. She was dressed in a blue tunic the same color as the pale spring sky, and she slipped off her soft-soled shoes for the pleasure of feeling the grass underfoot. There were small white flowers in the coronet of her dark hair, and though she was unaware of it, the aura of strong magic sparkled all around her.

Barefoot, Calwyn ran across the wooden bridge that spanned the river. The water churned white as it roared below, only an arm's span beneath the bridge, and her feet were splashed with spray. Once, that would have terrified her, but now she felt only delight at the cool water on her skin.

Tomorrow, before dawn, they would begin the long journey back to Merithuros. Darrow had been away too long, and they had all agreed, as they sat talking in the great hall the night before, that Merithuros needed their new knowledge more urgently than any other land in Tremaris.

It will be a great joy to see life breathed into that dry land. Halasaa had smiled.

"I'm so glad you're coming," Calwyn had replied. "I thought you might go back to the Wildlands with Briaali and the others."

I could not be parted from my sister so soon. I only hope I will not be in your way. His smile broadened.

"Never," said Darrow. "And if you are, we can soon be rid of you." With a throat-song of chantment, he tipped Halasaa's straw hat abruptly over his eyes.

"You make sure you do get in their way, Halasaa," growled

Tonno. "I don't want to see these two mooning around *Fledgewing*, tripping over ropes and staring in each other's eyes. Nothing worse than a pair of lovers on board ship."

"Then you'd better be careful yourself," said Darrow, with a pointed glance toward Keela. She was deep in conversation with Lia in a far corner of the hall, earnestly discussing matters of statecraft; as if she'd heard her name, she looked over and gave them a smile that lit up her face.

"Don't know what you mean," muttered Tonno, but a scarlet flush spread up his neck and turned his ears red.

That's enough! warned Calwyn quickly, but it was too late. Trout had scrambled up and walked out of the hall.

Tonno shook his curly head. "Curse my tongue!"

"I can only imagine how I would feel if —" Darrow stopped. "I didn't know that he loved Mica so much."

"He didn't know it himself," Calwyn had said softly.

Time will help him, said Halasaa soberly. *It will not dissolve his grief, but it will help him to bear it. It will help us all.*

Calwyn had said nothing. But she knew, and she had felt it freshly as she stepped through the Anary graveyard; her own grief for Mica was a wound that would never completely heal. It was lodged inside her like a dark stone.

They had buried Mica next to Marna, beneath the whispering spander trees with their drifts of white blossom and soft mist of new leaves. The bees were frantic among the blossom, as if to make up for the time they'd lost. It had seemed wrong, at first, to leave Mica here, so far from the ocean that she'd loved. But as Calwyn gazed out across the valley, she saw it rippling with wave after wave of wildflowers, dark blue and white and green. Every spring, at least, Mica would be near the sea. And to mark her grave, Trout had built a special which-way, whose arrow would point forever to the Isles where she was born.

Calwyn sat down on the sun-warmed grass. There were plenty of wildflowers, but only the goats could eat them. The hard times were not over yet for Tremaris; many people would go hungry before next harvest. But that harvest would be a good one. They had held two more Dances of Becoming in the sacred valley, and with each healing ceremony, the land seemed to stretch and purr like a roancat soaking up the sun. Everywhere she looked, Calwyn saw life bursting from the soil, shoots thrusting eagerly upward, leaves uncurling. Lia would continue the Dances after they had gone, a new ritual to add to the calendar of the Goddess.

And now that Briaali was bearing knowledge of the Dance back to the Tree People, there would be rituals performed again in the cave by the Knot of the Waters. A handful of priestesses had gone with the Spiridrelleen to call up the healing magic. *Perhaps the gift of Becoming will be born in our children anew.* Briaali's eyes had glittered at Calwyn when she'd said good-bye. *Or you might send your daughter to us, or your son.* She'd laid her hand briefly on Calwyn's belly, and her eyes wrinkled with secret amusement. *In time, child, in time!*

Calwyn stretched her legs in the soft grass. "We'll name our first daughter after you, Mica," she whispered and stared away across the sea of flowers to the mountains on the horizon.

There was so much to do. Taking the news of the Dance of Becoming to every corner of Tremaris was the most urgent task. But there was also the work of bringing back chantments of all kinds to daily life, finding the chanters in every land who had been despised and scorned and feared for so long, teaching them to be proud, teaching them the songs that were almost forgotten. And there was a new power to teach, not just to chanters but to everyone: the Tenth Power, the Power of Signs. As Darrow had said the night before, "There is a lifetime's work ahead for the Singer of All Songs."

Everyone had gone and for once they were alone. Calwyn had leaned against his shoulder. "I thought — I thought when I became the Singer, that everything would be easier. But it's harder with every step. Lia won't say it, but she's angry with me; she thinks I should stay in Antaris and be High Priestess, as Marna wanted. And Sibril still doesn't believe we're right! He'll go back to the forests and tell the Spiridrelleen that I'm arrogant, a false prophet, using the magic of the Tree People without any right."

"For every Sibril, there is a Briaali, and a hundred others, to contradict what he says. Don't worry about Sibril."

"I've made so many mistakes already." She fell silent; there was no need to mention Mica. She said in a low voice, "I think I did wrong, when I sent Samis — sent the ship away. There were so many records, chantments, and histories, so much knowledge we could have used."

"We will make our own records, we'll replace what's been lost. Trout must invent a way of writing for us, a better way than scratching on stone or tablets of wood. We will travel all over the world, recording the knowledge of every land, and sharing what we learn. The portent of the star was a true one. This is a new day for Tremaris."

"But —"

Darrow shook his head. "Everyone makes mistakes, my love. Even the Singer of All Songs. If you hold back for fear of making a mistake, you will never accomplish what you must. And with each challenge, you will become stronger. I will help you, we will all help you. Even Keela — she has her own wisdom, you know. After all those years scheming in the court of Merithuros, she is as shrewd a judge of character as anyone. You will see." He smoothed back a strand of her hair. "Do you know what Gilly is telling the younger ones? That you are the Goddess, come down from the skies to dwell with mortals."

Calwyn sat up. "I never heard anything so ridiculous! How can Gilly talk like that, when we grew up together? We shared a washing-basin, we threw rotten apples at the goats, and Tamen gave us such a scolding! I'm no more the Goddess than she is!"

Darrow smiled his crooked smile and raised her hand to his lips. "Perhaps there is something of the Goddess in everyone. Only in you, it is easier to see."

"It would be a lonely fate, to be the Goddess," said Calwyn.

"But you are not alone."

"I know." Calwyn leaned back, and they sat for a time in silence.

But for this morning she was alone, with no sound but the breeze rustling through the grasses. This might be the last solitary morning of her life. She had seen how Darrow, when he became Lord of the Black Palace in Merithuros, was besieged by petitioners and officials, people wanting something from him, people wanting to do something on his behalf. It would be the same for the Singer of All Songs. She shrank inside; she had never felt comfortable in crowds. Well, she would have to learn.

All the peoples of Tremaris were her people, now: Tree People and Voiced Ones, chanters and those who did not sing. Those who sang would become dancers too. Those who neither sang nor danced would watch and listen. Everyone could play a part in weaving the health of Tremaris, if they chose. But Calwyn knew that the most important responsibility was her own. She reached up and plucked a spray of white blossom from the spander tree, and laid it across the grass of Marna's grave. "I will do my best, Lady Mother," she murmured.

Samis had pointed out to her that every new kind of chantment was easier to learn than the last. She knew that she still had many lessons to learn, lessons of judgment, and compassion, and persuasion, and reflection. She was not at the end of her journey; it had only just begun. For an instant she wished it could always be spring, the beginning of everything, fresh and new and unspoiled . . . But then the wish passed from her like a petal of blossom drifting on the warm breeze.

The memory of Samis reminded her of something else that troubled her. Had he pulled off one last tremendous bluff on that final night? Even now, she scarcely knew why she had sent the ship away: It was part ruthlessness, part pity. But perhaps she had done what he wanted after all. Perhaps he had tricked her one last time. What if he learned to sail the silver ship? She spoke aloud, as if Marna could answer. "What if I was wrong? What if he does come back?"

In her own mind, she seemed to hear the echo of Marna's voice. *You have the dark chantments, little daughter. If you must, you will defend yourself, and all chantment, and the well-being of the world.*

Calwyn could not say that she would never use those chantments again, that the secrets would die with her. That dark magic too was easier to use each time. That was another lesson. The dark was a part of her now, as well as the light.

There were times, when Darrow kissed her, that she could feel the ghostly print of Samis's lips on hers, and the phantom touch of his hand on her hair. Those memories too would always be a part of her, however she might try to wish them away.

Something caught her eye overhead: a swift dazzling flash of white. Before she could focus her gaze, it was gone. She shook herself. The Singer of All Songs could not shy like a startled bird at every little thing. No doubt it was only the sunlight on a scrap of cloud or the white belly of a snow-throat flying over the valley. But somehow she knew that as long as she lived, she would always be glancing at the sky.

What if Samis managed to sail all the way to the home of the Ancient Ones, hidden between the stars? What if he brought the ship back to Tremaris, laden with strangers from another world, for a second invasion?

For they would be strangers: The Ancient Ones who had arrived here so long ago were not the same people as the Voiced Ones who lived in Tremaris now. The Voiced Ones belonged here as much as the Tree People; Tremaris had changed them, claimed them as its own. From now on, the peoples of Tremaris would find their way together.

Calwyn looked up and saw a figure walking toward her across the wide, rippling valley. She stood up and waved to Halasaa as he came nearer, and he raised his hand to greet her. His arms were spread wide, his fingertips brushing the blue and white flowers. He threw back his head to gaze at his sister where she stood beneath the trees, at the pale green buds that danced to and fro above her head, and beyond, to the dim silver shadows of the moons on the wide blue sky. Steadily he came wading through the ocean of wildflowers, and the breeze carried a sound that Calwyn had never heard before, and had never dreamed of hearing. She began to run, faster and faster, down the slope toward him.

In a husky voice, unpracticed, but surprisingly clear, Halasaa was singing.

This book was art directed and
designed by Elizabeth B. Parisi.
The text was set in Centaur,
created by Bruce Rogers in 1914.
The display type was set in Civilite,
originally designed by Robert Granjon in 1557.
The artwork for the chapter openers and
cover was created by Matt Manley.
This book was printed and bound
by RR Donnelley in Crawfordsville, Indiana.
The manufacturing was supervised
by Jaime Capifali.